DEAD IN THE MARKET

A neurotic, barren wife of a British serviceman in Germany acquires a baby illegally. Seventeen years on, with her husband now a prosperous Welsh businessman, someone discovers her secret. The result is blackmail, to be followed by murder, on a Saturday morning, in Cardiff's vibrant covered Central Market in front of a thousand shoppers – except, astonishingly, there are no witnesses.

Chief Inspector Merlin Parry, again supported by Sergeant Gomer Lloyd, here tackles a baffling human drama, staged in the heart of the Welsh capital, and which intrigues right up to the nail-biting denouement, the whole leavened with masterly characterization and polished wit. 'The promise of the first book is enhanced by a robust sequel of superbly crafted thriller writing,' wrote Michael Boon, reviewing the second Inspector Parry mystery in the *Western Mail*. With the third, *Dead in the Market*, David Williams, creator of Mark Treasure, has unassailably established yet another enduring sleuth on the popular whodunit scene.

DEAD IN THE MARKET

David Williams

For Mike & Mary
another medically immaculate story
from the ditto author!

Love

David Williams

HarperCollinsPublishers

Collins Crime
An imprint of HarperCollins*Publishers*
77–85 Fulham Palace Road, London W6 8JB

First published by HarperCollins*Publishers*
in 1996 by Collins Crime

1 3 5 7 9 10 8 6 4 2

Copyright © David Williams 1996

The Author asserts the moral right to
be identified as the author of this work

A catalogue record for this book is
available from the British Library

ISBN 0 00 232589 6

Set in Meridien and Bodoni

Set by Rowland Phototypesetting Ltd
Bury St Edmunds, Suffolk
Printed and bound in Great Britain by
Caledonian International Book Manufacturing Ltd,
Glasgow

This one for
Nanette Newman and Bryan Forbes

1

_____

'I don't know why we said we'd leave at half past five in the morning,' the tall, sandy-haired Welshman complained with a sigh that was nearly a groan, but a good-natured groan. He had been rolling open the passenger door of the new, white Volkswagen camper as his wife Dilys joined him from the house.

'To please me, love, that's why,' she said, giving him an unexpected quick kiss, and squeezing his hand tightly. She wasn't normally quite so demonstrative. She was carrying a tightly closed, small, bulging holdall which she now pushed on to the floor in front of the van's bench seat. 'And we couldn't have left it any later, Huw, could we? Not if we're getting the four o'clock ferry. Not on top of everything else,' she completed firmly. Nor did he attach any particular significance to her last comment. She was looking behind the seat now, to check that he had stowed the last of the gear they had brought out earlier.

'It's still not civilized. Getting up at the crack. _Before_ the crack,' he added, with a grin. 'And if this is a foretaste of life in civvy street, give me the RAF any day. Still, it looks like being fine, doesn't it? Good day for a long drive.' He went to see that the rear door of the van was properly secured.

'Mm. Good day for a lot of things. One thing specially,' she ended quietly, and not loud enough for him to hear.

It was Sunday, April 8th; a week before Easter. The sky was cloudless, with a nearly full moon, stars still shining brightly, with the just pre-dawn air crisp and invigorating.

He couldn't know it yet, but this was the morning on which the thirty-eight-year-old Flight Sergeant Huw Madoc

Bevan would have to make the most major, momentous, most ineradicable decision of his whole life – a decision with a following commitment a hundred times more irreversible for him than his marriage vows had been.

'So is that absolutely everything?' he asked blandly, oblivious still of what was in store for him.

'Everything except me.' She smiled, kissed him again, more fondly than before, and stepped into the vehicle.

Huw was glad to see she was happy, for now, at least. He supposed her spirits were high because this time they were going back to the UK for ever, not just on leave. He only hoped the mood would last the journey. Probably she'd taken one of her tranquillizers already, though he hadn't seen her do it. He'd have liked it if she had kept them in reserve still. He'd have liked it even more if there was any prospect of her leaving them off altogether, but there was no chance of that yet, not so far as he could judge.

Dilys had suffered two miscarriages in the previous year, both around the twelfth week of pregnancy. The last one had been in early October. When, in the previous August, she had found she was expecting the second time, she had made Huw promise that none of their relatives and friends at home would be told about it. He had kept his word. The subsequent second miscarriage had upset her a lot mentally, much more than the first one, and the effects had endured.

The same woman medical officer, a flight lieutenant, had treated Dilys for both pregnancies. After the second failure, she had referred her patient on to the air base psychiatrist, a squadron leader. He hadn't done her much good, except for the pills.

Dilys was the same age as her husband. Immediately after the October experience, she had convinced herself that her chances of having a baby were now nonexistent, not the least, she believed, because they had left it too late in the first place. She had badly wanted children, and the guilt she had brought upon herself then was as enormous as it was unjustified, but no one seemed able to convince her of that. Recently, though, she seemed more to have come to terms with the situation. At least she had stopped reiterating that she was doomed to remain childless.

Huw had never been as anxious for children as Dilys. His concern had been solely for her, for her wellbeing. He had never admitted to her that, so far as he was concerned, they could live as happily without kids as with them – and live better too, most likely, children costing as much as they did.

Today it had certainly been Dilys's idea that they should do the drive from Rheindahlen, in Germany, to Calais by teatime. Then, after crossing to Dover on the ferry, they were to press on to her mother's house in Cardiff, all before nightfall. Huw would have preferred it if they'd taken their time, done some sightseeing *en route*, stayed a night somewhere, even two or three nights. If it hadn't been for the camper van, of course, they could have flown home for nothing, courtesy of the RAF, all the way to the St Athan base in South Wales, probably. But since they were driving, it was a shame really not to be making a holiday of the journey. Well, that was Huw's view, and, curiously, Dilys had shared it until a week before this when, suddenly, she had come up with the other plan, and doggedly insisted they adopt it. Huw, twenty-one years in the Royal Air Force, and only four weeks away from his honourable discharge, might have resisted the plan: he could be quite stubborn when he chose. Nowadays, though, he tended to give way to his wife on most things, for the obvious reason: it made for a quieter life, for both of them.

Involuntarily, he turned now to take a last nostalgic look in the semi-darkness at what had been their home for the previous three years. It was an end house in a short, grey stuccoed terrace, part of the married quarters on the Rheindahlen RAF base. For a moment, he felt a pang of uncertainty in the pit of his stomach. It wasn't that he was sorry to be leaving the service, even though he would have been the first to admit that the service had treated him well.

Huw Bevan was a well-qualified electrical engineer, with a good civilian job waiting for him in Cardiff, and plenty of prospects beyond that. It was the camaraderie he was going to miss. On top of that, what he was feeling now, he conceded to himself, was just a touch of natural apprehension – about how he would cope outside the security of service life. He'd be technically on leave for a month, until his formal discharge came through. So, in effect, this was his last day, his last hour, his last few minutes, really, as a regular serviceman. And he wasn't even wearing uniform. He was in a polo-necked sweater, and grey trousers flared at the bottoms in the current style, with comfy sneakers on his feet – hardly appropriate dress for an official farewell.

But there would be no formal goodbyes, not at this time in the morning. When he thought about it, that was some-thing he was sorry to be missing in a way. Twenty-one years was a long time.

'Come on then, love.' Dilys interrupted his reverie, speak-ing through the open window. She was small, with fluffy black hair, and expressive, soulful blue eyes. Her figure was nearly as full and cuddlesome now as it was when they had married. She had lost a lot of weight before Christmas, but had started to put it on again in recent weeks.

He turned about and shrugged. 'Right you are.' He hurried around to the driver's door, got in, and started the engine. 'Going to wake up everybody in the street, this is. On a Sunday, too,' he said, as he backed the camper out of their parking spot in front of the house. 'You got the house keys handy? I promised the adjutant's office we'd give them in at the gate.'

'Of course I've got them. Both sets. Good riddance, as well.' Her voice was a touch less relaxed than it had been only moments earlier. Also, her husband found the sentiment she expressed to be unexpectedly acid: she had never complained about the house in the past, or about their life here. She was smoothing her check skirt over her knees with one hand, or rather kneading it without pause, a habit of hers when she was impatient, or worried, or both.

Huw rationalized that perhaps she was really a bit sad at leaving too, and implying the opposite was her way of disguising how she felt. She was often hard to fathom these days.

'Well, Cardiff, here we come,' he offered, with forced

10

enthusiasm, as they turned out of the cul-de-sac on to the main camp road. Her only response was a low affirmative murmur, and, glancing sideways at her, he could see from her expression that her mind was on something else. When they stopped at the main gate, he almost had to wrest the keys from her hand.

'Good luck, Flight. Wish it was me leaving this lot,' called the guard room corporal as he took the keys.

'Don't you be in too much of a hurry, *bach*. It's a great life in the RAF,' Huw responded lightly, waving to the other man as he drove off, and, after all, getting a half-jocular, but still smart salute in response: he appreciated that salute. The exchange had improved his own mood. As he drove the camper under the raised pole barrier, he was unexpectedly affected by their emergence into the world outside. If he had been more erudite, he might have termed the experience symbolic – and challenging with it.

'Turn left at the bottom, love, will you?' said Dilys in a curiously breathless voice.

'No, no, not left. Right. The autobahn's the other way,' he answered, surprised at her mistake. It was a route they both knew backwards.

'Turn left, Huw,' she repeated in the same tone as before. 'Just do as I say, will you?'

They were close to the junction now. 'But that'll take us into town. We don't want to –'

'I have to make a quick call,' she interrupted, still breathing heavily. 'Something important. It . . . it won't take long. At a house in the Walterstrasse.'

'But that's nearly the centre of town. Who do we know in the Walterstrasse?' he questioned, slowing the vehicle to a crawl.

'It's a friend of mine. Frau Heller. Sonya. You don't know her. She lives at number eight. It's this end.'

'And you think Frau Heller is going to be up at this hour on a Sunday morning? Look at the time. It's still only twenty to six.'

'She'll be up, waiting for me. I called her. It's important. Turn left, Huw, for God's sake.'

11

Now he did as she said, uneasy at her vehemence. Since there was no other traffic, they were turning into the Walterstrasse in less than three minutes. Even so, Huw was put out over the diversion, unscheduled and so far not properly explained.

It was a big, old house, set well back, and, like the rest in the residential avenue, semi-detached, and ponderous under heavy gables on the two visible sides. There were steps up to the porticoed front door. He made to draw up the vehicle outside in the street.

'Oh, could you turn into the drive for me, love?' she said; her voice had now turned plaintive, as well as unaccountably exhausted.

Huw made an irritated shoulder movement, reversed a few feet, then swung the camper up the concrete pathway beside the house. There was no garage, the space was too narrow for that, but the dipped headlights revealed a small car already parked at the end, against a high wooden fence with a gate in it.

'Go as far as you can, Huw, will you?' There was definitely something different about her tone. It was as though there was a weight on her chest, and she was forcing out the words.

'Are you all right?'

'Yes, fine.' She took a deep breath, then let it out slowly. When he stopped, she opened the passenger door and began to get out awkwardly. There was very little room between the camper door and the house wall. 'Hang on,' he began. 'I'll back up again, and –'

'I'm OK, thanks,' she put in quickly. 'We got here in time, that's the main thing. I'll be a few minutes.' With that, she moved slowly to the side door of the house and rang the bell.

There was no immediate response. So much for Frau Heller's readiness, Huw thought, watching his wife waiting in the gloomy doorway. He wondered why she had slipped on that tent-like topcoat before she got out. It wasn't that cold, and it was a garment he had never liked: it made her look gross. It was another thirty seconds before the door was

12

opened and Dilys was illuminated in the light shed from inside. She waved back to him, and, for some reason, blew him a kiss, before going into the house. He noticed the expression on her face had been radiant.

It was more than five minutes before Dilys came out again. She was holding a long rounded parcel in front of her, but despite this, she was moving more easily than before.

'Took you long enough,' he complained as she got in. 'What've you been doing?'

'Yes, well, I'm here now. So let's go,' she said, without answering his question. Still holding the blanket-covered bundle, she had pulled the door shut.

Her husband, impatient and irritated, hadn't needed any bidding. He had already started the engine. Without showing further interest in Dilys or her doings, he backed the camper on to the street fast, swung it around in the direction they had come, and moved off. He was busy calculating how to make up the quarter of an hour they had wasted. It wouldn't be that difficult. The itinerary he had planned had allowed for a longer than strictly necessary stop for lunch: so the stop would need to be that much shorter, but it wouldn't be his fault. Now he concentrated on getting out of the town before more of it came awake.

'So what was the Walterstrasse call all about?' he asked a few minutes later as they joined the autobahn. He was still keeping his eyes on the road, but his mood was mellowing.

'Go on, you're joking, Huw. You know very well what it was about. After you got us there so fast, too.' She paused before continuing. 'Having our baby was what it was all about. Our beautiful Barbara Anne. Wasn't it, my lovely?' She was looking down into the bundle she was cradling, rearranging the folds of its outer wrapping.

'What d'you mean, having a baby?' He snatched a quick, sidelong glance at her. 'That's not another German doll you've bought for Megan, is it?' Megan was the oldest of his two nieces.

'Daddy doesn't know what he's talking about, does he, Barbara Anne?' she answered, widening the upper opening of the bundle. 'That's because Daddy forgot the date, I expect.

April the eighth, the day the nice lady doctor said you'd arrive. And she was right, wasn't she? She'd said you'd be with us on Palm Sunday, and you are, aren't you? My lovely, gorgeous daughter. Right on the dot, you were.'

The bundle coughed.

Huw heard the cough. This time he was suddenly suffering much more than a pang of anguish in his stomach: the whole of his innards had started to churn, and his heart was tolling hard against his ribs. 'It's really a baby you've got there?' he said, slowing the camper, and looking across again, but for longer this time.

'Of course it's really a baby. It's *our* baby, born at five forty-two this morning. Weight seven pounds, six ounces. Aren't you just over the moon? I am. Oh, and I feel so well already. It's amazing, really.'

In a panic now, he pulled on to the hard shoulder, meaning to stop, before he remembered it was against the law to do that on the autobahn, except in an emergency. This was an emergency all right, but he sensed it might not be one to risk involving the police in. The next junction was thirty kilometres ahead. He gunned the accelerator. 'Where did you get the baby?' he demanded. It was a baby all right. He'd just seen it move as well as heard it cough.

'But you saw exactly where I had our baby. You rushed us there, and waited. Nurse Heller, the midwife, she said it was such an easy first birth. She couldn't believe it.'

He swallowed hard, sensing he was out of his depth, knowing she needed help – knowing they both needed different sorts of help. 'Dilys, whose baby have you got there?' When she didn't reply, he tried again. 'Did you buy the baby?' Still there was no response. 'Look, it's no use, love. I'm sorry, but we're taking it back. Now. I'm getting off at the next junction, and going back to town. To the Walterstrasse.'

The strange noise in Dilys's throat began as a long, frightening, ghoulish rattle. Then it broke up into a string of unnatural, shorter moans before she burst into agonizing sobs while rocking her body forwards and backwards in the seat. 'It's my baby ... I'm telling you ... why can't you believe me? You were there, outside,' she uttered through her tears, then gasped for breath as though she were suffocating. 'You can't give my baby away. Why are you being so cruel to me?' She clasped the bundle tighter to her bosom, shifting away from him, towards the door. 'If you give her back, I . . . I'll kill myself. I mean it. I mean it, you'll see.'

At that moment he believed her. 'Give her back to who, Dilys? Tell me, love,' he asked, but very gently this time. At least he'd got her to admit part of the truth.

Her sobbing stopped quite abruptly. 'The . . . the other woman, she didn't want her,' she offered coherently. 'She's got three children already. This one's mine. Ours. This one's Barbara Anne.'

'It's Frau Heller's baby, then, is it?' he questioned, his tone still coaxing.

'No. The other woman was a patient of hers.'

'In the hospital where Frau Heller works? But they'll know –'

'Not in a hospital. The other woman . . . she was having her baby at home. Nobody knew about it.'

'But somebody must have known. The other woman's husband, for instance?'

'She's not married. The father's married to someone else. He's very intelligent, Nurse Heller said. An important business executive. But the other woman didn't want another baby. It's only fair this one's mine.'

'I see. Did you, er . . . did you pay for the baby?'

She was silent for a moment. 'Not much. Only . . . only expenses. It won't cost you anything. It was out of my savings, I can –'

'I don't care about the cost. Perhaps we can adopt the baby?' he said. They had talked of adoption before, but the red tape involved had put them off, and anyway, Dilys had been against it. 'Perhaps, in the circumstances,' he went on, with more conviction than he was feeling, 'perhaps we can adopt it officially later, that's if we take it back now.'

'No.' Dilys was shaking her head violently. 'They won't let us adopt her. Because we're not German. It's over the nationality. It's got to be this way. Unofficial. But nobody minds this way. Please, Huw. Please.'

He hesitated. 'But, love, we're not going to get away with it.' He couldn't credit that for a second he had found himself half entertaining the opposite premise when his every instinct told him the whole concept was madness.

'Yes, we will get away with it. It's all worked out. We'll say we left Rheindahlen yesterday. That I had the baby last night, here, in the camper. That we got help from the midwife in a village we were passing through. That way there's no record. When we get home, we'll tell the family we kept the pregnancy a secret, like we said we would in the first place. What's the difference? Mum'll be so happy for us. Your mum and dad, as well.'

'But what about the baby gear, the feeding stuff, the clothes, and all that?'

'All packed. Ready-use stuff in the holdall. The rest in the back. There's a carrycot there as well, but I'd rather hold her for now,' she said.

He might have known she'd come totally prepared. 'And when we get to the Belgian and French borders, and the ferry?' He supposed she'd work that out as well.

She had: 'A new baby wouldn't be in our passport yet,' Dilys returned promptly. 'Or even registered. Not if she was born yesterday. Anyway, no one'll be bothered about our tiny baby. When we get home, we have to tell the District Health Office what's happened. That Barbara Anne was born a bit earlier than expected, on the journey home. We can register the birth in Cardiff as well. That's the way it's done. No questions asked. It's worked before for other people. Plenty of them.'

'I don't know,' he said, but thereby incautiously advertising which way his sympathies were moving. It was all so clear now – the way she had suddenly needed to change their travel arrangements, her high spirits when they had first got up this morning, the whole charade she had played out when they set off, making believe she'd started her labour, then actually kidding herself that she'd given birth. He'd read about the elaborate fantasies of desperate women who ended up stealing babies. Thank God, at least, she hadn't done that. And her planning had been perfectly rational and thorough, even down to it all happening the day her last pregnancy should have come to term.

She had moved next to him on the seat, pressing herself against him, dropping her head on to his shoulder. 'Darling, darling, Huw, I promise on the Bible I'll never ask you for anything again. Only let me have my baby. Our baby.' She snuggled even closer. 'You won't be sorry. It'll make me whole again, can't you see? Because I've been going mad. You know that? Please make me whole again, Huw. Sane again.'

It was the break in her voice that decided him.

2

It was more than seventeen years later that Dilys Bevan was run over, and injured, while she was out shopping. The accident happened on a Friday morning in mid-August. Dilys had been picking up some things at the dry cleaner's. She was in a hurry because she had arranged to drive into Cardiff with Barbara later. They were going to look at dresses together in the fashion department of David Morgan's. Dilys told everyone she relied on her daughter's advice when she bought clothes for herself: this wasn't strictly true, because Barbara's taste was much too daring, but Dilys believed it pleased her daughter to hear her say it was. This made a positive point of contact between them – and there weren't so many of those.

Just before the accident, Dilys had been rushing back to her car. It had been parked on the other side of Station Road, the narrow main shopping street of Bryntaf, the leafy, elevated suburb, north of the city, where the family now lived. With her arms full, and forgetting to put her glasses on again after leaving the cleaner's, she had stepped out between two parked cars, and been hit a glancing blow by an accelerating delivery van. Miraculously, most of her injuries had been superficial, though not the ones to her abdomen.

'Quite comfortable now, are you, Mrs Bevan?' the surgeon asked when he visited her again in her private room, two days after the operation. Gently and methodically he ran a hand over her bared middle.

'Oh, yes. I'm feeling fine this morning. Ever so much better. All thanks to you, Mr Tranter.' Slightly embarrassed, which showed she was back to her normal self, she continued to give close attention to the ceiling above her bed. She was thankful at least to be lying on her back, a position that served to flatten her out somewhat. Not that there was truly much point in her worrying about how she looked at this stage, not since she still had a black eye, bruising to neck, right shoulder and arm, and a light bandage around a twisted ankle: all this, of course, was in addition to the stitches in her lower stomach. Even so, in the last decade, she had spent a good deal of effort, as well as a significant amount of her husband's money, on delaying the ageing process, and while the result was more in her own perception than in other people's, she took pride in it.

'Oh, I don't know about the size of my contribution,' Tranter replied modestly, but not so adamantly perhaps that he might have been expecting Dilys Bevan to take him literally at his word. 'Right.' With professional diffidence, he pulled the patient's fancy pink nightdress decorously back over the flaccid flesh. He was middle-aged, and highly competent, while his sage, reliable expression and considered manner might easily have got him cast as a surgeon in a TV soap opera. 'You've a sound constitution, Mrs Bevan, and you're very fit,' he continued, while forbearing to add, 'for a woman of your age.' In his experience, that usually damaged the compliment for a woman over fifty. Instead he ended with: 'That helps a lot with recovery, you know.'

'In my case, the fitness will be from tennis and swimming, I expect. We've got a court at home. *En tout cas*, it is. And an indoor heated pool,' Dilys elaborated rapidly. She had a compulsion always to impress strangers with the range – and often the cost – of the family possessions. It was a necessary boost to her confidence, increasingly so over the last few years when that confidence had reached a very low ebb, for determinable reasons.

'Have you, now?' Tranter responded. 'Well, they should come in handy quite soon, especially the pool.' The information the lady had volunteered wasn't anything that would materially alter the size of his ultimate bill. It was good, though, to have it affirmed that a patient owned better than the basic wherewithal, if his fees exceeded what her health insurance company considered seemly.

To his credit, even after he had studied the X-rays and scans a second time, Mervyn Tranter had been hesitant about moving Mrs Bevan from the hospital where she had first been taken as a casualty, and across to St Olaf's Private Nursing Home. If she had stayed where she was, she could have had the operation performed free through the National Health Service by one of the consultant surgeons there. But her husband had wanted her switched to St Olaf's, which was much closer to their home. There she could command the services of a chosen surgeon, and comforts as good as those of a four-star hotel, while also enjoying more frequent visits from her family doctor. Despite his continuing unease because of the unpredictability of internal bleeding, in the end, Tranter had sanctioned the move. The operation had happily been completed without mishap.

'So when can I go home, then?' the patient enquired, plaintively.

'Oh, let me see.' He frowned. 'Where are we now? Monday, is it? Yes, well, with luck and a following wind, I should think we can have those stitches out on Thursday, and set you free the same day. Yes, Thursday. That's so long as you go on improving at the rate you're doing at the moment. I'd like you to walk in the corridor as much as you can today. Use a stick, if you need, for the ankle. Sit up in a chair afterwards, so long as it doesn't tire you. And do remember to keep those elastic stockings on.' He gave an understanding smile, and pulled the stethoscope away from his neck. 'Anyway, I'm sure Sister and her team will keep an eye on you, won't you, Sister?'

'Oh, yes, Mr Tranter, you can rely on that, all right.' Sister Pansy Watkyn, in voluminous, crisp white uniform and starched cap, was a thirty-six-year-old, triumphant brunette of formidable proportions, with a wide halo of frizzed hair, a busy pair of eyes, dimpled cheeks, and Cupid's-bow lips. Despite her impressive girth, she moved with the grace of a battleship breasting still waters. Studiously, she rearranged both her expression and the sheet covering her patient.

Before this, she had been exhibiting the deference proper in a senior nurse when in the presence of a visiting surgeon. Now she projected a nice mixture of active comprehension of orders received, with a determination to carry them out with thoroughness as well as compassion. Well, you could scarcely ask for more.

Tranter knew Sister Watkyn well, and admired her professionalism. He did a lot of private operations, in addition to his NHS contract work at one of the county hospitals – though not the one where Dilys had been taken after the accident. He liked operating at St Olaf's, which was a fairly new establishment, with two well-equipped theatres. It also seemed to get more than its fair share of good local nursing staff.

'The patient had a lucky escape,' the surgeon confided later to the sister, as he wrote his report and orders, standing at the high desk in the third-floor nurses' station along the corridor.

'You said she has a good constitution, Mr Tranter.'

'Hm.' He put the top back on his fountain pen. 'What probably saved her life was never having had a baby. Internal bleeding in a pelvis full of adhesions is always tricky.'

'Due to long-standing endometriosis, was that?'

'Quite right, Sister.' He looked up from his rereading with a commending expression.

'We've kept Mrs Bevan on the maximum dose of doxepin. That's her regular antidepressant, sir.'

'Yes. I remember that was at the request of her GP.' He looked at the patient notes again and pouted. 'Her spirits seem high enough.'

'I thought that, too, sir.'

'Might be in her long-term interests if we try reducing the dose from tomorrow, perhaps. I'll have a word with the good doctor.' He smiled at Sister Watkyn. 'I remember your telling me, you used to be a theatre nurse. We can't tempt you back again?'

'Not to the NHS, sir, no. And the private sector would mean late evening work. I can choose the hours in my job here.'

'I understand.' There was no wedding ring, he noticed, but that didn't mean anything these days. Her reply implied she might have a child at home, or an aged mother, perhaps. Pity, the surgeon mused – pretty face, too: he liked buxom women.

'It's Barbara Bevan, isn't it? Fancy a cup of tea or something before you go up? Your mother's having a nap at the moment. She's only just dropped off. I'd give her half an hour, if I were you.' Sister Watkyn smiled at the slim, pretty teenager who had been waiting for the lift on the ground floor as she got out of it herself. The sister was still wearing uniform, but now under a light, open raincoat. She had removed the white cap, and was carrying a big, black leather handbag. It was just after four o'clock.

'Oh, I'd love a sandwich,' said Barbara, pushing a lock of long flaxen hair away from her face, while moving from one foot to the other. She was a study in nervous energy. 'I missed lunch because of a French lesson. Can I get something here?'

'There's a self-service coffee shop in the basement, didn't you know? It's not bad. I'll keep you company for a bit, if you like?' the sister volunteered in a convincingly ingratiating manner. 'We can walk down. It's quicker.' The lift door had already closed.

'But aren't you going off duty?'

'Yes, but I'm not in any hurry. Got a bit of shopping to do on the way home, that's all. Why don't you call me Pansy? Silly name, but I've had it too long to change now.'

'I like it. It's original.' The girl moved half sideways as she descended the carpeted stairs, springing the lower foot up again each time it touched down, as if she were exercising rather than just aiming to reach the bottom.

'Names of flowers used to be all the rage for girls years ago,' said Sister Watkyn. 'I'm talking of long before my time, of course. But I had an auntie called Pansy. She was my mother's favourite sister. She died early, and I was named after her. I've always liked your name. Do you have another besides Barbara?'

'Yes. Mummy always says it was Barbara Anne pretty well from the day she conceived me.'

'I see,' the sister responded thoughtfully. 'So what are you going to have? There's hot food if you want?'

The two were now at the counter in the nearly empty coffee shop. The low, indirect lighting, grass-papered walls, and wooden tables, with basket-weave armchairs around them, gave the place much more the atmosphere of a village tea shop than a hospital cafeteria, allowing only that it was windowless.

'A cottage cheese sandwich and a yoghurt will be fine,' said the girl, picking up a plastic tray and zestfully fanning herself with it before placing it on the counter rails.

'Not difficult to know how you keep that svelte-like figure,' mused her overweight companion. 'Well, I'll just have tea, I think, and perhaps a chocolate biscuit,' she completed, making a face – mouth and button nose squeezing closer together as though it had hurt her to utter the last words.

'Please let me pay for both of us.' Barbara had produced a purse from a breast pocket of the cream blouse she was wearing, over tight-fitting blue jeans and open sandals.

'No, no. We'll go Dutch,' the nurse insisted firmly, opening her bag.

When they were seated at a corner table, Barbara said, 'Mummy told me on the phone this morning she'll be out on Thursday.'

'No reason why not. She's a model patient, your mother. And she's come through a nasty experience with flying colours.' She sipped her tea before continuing: 'Your mother was telling me you'll be going to university next year.'

'If I get enough high-grade A Levels, yes.' The girl was consuming her sandwich with obvious relish.

'I'm sure you will. How many GCSEs did you get?'

'Eleven.'

'Eleven? That's very good. Which school d'you go to?'

'You wouldn't know it. It's not the one I'm at now.' Barbara wiped her mouth with a paper napkin, and sat up even straighter than before. 'My new one's not a proper school. It's called Prince's Academy. Just a small, sixth-form crammer.

Daddy took me out of the other one. He said they weren't stretching my mind enough. He was right, probably. He usually is. I'm having extra lessons in the hols, too. From tutors at the crammer.'

'Like you did today?'

'That's right. It's a drag, really. But Daddy's keen on me going to university.'

'Which one?' She had unwrapped the chocolate biscuit, her eyes devouring it ahead of her lips.

'Well, I'll try for Oxford or Cambridge. That's Daddy's choice again. But if I don't get either, I'm putting down for Manchester first, with Bristol second. Daddy wants me to read law.'

'And eventually become a lawyer?'

'Yes.' The word came out with no enthusiasm as the girl shifted in her seat and took the top off her yoghurt carton.

'But you want to do something else?'

Barbara looked up, her eyes sparkling. 'I want to act. But you see, you can do a drama degree at Manchester or Bristol. Daddy's agreed if I end up at either of them, I can apply to switch to drama in the second year. That's if I pass the first year law exams, and if I still want to switch then.'

'He's hoping you won't, I suppose?' questioned the nurse, munching her biscuit.

Barbara shrugged. 'Yeah. He says he's never met a starving lawyer.'

'That must be true enough. What does your mother think?'

'Mummy?' Barbara looked momentarily nonplussed, as though the question had more than just surprised her. 'Oh, I see. Oh, it doesn't matter really what Mummy thinks. It's Daddy who calls the shots in our family. He's super, though. A super father.' The first super had been half defensive, the second, heavily emphasized, was almost aggressively affirmative.

'I'm sorry I haven't met him yet,' said Sister Watkyn, who was nevertheless determined to do so soon.

'He came to see Mummy yesterday, about this time, or a bit later probably.'

'After I came off duty, I expect.'

Barbara scraped the bottom of the yoghurt carton with her spoon. 'He couldn't stay long. He never has much time to spare. Not even on Sundays.'

The sister smiled. 'Except for you?'

'Me, and the business,' the girl returned, bashfully, and omitting to include her mother in her father's priorities. 'You know he owns one of the biggest electrical contractors in Wales?' she continued. 'Built it from practically nothing, as well. That was when he came out of the RAF, after twenty-one years. He always says he was lucky then. Being in the right place at the right time. That was seventeen years ago, at the start of a building boom. But I don't believe it was luck. I think it was because he was ready to work harder than anyone else.'

'So this all happened soon after you were born?' Sister Watkyn drank some more of her tea.

'Yes. I was born in a camper van, somewhere in Germany, on Palm Sunday, April 8th. Nobody knows exactly where. What a zany start in life. They were coming home on Daddy's last leave.'

'Fancy that,' said the nurse, memorizing the date. She had already worked out the year 'And did your father start the electrical company himself?'

Barbara frowned. 'Well, not exactly. It'd been started already by an ex-RAF friend. He'd asked Daddy to go in with him as soon as he left the service. I think the business had been going about two years before that.'

'Here in Cardiff, was it?'

'Yes, in Ely somewhere. That's why it's called Ely Electrical Contractors. It's moved twice since then, further out.'

'Because it got bigger?'

'Oh, miles bigger. At the time, the friend was doing pretty well. That's why he needed a partner. Then the friend died, and Daddy was left to run everything on his own.'

'He couldn't have known much about business if he'd been in the RAF all that time,' Sister Watkyn observed sympathetically.

'He didn't. Had to learn it by doing it, he says. But they'd just landed two big contracts. One was to do all the electrics on a huge housing estate in Newport. The other was to do the same at a big new factory somewhere. Bridgend, I think.'

'And after that, your father never looked back?'

'That's what everyone says. It's a wonderful success story, isn't it?'

'I'll say. You must be very proud of him.' The nurse was becoming increasingly aware that Barbara simply idolized her father. She found it wholesome, in these times, that a girl of that age, intelligent, possibly a bit headstrong, and certainly with a determined streak, was prepared to defer to her father's wishes over the direction of her whole future career. There had been no resentment in her voice when she had explained what she had agreed about first reading law at the university, and only hopefully switching to drama later, all at her father's behest. This was despite her own clear yearning to become an actress. 'Do you think you look more like your father than you do your mother?' Sister Watkyn continued, changing the subject slightly. She had already noted that the resemblance to the so-called mother was nil.

The girl hesitated. 'Probably. I never think I look much like either of them, really. I'm more Daddy's colouring, I suppose. And I've got more of his temperament. We're both kind of, well, get-up-and-go people.' She was fingering a glass container in the centre of the table, and the corners of the small packets of sugar it was holding. 'Mummy's quieter. Well, you know her.'

'Less demonstrative, you mean?'

'Right.' Barbara looked up, and at the same time again brushed the long hair back from her forehead, exposing one of the pair of plain gold earrings she was wearing. 'She wasn't always like she is now,' she went on, playing with the earring. 'Or so Daddy says. She was . . . she was ill. Not long after I was born. Well, about two years after, I think.'

'What kind of illness was it? Something serious?' Sister Watkyn sounded professionally solicitous rather than merely inquisitive.

'I think it was a nervous breakdown of some kind.' Barbara frowned, and folded her arms tightly across her boyishly flat chest. 'She was in a . . . a special hospital for a long time.'

'But she got over it, all right. That's obvious,' said the sister cheerfully.

'In a way. She always says she's been less certain of herself since then. Is that the way a nervous breakdown affects people?'

'Sometimes.'

'She's not stupid or . . . or anything,' the girl went on, watching the other's eyes. 'And she's a terribly caring person. I mean, she does a lot for charities. Only she never takes any credit. She leaves that to other people. Oh, and she's always giving blood. Is that OK at her age?'

Sister Watkyn smiled. 'Of course it is, and for a long time after her age. I hope you do the same thing.'

'Yes. Are they as short of blood as they're always saying?'

'Mm. Especially of the rarer groups.'

'I'm just boring old O negative. Everybody's that, aren't they?'

'Not quite everybody, no.' Not your mother, for a start, and not your much-loved father, either, Sister Watkyn thought to herself. Their uncommon but mutual blood group had been recorded on Dilys Bevan's hospital data sheet, at her husband's insistence, in case Dilys had needed an emergency transfusion. By volunteering her own blood group, Barbara had affirmed something as beyond further doubt in the nurse's mind.

Sister Watkyn had once done a course in haematology. Whether or not Mervyn Tranter could have been mistaken when he said that Dilys had never had a baby, because of their common blood group, neither Dilys nor her husband could possibly have been a parent to Barbara.

3

'I'm home, my lovely, scrumptious, sexy lover,' Pansy Watkyn called, as she struggled to pull the key out of the front-door lock. Her arms were full of shopping.

'Hello, my purring puss. You're late. I had to make my own tea,' a rich bass voice responded from the living room at the rear of the bungalow. As Pansy bustled in from the hall, Evan Rees, the beefy owner of the voice, looked around from the depths of the sofa where he was watching cricket on the television. As he moved, a lock of dark, wavy hair fell languidly over his broad brow, while the narrowed eyes set in a sort of seductive leer above the strong mouth and jutting, film-star jaw.

'You did say you'd be working, my angel,' she pleaded.

'I was. I am.' He waved an arm dismissively. 'I just stopped to see the score, that's all. After I finished tea.' The accent was a mix of acquired upper-crust English and native Welsh, affected but still melodious.

'That's why I didn't hurry back. Not to interrupt.' She sounded contrite, this normally assertive woman, known to her underlings for her arrogant ways.

Rees was two years younger than Pansy. He was tall, as well as ruggedly good-looking. The clothes he had on – a jazzily designed, short-sleeved sports shirt, open to the waist, blue linen shorts, and backless canvas slippers – were exposing a good deal of his bronzed, hairy body. 'So come here and be ravished, you naughty nurse,' he said, opening his arms to her, but almost immediately regretting his loose, unguarded use of the term ravish.

Her face had lit up with pleasure. 'Oh, Evan, I'm ever so

28

sorry about your tea. I should have been here earlier. I don't really deserve ravishing,' she giggled, hurrying across the room to him, kicking off her shoes *en route*, and already starting to breathe like an espresso coffee machine building for a climax. She fell on top of him, bringing some of the shopping she had balanced on the back of the sofa down with her. They kissed, with hands exploring and caressing, his hands with a good deal less insistence and facility than hers. 'Take me now, Evan, please,' she pleaded urgently, her lips close to his ear. Since her whole formidable weight was upon him, he was in too restrictive a position to do much about the request, even if he'd wanted, which, as it happened, he didn't.

'No, let's be strong-minded, and save that for later, my wonderful one,' he uttered, imitating a man selflessly depriving himself of his deepest desire, and in support of a finer purpose. 'I want you dearly, but I must work.' That was the finer purpose. He was using his last, but invariably effective resort. His work was the only reason she ever accepted for leaving him alone.

They had been lovers for two years. Rees's attitude towards her was suspiciously close to condescension. Pansy's attitude to him made it plain that he was her whole world, and that he could condescend as much as he liked, so long as he stayed with her.

They had met in a Cardiff singles bar when she had been at the stage, and the age, of despairing about landing a man of her own, especially one as young and dishy as this one. To her he was truly an Adonis who needed someone to care for him. He was well educated, witty and intelligent, with a glamorous occupation, and a sexual thirst seemingly as voracious as her own.

Pansy had accepted in about thirty seconds that this paragon met her dream specification, and he, lacking any vestige of modesty, had been the first to agree with her. But the sexual thirst was the one he would never be content to quench at the same fount for ever – or even for a reasonably lengthy period. It was true, though, that, at the time of their meeting, he had been nearly as desperate on his own account as Pansy had been on hers – which was why he had been frequenting singles bars.

After university, Rees had begun a quite promising career in journalism, working as a reporter on local, then national, newspapers. He had later unwisely opted to become a free-lance feature writer, an occupation for which he lacked both the special talent and the self-discipline to succeed, though he had been as unready to admit the fact then as he still was now. His besetting problem was indolence, a shortcoming that seldom matches the lifestyle of the self-employed.

Rees had known – and still knew – a clutch of women keen to sleep with him, but not one who was ready to main-tain him financially until his career took off again, which, in practice, most of them reluctantly accepted, was a prospect to be encouraged if unlikely to be achieved. Too many of his admirers were comfortably married, to all-providing hus-bands, to make life with an impecunious, self-employed writer a practicable proposition in any context, no matter how great his manly attributes. Indeed, there had been none, married or single, prepared even to try, before he had lighted upon the outsize Pansy, who made up in several other ways what she lacked in basic glamour – gratitude and generosity being only two of those ways. The overaccommodating nurse had even been close to accepting that it was unlikely he could ever marry her. Along the way, he had already married, and subsequently deserted, a woman who, he claimed, refused to divorce him for religious reasons.

'All right, my love, we'll save it for later. And it'll be mar-vellous. I'll make it marvellous, I promise,' Pansy whispered again, this time so close to his ear that it did something unnerving and peculiar to the inner membrane. Her heaving bosom was still pressed against his chest, while the hem of her uniform dress had remained pulled up to a level his sensitive nature found not so much indecorous as actually obscene.

'Bless you. I can hardly wait,' he answered, while the effort he was making to unpinion himself from under her made it clear that this last comment was not meant to be taken liter-ally. Sensible of this, Pansy rolled off him to the inside of the sofa, pulling the skirt down, and fluffing up her hair.

'You know, spontaneous sex is very good in prospect, if sometimes a trifle too athletic in practice,' he continued, with a grin, and in the lofty tone that usually amused her. He had not made the same comment to the woman visitor he had entertained here, on the sofa, earlier in the afternoon, but she had been pencil slim and more adapted to limited confines, also she hadn't been able to stay long. He rescued some of the shopping – a split bag of apples and a cellophaned stick of celery – from between the cushions.

'You used to say you liked it best spontaneous,' she replied, backing to the end of the sofa and swinging her feet to the floor. 'Anyway, you're marvellous wherever, and I can wait till tonight.' She leaned over and kissed him again, before taking charge of her abandoned purchases.

He gave a modest chuckle, justifiably modest since any strenuous physical effort in their love making was nowadays usually hers. 'Did you have a good day?' he asked, hoping she would soon find things to do in the kitchen.

'Yes. Oh, and I got you the cigarettes. Two hundred Gold Leaf, was that right?'

'You're spoiling me, as ever,' he replied, and meaning it deeply.

'Something interesting happened, too.' Her expression clouded momentarily. 'Oh, you didn't cut the grass, then?' She had just looked out beyond the open French windows. There was a sun lounger on the patio, though, and a book beside it, also an empty beer glass, and a tray with tea things on it.

He made a tutting noise. 'God, I knew there was something. But honestly, I've been so busy all day on the computer.' He checked the direction of her gaze. 'Or thinking outside,' he added quickly. 'But I'll do it before supper. Promise. I just need to bash out another five hundred words of deathless prose.'

'No, no. I'll do the lawn.' The disappointment hardly showed in her voice, and she had accepted once again the absolute priority of his work. But it was quite a small lawn, and he had promised.

31

Rees's hand now moved to his brow, and his eyes half closed as if he was finding the late afternoon sun too strong, or his previous exertions too debilitating. The last reason was the true one, but not in any sense that he could explain to Pansy. 'I only switched on the telly as you came in,' he added defensively.

'What are you writing today?' She made a show of looking around the room. 'I must dust in here before supper, as well,' she went on, before he could answer, and justifying her inspection which had really been to check that his desk computer in the corner was at least switched on: it was. Again, she inwardly upbraided herself for thinking it might not have been. 'It's always the same when the weather's dry and hot, isn't it?' she said. 'When the windows are open all day. Dust gets everywhere.' She looked about her once more. 'God, I'm so sick of this old furniture. It was contemporary when my mum and dad bought it, but that must have been forty years ago.'

'Oh, it's all right. Very . . . very serviceable, really,' he said, lighting the last cigarette in the packet, confident he now had two hundred free ones in hand. He put an arm across her shoulder, while surreptitiously still following the cricket. Although he had said the opposite, he agreed with her about the furniture. He considered it all to be in unspeakably bad taste, but he avoided subjects that might lead to any of Pansy's disposable income being diverted to inessential channels – a heading that broadly encompassed everything that didn't include his own upkeep. 'No more news about the development?' he asked casually.

'No. But I still don't think it'll be approved,' she answered. Pansy had inherited the bungalow, number 5, Carmen Lane, from her parents, who were now both dead. The lane was a potholed cul-de-sac, unadopted by the local authority, and leading off the lower end of Station Road, Bryntaf. There were only the three bungalows in it, numbered 1, 3, and 5, and all on the eastern side of the road, which terminated in a field gate just beyond number 5. Like Station Road itself, the lane was part of the old, pre-salubrious Bryntaf. It was some years after the Second World War that developers had expanded the upper boundaries of the old village, making it into a well-elevated dormitory suburb of substantial houses, some of them *very* substantial, and allowing Bryntaf to compete in affluence with nearby modern Radyr and ancient Llandaff.

The twin-gabled bungalow was grey rendered, with a paved area behind a low wall at the front, with a concrete drive up to a wooden garage on one side. There was a modest-sized, oblong garden at the back, and the whole property was sheltered from number 3, the only immediate neighbour, by tall bushes – a convenient feature from Rees's viewpoint, since it stopped prying eyes from watching when he had a visitor during Pansy's absence. The fenced wasteland to the east and south of the property ran down to the curving railway line that ran along the valley bottom, a section that had not been considered for development until recent times because it was too close to the trains.

Pansy had sometimes thought of selling the bungalow, but not since she had joined St Olaf's. Despite its being in Bryntaf, a bungalow in Carmen Lane wouldn't fetch enough to buy anything better in a less exalted area, and the nursing home was only five minutes' drive away – or ten stops on the bus, if Evan needed her car. In a curious way, she would have felt uncomfortable about leaving the place, as well – ungrateful to her parents. This was why she was torn over her attitude to the current application of a property company to develop the area, while still accepting this might increase the value of existing properties if it went through.

Evan Rees had been the reason for Pansy's pressing need to increase her income a year before this, something she had eventually succeeded in doing, but without reducing the amount of time they could spend together. If it hadn't been for the last consideration, she could certainly have gone back to specialized theatre nursing, which paid better than her present job, except the hours didn't suit. She needed to be sure she could be with her Evan at times of day when he might otherwise find himself in singles bars.

It had been quite early in their relationship that Rees had come clean about his failed marriage – though not so early

33

that he judged it could have spoiled her ever-deepening regard for him. He had left it a bit longer before he explained to her that he was having difficulty in selling his work, due to a temporary recession in the market for good writing. That had been after he had left his small Cardiff flat and moved in with her, explaining at the time that what he needed most in the world was a quiet but fairly central base where he could write lucrative features in peace. She still believed that.

'So, is it the article for the *Daily Telegraph* you're doing?' she asked now, getting up and going to collect his tea tray and beer glass from the patio.

'Yes. I've nearly got it right, too. They'll love it.' It had been a long time since he had placed anything in the *Daily Telegraph*, just as he had never been directly commissioned to do anything by that paper or any of the other nationals. All his work was speculative. His forte was the production of whimsical commentaries on everyday topics, like gardening, home decorating, keeping cats, planning holidays, and easier ways of getting to work – he had rung the changes on the last topic with a commendable degree of inventiveness for a man who seldom actually went out to work himself, unless it was to visit a Cardiff library to check a fact. He had sold a few articles in the last year, mostly to regional magazines, but not nearly enough of them to justify the occupation he boasted.

'Can I see what you've written?' Pansy asked, as she came back from the kitchen, a yellow duster in her hand.

'Not yet, my petal. Not till I've had a chance to polish it.' He got up, switched off the television and began to move towards the computer. 'So what was this interesting thing that happened in your young life today?' he asked. Then he changed direction suddenly, swinging about and taking her in his arms. 'I know. A consultant groped you in the intensive care unit, giving new meaning to the expression. God, what you must have to endure, with a body as fetching as yours. Would you like me to knock his head off, the swine?' He began covering her face with kisses.

'It was nothing like that, Evan, honestly,' she answered with another giggle. 'And let go of me, I've got work to do.'

But he could see the compliment and the embrace had pleased her. He was mindful of the courtesies due, even though he had tired of Pansy physically some six months before this: intellectually he had found her a bore from the start.

Pansy had been pleased by her lover's extra attentions, and almost more so by what he had said about the consultant – which had made her redden guiltily. She had imagined that Mr Tranter just might have been about to make a pass at her this morning. When Rees released her, she went on with the dusting before asking in a matter-of-fact voice, 'By the way, where did you say that German reporter friend of yours works? You know, the one you had to give dinner to last month. That night you were so late. Freddie somebody.'

He had looked momentarily confused – then a touch apprehensive. 'Oh . . . oh, yes, Freddie Metz? He's on a paper in Frankfurt.'

'I thought so. You said you had to butter him up, because he could do you favours,' she went on, while removing the ornaments from the top of a bookcase one by one for dusting.

'That's right.' He remembered saying it, of course. He had been stony broke at the time, and had needed to say something convincing to get Pansy to give him the money to entertain the visitor in Cardiff.

'So could he find out about something that happened in Germany seventeen years ago? Something unusual. In the Düsseldorf area.' She had consulted an atlas in the Bryntaf bookshop on the way home, to find out where Rheindahlen was located.

Rees shrugged. 'I suppose so. If it was something that got in the newspapers.' He was seated in front of the computer now.

'I think it would have done.'

'And this is the interesting thing that happened today?'

'Part of it.'

'Have you got the date of this . . . this happening?' He was not particularly interested in what he assumed would be some parochial news item.

'Yes. Well, near enough the date. To a day or two. And

the place. It was a town near Düsseldorf, not Düsseldorf itself.' She had been polishing the face on a cheap toby jug which she now replaced on the mantelpiece as carefully as if it had been a Dresden shepherdess. 'It's to help a patient at St Olaf's,' she went on. 'Her husband used to be stationed near Düsseldorf. In the RAF. A very young baby disappeared a few days before they left.'

He looked up sharply. 'A baby snatch?'

'She thinks so.'

'So what's it got to do with the patient?'

Pansy swallowed. 'She was half sure her German cleaner was involved. She's always wanted to know if the baby was found, and . . . and if the cleaner was arrested . . . got sent to gaol . . . that sort of thing. I think she'd want to help the person if she'd been in trouble.'

'Taken her long enough to do anything about it. Seventeen years, you said?'

'It's because she's well off now and wasn't before. She'd pay for the information. Only she wouldn't want anyone to know she was making enquiries.'

Rees's interest was kindled at the prospect of reward. 'Well, if it's a research job for a rich do-gooder, I daresay I could handle it for her quietly, through Freddie. He'd need to go through a lot of newspapers. Back issues. Could be time-consuming. Expensive.' He paused, his brow furrowing. Of course, it would cost his friend nothing to have the paper's information department do the search, saying it was neces-sary background stuff for a current story. They'd most likely have everything logged on computer by subject in any case. It shouldn't take more than five minutes to check through every baby snatch in and around Düsseldorf over a year, let alone over a day or two. It wasn't that common a crime. So the expense would be whatever the client was good for. 'You sure that's all it is?' he pressed.

'How d'you mean?' She was dusting the top of the tele-vision set, her face away from him. She never had been good at lying, but she didn't want to tell him the truth now, or ever, come to that. She had pulled off the other business a year ago without Evan knowing anything about it. This was potentially much more promising.

Rees shrugged. 'I didn't mean anything, really. Just wondered.' He looked at his watch with some ceremony. 'Bad time to ring Freddie now. I'll do it in the morning. Just put down the date and place for me. Did the patient give you her cleaner's name?'

'Yes. It's . . . it's Carla Resen.' She spelled out the name for him to write down. She had made it up on the way home. There had been a German girl at her school called Resen.

'Shouldn't be a problem,' he said.

'You won't forget, in the morning?' She was obviously hinting that she'd have preferred him to ring now.

'Of course not. Promise.' He made a kissing movement with his lips, followed by a big smile. He needed to make the call to Germany when Pansy was out of the house for several reasons – not the least being that his friend Metz's first name wasn't Freddie; it was Freda.

4

'Sister Watkyn. Well, I never. So lovely to see you. It's Pansy, isn't it? Come in,' said Dilys Bevan, opening the front door wider.

'I was on my way home, and I thought I'd just pop in, on the off chance. To see how you're getting on, Mrs Bevan. I can't stay long.'

'Oh, it's so kind of you to think of me. You'll have a cup of tea?'

'No, thanks. And I'm not interrupting anything, am I? You haven't got visitors?'

'No, no. I'm by myself for once. I'm sorry Barbara isn't here. Or my husband. He's in Hereford today, on business. And Barbara has extra tuition on Tuesdays. They'll be ever so sorry not to see you.'

'Never mind. You're the important one.' Pansy hadn't needed telling about the others. She knew about Barbara's tutorial arrangements, and a call to Huw Bevan's office had established his movements for today. She had found out from Barbara, some weeks back, that Mrs Bevan's cleaning lady didn't come on Tuesdays.

'You'll excuse me being in this robe. I was going to swim later.' Dilys smoothed the sides of the elegant, long blue-grey garment with both hands.

'Nothing to excuse. Looks lovely on you. Shantung, is it?'

'That's right. I got it in London. Harvey Nichols.'

'You can always tell good clothes, can't you, Mrs Bevan? By the cut as well as the material. And I'm glad you're swimming. How long now since you left St Olaf's? Over two weeks, isn't it?'

'Nearly three.'

'Time flies. But you're looking fine, and moving well, too. No problems, then?'

'None at all.'

'Are you still on the smaller dose of your old pills?'

'My pep-up pills? Yes. I only take the one at night now. None in the daytime. And I'm feeling wonderful,' Dilys responded, touching the younger woman's well-nourished arm. She had closed the door and was guiding the visitor through the wide, close-carpeted hallway of Hill House, the most substantial of the six superior, individually designed properties that made up Hillside Rise, a road which the local estate agent's invariably referred to as Bryntaf's most exclusive section. And if wealth equated with exclusivity, the last description was certainly warranted.

The Lutyens-style Hill House stood in over three acres of grounds, with a fifteen-foot cupressus hedge marking the boundaries. The cupressus trees had been planted only six years before, and they were expected to double their present height in a further six, giving their owners even more exclusivity than they enjoyed already – by excluding even more sunlight from sections of their domain. It was immaterial that anyone able to overlook a fifteen-foot hedge would have to be riding on the top deck of a double-decker bus, and standing up as well – except no conveyance as plebeian as a double-decker bus, or even a single-decker one, ever passed along Hillside Rise, with its specially laid deep-pink road surface, and carefully manicured wide grass verges.

'The good weather's helped with my recuperation, our doctor says,' Dilys continued. 'I was sitting outside when you rang. Shall we go out again now? It's such a lovely afternoon still.' They moved through the opulent, low-ceilinged drawing room more slowly than the hostess's ambulatory state prescribed, but she was anxious that the room's merits and contents should be properly appreciated.

'Lovely lounge you've got,' Pansy offered, on cue.

'Yes. We like it. Elegant but cosy.' Dilys's approving gaze moved from the heavily framed landscape of heroic proportions hanging above the marble fireplace, to the immense

Persian rug in the centre. Elegant armchairs and occasional tables were set to approach, but not to encroach upon, this last pristine, untrammelled oriental surface. 'That's my important collection of snuff boxes in the Louis Fourteenth cabinet,' she went on, her hand indicating the two prized possessions she had deftly advertised in one breath. 'And through there's the conservatory,' she continued, now pointing to the right. 'It's one of a pair, actually. The swimming pool's in the other one, on the left of the terrace. The pool's on its own so as not to get condensation in the house. I don't understand how that works, but it does.'

'Fancy.' The nurse, who had never been inside the house or the grounds before, was pleased that she had under rather than overestimated the family's wealth.

A few minutes later the two women were on the terrace ensconced in white recliners with deeply padded blue cushions. This was a wide area partly shaded by a long blue and white canopy. The canopy also gave protection from the sun to the southern aspect of the drawing room behind it.

'Your husband must have been very successful to have earned a house as beautiful as this,' said Pansy.

'Earned is the right word, too,' agreed Dilys proudly. 'He built his company on his own, you know?'

'And before that, I remember you saying Mr Bevan served a long time in the regular RAF?'

'For over twenty years, yes. You're sure you won't have some tea, Pansy?'

'Yes, positive, thanks, Mrs Bevan. I had a cup before I came off duty.' She smiled, while urging herself to get on with the business that had really brought her here at this carefully judged time. 'And your husband's last posting was in Rheindahlen, Germany?'

'Yes. West Germany, they called it then. I expect Barbara told you that, did she? She's very proud of her daddy. They have a . . . a wonderful relationship.' Dilys hesitated for a moment, evident indecision reflected in her eyes. It seemed that she had it in mind to enlarge on the last point, but if that was so, the intention had been abandoned before she went on: 'Barbara was born the day we left Germany. On the way home. It was quite a drama. Did she tell you about that as well?'

Pansy frowned. 'As a matter of fact, it wasn't Barbara who told me any of it. It . . . it was a German reporter. He came to St Olaf's last week. He asked me about your husband. And you.' She paused. 'That's the other reason I dropped in today, really. To tell you. Well, to ask you what you want me to do about him.'

Dilys blinked several times. 'I don't understand. Why would a German reporter want to know about my husband and me?'

'And about Barbara, as well. Where she was born. He knew her date of birth. He'd looked that up, he told me. Anyway, I couldn't help him about the other, even if I'd wanted to, which I didn't. Well, not till I'd spoken to you first.'

There was a stiffening in the older woman's facial muscles. 'But how did he know anything about us in the first place?' she demanded.

'I think it was through the report in the *Western Mail*. About your accident. Someone told me it was quite a long report, the family being so prominent in South Wales. I didn't see it myself. Did it mention about Mr Bevan being in the RAF?'

'I think so, but –'

'So it probably said about him serving in Germany. In Rheindahlen. And about Barbara being born on the way home.'

'Yes, perhaps.'

'Well, I think the Rheindahlen paper must have picked all that up. This reporter was from Düsseldorf. That's not far from Rheindahlen.'

Dilys looked confused. Her hands were tightly grasping the plastic arms of her chair. 'Who did he talk to besides you, Pansy?'

'It was only me, Mrs Bevan. He was waiting for me in the car park last Friday. He'd found out I'd looked after you, after the operation.'

'How did he do that?'

'Oh, you know what reporters are. They're into everything, aren't they? There's no privacy where newspapers are concerned.'

Dilys appeared bewildered but not convinced. 'But why didn't he come to me? Or my husband?'

'Because he doesn't want you to know what he looks like, or his name, or anything.'

'How d'you mean, Pansy? You're making it sound as if there's something, er . . . what's the word . . . sinister in it all.'

Pansy steeled herself even more. This was it – the moment when she had to expose everything, with no turning back afterwards. 'There is something sinister, I'm afraid. To be honest, I believe this man could make terrible trouble for you and your family. Only don't worry, I can stop him if you want. I know that for sure. Tell me, do you remember a woman called Heller? Frau Sonya Heller. She's a midwife. She says she knows you.'

The effect on Dilys of this deliberate lie was devastating. She fell back in her chair as if someone had struck her a heavy body blow. The blood had drained from her face. 'Oh, no. Please God, no,' she uttered despairingly. She tried to swallow, but failed. Her breathing suddenly became loud and irregular, her eyes staring about wildly. Then, suddenly, her hands flew to cover her mouth, as she bent forwards, gagging, and on the brink of throwing up.

The nurse was beside her in a second, arms around her erstwhile patient. 'Lean over, Mrs Bevan. Deep breath. Now out slowly . . . And again . . . Well done. Better now, are you?' Dilys looked up at her plaintively as Pansy went on. 'Good. Now relax those tight tummy muscles. Do that breathing movement the physio showed you at St Olaf's . . . All right, now? So lean back again on the cushions. Take it easy for a bit. We can't have you undoing all the good progress you've made.'

It was nearly a minute before Dilys spoke, and the words she uttered were only just audible – delivered in a low, breathy tone. 'He said Frau Heller knew me? This man. The reporter?'

'Yes. You did know her, didn't you, Mrs Bevan?' Pansy

42

waited for a reply, and while the other woman offered none in words, there was a kind of eloquence – and answer enough – in the tears that were now coursing down her face.

'Well, don't worry. It's not as bad as it seems.' Pansy gave a comforter's smile, while she was scarcely able to disguise or contain the rush of satisfaction welling inside her. From the moment it was clear that this first part of her deduction was true, she knew that the whole of it had to be. The scam was going to be a piece of cake, much easier than the last one. She was glad she hadn't waited till Dilys Bevan had been stronger. She had considered delaying longer, but eventually dismissed the idea, despite professional misgivings. The woman was physically quite strong enough already to withstand a mild shock. Going back to the old dosage of her antidepressant pills would bridge any gap, and do her no harm. After all, it was Pansy herself who had suggested the doctors reduce the dose postoperatively, something that helped quash her lingering professional qualms now. The hard fact to be faced was that if Mrs Bevan hadn't been emotionally a bit unstable, she might never have capitulated the way she had done, with guilt written all over her face.

'There's really nothing for you to worry about, Mrs Bevan,' Pansy reiterated. 'You or your family. Let's get that clear from the start. You're quite safe.'

'But Frau Heller –'

'Has been to prison,' Pansy interrupted.

'To prison. What for?'

'For kidnapping a newborn baby.'

Dilys drew in a breath sharply, as though she was in pain. 'When did she do that?'

'Sixteen years ago. When she was released, still protesting her innocence, she tried to sell her story to the newspapers. But no one was interested. At least not as the story stood.'

'Was . . . was the baby she took found again?'

'Oh, yes. Within a week. Unharmed, of course. They always are, aren't they? Looked after so carefully, too.'

'But . . . but she didn't steal it for herself?'

'No. It was for a woman who desperately needed a baby. She paid Frau Heller.'

Dilys made a whimpering sound. 'And this was sixteen years ago?' Repeating the fact seemed to provide her with some kind of consolation.

'Yes. Frau Heller served eighteen months of a three-year sentence. The woman she sold the baby to was treated more lightly, because they thought she was . . . mentally disturbed. She was detained in a state institution and given compulsory psychiatric treatment. That can last a long time, of course.' She paused for the fact to sink in. 'Still, she was lucky not to go to gaol proper.' Pansy noted the other woman's pained reaction to her last words as she went on: 'They weren't so understanding to Frau Heller. She had no excuse for what she'd done. The judge said she should have known better, being a qualified midwife and everything. He said she should have persuaded the woman to have counselling.'

Dilys nodded slowly. 'But this has nothing to do with my husband and me. It can't have,' she said, but in a voice singularly lacking in conviction. 'What reason did this man have for saying we knew Frau Heller?'

'There have been two other previous cases of baby snatching from hospitals in the area where he lives, and he believes you . . . well, that you may know something about the first of them. It happened seventeen years ago.' She was offering something nearer to the truth now, and in the way she had practised, putting the case that was going to earn her a fortune. 'Frau Heller had connections with both hospitals at the times of the kidnappings,' she added.

'The babies were both taken from hospitals?' Dilys interjected, despite herself, then wished she had stayed silent.

'I think so. Do you think they weren't? Is that because you do know something about them? Or one of them? The first one?'

Dilys shook her head, but made no audible reply.

'The police tried to connect Frau Heller with the other two crimes when they investigated the third, but they couldn't find any evidence, except she was on the spot when they happened. She went on denying she was connected with any of them.'

44

'I don't understand. The other two babies, they were found as well?'

'One was. But not the first to be taken. That was a girl, and she's never been seen since.' The speaker paused for a second. 'After reading about your accident, and all the other details about the family, this reporter who came to see me, he did some research on his own. He knows the baby girl was stolen the day before you left for the UK. He got the baby's profile from the records. Her blood group, and distinguishing marks. From that, he knows the baby had a pear-shaped birthmark on her upper left arm, like the one he's seen on Barbara's arm.'

'He's met Barbara?'

'Not properly, he hasn't. He got one of her schoolmates to point her out to him on some pretext, then he stopped her in the street and asked her the way to somewhere. But he saw the birthmark all right. He hasn't been able to check where you and your husband say she was born, the village where you said the local midwife helped you. But even you don't know the name of that, do you, Mrs Bevan?'

'No. It . . . it was quite small, and . . . and dark when we got there . . . and, and –'

'Well, I'm afraid the reporter doesn't believe it exists.'

'He has no right –'

'Of course he hasn't. But I've told you, there's no need to worry. There's a simple answer to everything.'

'What is it?'

'Let me finish, and I'll tell you. But you'd better know all the facts first. The reporter also has the names of two other RAF staff sergeants who served in your husband's squadron with him. Both lived in married quarters at the Rheindahlen base the same time as you. He hasn't got their UK addresses yet, but it probably wouldn't be hard to find them through official channels.'

'But why would he need them?'

'To find out if they remember you being nine months pregnant when you left the base. They, or their wives, more likely. It's not something you could have hidden very easily, is it? He also has the name of the RAF woman doctor who

45

would have supervised your prenatal care. According to the Medical Directory, she's in practice in Northumberland now. Don't worry, he hasn't tried to contact any of these people. Not yet.' She paused. 'Lastly, before he came here, he went to see the real parents of the kidnapped girl. They live in Zürich now. He wouldn't tell me their name. The stolen baby was the wife's first born. She's had two more children since.'

'She was married? It was her first baby?' Dilys half whispered, in evident surprise.

'That's right. She still wants her child back, too, and punishment for those who took her. She's very bitter, apparently.'

'Has the reporter told her what he's found out about . . . ?' Dilys couldn't bring herself to finish the question.

'About Barbara? No.'

Hands clasped tightly across her bosom, Dilys begged: 'What can I do to stop him, Pansy? I've got to stop him, you see? You'll help me, won't you?' Her upper teeth bit harshly into her lower lip. She was afraid and in a panic – and so blinded by her plight that she hadn't yet thought of others she should turn to besides the woman at her side. This was exactly as Pansy had planned.

The nurse knew that her victim's words had been as good as a confession. A large part of the story she had told had been invented. But it had been built upon a supposition which had now been confirmed as a horrendous truth.

The visiting German reporter Pansy had described didn't exist. The genuine information she owned had been unearthed by Evan Rees's journalist friend in Düsseldorf, and under a quite different pretext from any she had been describing. Fifteen years ago the Rheindahlen midwife Sonya Heller had been convicted of trading in babies – not kidnapping. She had been heavily fined, and gaoled for a short term. Pansy didn't know whether she was alive or dead. There had been no kidnaps, and no family that moved to Zürich, but the contemporary newspaper reports had shown that Frau Heller had been suspected of carrying on her secret trade for many years, and unsupported evidence had been offered that she had sold babies to foreigners.

There remained no doubt in Pansy's mind that Barbara Anne Bevan had been bought at birth and sold to a couple who couldn't let the fact be known today, any more than they could have done when it had taken place. And now the scene was set for the kill.

'Oh, we can stop him easily, Mrs Bevan,' the nurse said with assurance, brushing imaginary dust from her snow-white skirt. She looked up and smiled. 'I'll handle everything for you. It's just a matter of money, that's all.' She watched as Dilys's faltering fingers withdrew a blue capsule from the silver snuff box she had taken from the pocket of her gown. 'Shall I get you some water to take with your pill?' It was certainly a good moment to reinstitute daytime doses, she decided coolly.

5

Only a Norman castle and a fourteenth-century church survive to witness that Cardiff city centre stands on old foundations. All other building there is post 1850, from the time when coal became king, and when the city grew to be the most important port in the world. It was between the middle and the end of the century that the Welsh capital's narrow medieval dirt lanes and alleys were gradually transformed into paved and covered shopping arcades, of which there are more such here than in any other British city. It was during the same prosperous period, too, that Cardiff acquired its covered central market, stretching between two of its principal, and oldest, streets.

The brashness of the market still balances the elegance of the arcades. Its huge ground floor, and wide upper gallery, offers thrifty citizens all manner of necessities and local delicacies. It's a bustling, dynamic, thundering emporium, under an echoing, single-span iron roof with alternating glass and wooden panels, and an abundance of mahogany as well as wrought-iron fitments. Trade has been brisk and elbow room at a premium here, for customer and stallholder alike, since long before the introduction of sell-by dates, and modern shopping malls with fancy atriums – and aisles that are the retail equivalent of motorways.

Just as eleven o'clock on a Saturday morning might well be the perfect time to experience the true vibrancy of the Cardiff central market, it's indisputably the most imperfect one on which to have to begin a murder investigation there. But this was what thirty-eight-year-old Detective Chief Inspector Merlin Parry of the South Wales police was ordered to do at shortly before that hour on Saturday, September 30th – nearly three weeks after Pansy Watkyn's visit to Hill House.

When the cellphone in his pocket burped at 10.45, Parry, and a colleague from uniform branch, had been attending an early-morning meeting with officers of the neighbouring Gwent Constabulary in Newport, together with chamber of commerce representatives, and officials from local banks.

The group was supposed to be examining ways to stem the growing number of ram raids on, specifically, tobacco shops and bank cashpoints – except purposeful discussion was being thwarted by two undeniable considerations. Modern South Wales is served by a network of fast, interlocking modern highways to facilitate trade and tourism, but which might easily have been designed by criminals for the purpose of expediting swift getaways. That was the first fact which militated against easy apprehension of villains in flight. The second was that if, in an endeavour to catch raiders in the act, the two already overstretched police forces staked out even half the target shops and banks, there would be no police left to do anything else like protect the very young, the very old, and the rest of the community, many of whose members, someone at the meeting had remarked wryly, didn't smoke, or own bank cards, or for that matter, bank accounts.

Parry had not been sorry to be given a pressing and irresistible reason for leaving the meeting. Newport is eleven miles due east of Cardiff, and he covered the distance in just over as many minutes.

'We've stopped people going into the market, boss. Inspector Powell, from uniform, he closed this entrance, and the other one in St Mary Street. That's when he got here at 10.46. The market superintendent's being very cooperative over that, and other things, but he's got his problems, of course,' provided the ample Detective Sergeant Gomer Lloyd, in nearly one breath, as Parry alighted from his car on the concourse outside the market's imposing eastern entrance. The sergeant had arrived some minutes earlier, but he had come back out of the building to meet Parry, with whom he'd been in touch several times already by phone. 'We've been making loud hailer announcements inside, asking people to come forward if they saw anyone leaving in a hurry earlier on. There's a police information point set up at both exits,' Lloyd went on.

'So what about people leaving the building?'

'We've just started letting them, boss, like you ordered. They're being asked if they've been up to the gallery, and we're taking the names and addresses of those who have. Anyone known to us, or suspicious-looking, is being questioned.'

'OK. Better announce out here that shoppers will be allowed in again soon. That should help the market superintendent. We'll need to keep part of the gallery closed for a bit, probably, but we'll be in trouble with traders if we keep people out for longer than needed.' The Cardiff Chamber of Commerce representative Parry had been sitting next to at the Newport meeting had been hinting about police imperviousness to retailers' problems. 'And we've got the victim's name confirmed?' asked Parry.

'Yes, boss. And we've got the weapon.'

'Right, so let's get on with it.'

The two moved off through the crowd in the wake of a burly uniformed constable who parted the way with the ease of a tank ploughing through opposing infantry.

Frustrated shoppers and curious idlers had gathered in increasing numbers here, in Trinity Street. Some were grumbling, or exchanging rumours, or embellishing unsupported fact. A few latecomers were convinced that they were involved in the filming of a fictional scene for television. These had expectantly watched a procession of uniformed and civilian participants carrying equipment, and emptying out of two police minibuses, assorted police cars, a dilapidated Land Rover, Lloyd's shining Ford Escort, and now Parry's maturing Porsche – all parked conspicuously in the wide pedestrianized precinct that lay between the market and St John's Church.

'She was found at ... ten thirty-four, was it?' Parry queried, as they went through the centre pair of heavy, half-glazed swing doors with their lyrically shaped, long brass handles. He looked at his watch. It was now 11.14. He was thinking that whoever had committed the crime would probably have left the market a minute later, and certainly before the police had arrived, even if they had been sent for immediately. But if the murderer had left in a hurry, police questioning at the doors just might produce a useful lead.

'That's right, boss. We got the first call at unit HQ at ten forty-two. I got here at ten fifty-four. Not bad going, eh?' The middle-aged sergeant had driven here from Cowbridge Police Station, ten miles to the west, with the determination of a fleeing ram raider – but on roads a good deal more crowded than they would have been in the middle of the night. Lloyd invariably advertised his own alacrity since his formidable weight suggested to many that he might be a slow mover.

Cowbridge was the headquarters of the force's now single Major Crime Support Unit, to which both men were permanently seconded. Even before the swift arrival of a substantial team of detectives from the unit there, the present incident had been handled by the fast response sub-group permanently positioned at Cardiff Central Police Station, and headed, in this relief, by recently promoted Detective Sergeant Linda Johns. 'By the way, I think the victim may have been dead for longer than we first thought?' Lloyd added guardedly, in Parry's ear.

'Not a lot longer, surely? Not in the middle of Cardiff market, in full view of everybody?'

'A few minutes longer, maybe, boss. Because of extenuating circumstances, like,' Lloyd responded, nodding pointedly, and searching for a peppermint in his pocket. There being too many tunnels on the last part of the road from Newport for perfect communication by cellphone, the sergeant had additional information he had yet to pass to Parry, but he didn't intend to do so while moving through a crowd of sharp-eared Saturday shoppers. 'Dr Maltravers is here already,' he added, in compensation. 'That was his Land Rover outside. He's, er . . . he's come up with something.'

51

They moved quickly past the fresh fish stalls, that physically and aromatically commanded the big entrance hall, before they went through to the main market. Here the uniformed constable turned sharp right and led them, past a colleague posted to prevent access by the general public, up the wide stone steps to the heavily balustraded trading gallery that ran around the whole of the rectangular inner hall. There were sets of stairs, matching the ones they were using – and guarded in the same way – at all four corners of the gallery.

'Weapon plunged straight into the heart, by the look of it. Lucky blow, possibly, or it could have been professional,' muttered the normally taciturn, sixty-year-old police surgeon, Dr George Maltravers. It seemed from his tone that his comments were being made as much to himself as in answer to the first question Parry had put, after the two policemen had joined him behind the orange plastic screens.

Maltravers had been doing his best to give the very dead body of a very stout young woman in a floral dress a more than cursory examination, including the taking of the deceased's underarm temperature. The task had been hard to achieve without disturbing the corpse's precarious position. 'Dr Ironmonger's on his way. He won't want anything moved, including the weapon,' he cautioned, straightening himself from the half-crouched position he had been in earlier, and removing one of the disposable gloves he was wearing. The movements served to release the very faint odour of pig farm that sometimes surrounded the doctor. He raised pedigree pigs as a hobby – sometimes transporting them in the back of his Land Rover, Sergeant Lloyd had been prompted to observe, after having once accepted a lift in the same compartment of the vehicle.

Like Parry and Lloyd, the doctor had also donned elastic-topped disposable covers over his shoes and trouser bottoms. The Dr Ironmonger referred to was a senior pathologist at the Royal Infirmary, a mile away, and known for his hands-on approach to suspicious death – which was the reason, Parry concluded, why he was coming out to the body, and not waiting for it to be brought to the mortuary.

'I'd say death was probably instantaneous, and almost

certainly caused by a stab wound,' Maltravers offered next, stating what seemed to be the obvious, but allowing for correction if the postmortem revealed that the victim had perversely suffered a fatal heart attack, or even swallowed a lethal dose of arsenic, a second before a knife had been plunged into her heart.

'You mentioned to Sergeant Lloyd that she might not have had time to cry out even, Doctor?' said the chief inspector.

'Perhaps. Perhaps not. Nobody seems to have heard her if she did cry out.' Maltravers looked about him. 'Pretty noisy spot at the time, of course. But still.' He frowned, without qualifying his last comment, and pulled at the hairs sprouting from within his left ear, which so far seemed the only reason why he had removed the glove.

'Do you know her, Doctor?' asked Lloyd.

Maltravers shook his head. 'No, never come across her. But your people have found out she worked in private medicine, not the National Health Service.'

'Can you give us an approximate time of death?'

'Yes, that's easy. Between ten twenty-six and ten thirty-four. And you can take that as firm.' The reply had come very promptly.

'That's going to be useful,' the chief inspector put in, smiling. Police doctors, or even pathologists, were rarely as precise in reply to that particular enquiry.

'But that's not on the medical evidence,' the doctor volunteered coolly, as though he was not intending to take credit where it wasn't due. 'One of the girls from behind that counter says she served the victim with coffee and a biscuit at ten twenty-six. A chocolate biscuit. Seems the till record shows the time as well as the date of transactions. The biscuit wasn't in sight when I arrived, so our late lamented customer may have eaten it. Or someone else did. Postmortem will show, of course.' He paused, glared at Lloyd who had just moved half a pace away, while the doctor produced a small notebook and pencil from his pocket. 'Her parlous condition was discovered at ten thirty-four,' he said. 'In the circumstances, though, she could have pegged out any moment in the previous eight minutes, quite possibly without anyone knowing.

53

The chap who finally raised the alarm had asked her to pass the sugar. Biggest surprise of his life, I should think.' He sniffed loudly, and began writing something in the book.

The Popular Café, which, Parry knew from experience, normally lived up to its name, was halfway along the north gallery from the staircase he and Lloyd had just ascended. Except for two cafés, this in the north gallery, the other in the south, the total gallery area was devoted to non-food trades, to the sale of such things as second-hand books, musical instruments, live pets, sports goods, and hardware. The Popular Café occupied both sides of the single aisle for some forty feet, which made it bigger than other gallery tenancies. The permanent section on the right, as the two had approached it, backed on to the market's outer wall. It was fronted by a high glass counter, with display shelves under it, and extending to almost the whole length of the establishment. Behind the counter was the serving and working area with its gleaming aluminium and white enamel fixtures – cooking and refrigerating equipment, worktops, and utensils involved with the preparing and serving of hot and cold food and drink. At present, the counter display was filled with a colourful and enticing selection of fresh sandwiches, baguettes, sausage rolls, pasties, cakes and pies, ready for the mid-morning and lunchtime trade which, under present circumstances, was now unlikely to materialize.

Across the aisle, there were movable tables, benches and stools for customers. This was an open sitting or standing area with an interesting view of the main market concourse below, but it was at present showing signs of the compulsory, swift abandonment of partially consumed refreshments.

The woman's body was balanced on a bar stool on the serving side of the café, beyond the far end of the long counter. The arms were slumped forwards, awkwardly, on to a chest-high, plastic-covered wooden shelf set into the wall, and occupying the last few feet of the establishment's own territory. The dead woman's left shoulder was collapsed against an upright wooden partition marking the end of those remaining feet – and also the end of the shelf, and was thus giving support to the head and upper torso, both of which

54

were inclining to that side. The impression, to a casual observer, might have been that the woman was dozing, or perhaps daydreaming, over her coffee. Even a closer look might not have revealed the wooden handle of a sheath or clasp knife protruding from the inner side of the left breast, near the lower part of the cleavage. The knife handle was partially screened from view by the large, brassiere-supported right breast, and which constituted what Gomer Lloyd had referred to, with unintentional accuracy, as 'extenuating circumstances'.

Apart from the screens around the body, the whole café had been taped off. Half an hour before, the area had been teeming with shoppers. Now, apart from the presence of Parry, Lloyd and the doctor, it was the preserve of six Scene of Crime Officers – policemen and civilians enveloped in white, spaceman-like overalls. The team was working under the earnest Detective Sergeant Glen Wilcox, senior SOCO, and a sociology graduate. Three of his men were, methodically and carefully, collecting, bagging and labelling detritus from the shelf and its surrounds, their haul including cigarette ends, the paper wrappings from sugar packages, used cups, glasses, plates, spoons and other plastic table implements. They had suction-cleaned the floor before even the doctor had approached the body. Another officer was collecting fingerprints from the counter, shelf and stool. A fifth was photographing the scene and the body.

Another team of detectives, led by the energetic, blonde and bespectacled DS Johns, was interviewing employees of the café, the staff of all the nearby stalls, and some conscientious citizens who had stayed to volunteer information – a group that included the young man who had asked the dead woman to pass him the sugar.

'Anything else useful in her bag besides the driving licence and credit cards?' Parry asked DS Wilcox, after moving across to look at the capacious, black leather handbag with a long carrier strap. This had been found lying on the shelf beside the victim's coffee. Then it had been bulging, but now, its contents removed, it was a quite slender item encased in a large transparent evidence bag.

'Depends what you call useful, sir. There's a thousand pounds in twenty-pound notes. Useful to the victim, but not much to us.'

'Used notes, are they?'

'Afraid so, sir.'

'So with those and the credit cards, the motive was definitely not robbery.'

'That's right, sir.'

'Anything else?'

'Yes, sir. The second look through produced this diary. It might tell us something. We missed it, first time. It was tucked in a side pocket. We've checked it for prints.' Wilcox handed Parry a small, cheap pocket diary with a red cardboard cover. 'The rest of the stuff may pay for careful examination later, sir. It was a real glory hole, that handbag. I've bagged up the employee identity badge separately,' he completed, as he presented this second item.

The badge had a colour photo on it of the dead woman, clearly discernible through the transparent film now encasing it. She had been Sister Pansy Watkyn of the St Olaf Nursing Home in Bryntaf. But Parry knew that already, and was quickly leafing through the pages of the diary, looking for today's date.

6

'I've just talked to the director at the nursing home, boss. She says Sister Watkyn finished work yesterday at four, and wasn't due in again till six tomorrow morning,' Sergeant Lloyd was reporting, half an hour later.

'Did she know if the sister lived alone?'

'No. The director didn't know anything about her private life.'

'Well, maybe some of the other nurses will.'

'We've got someone on the way there now. According to the council's electoral role, Sister Watkyn is the only resident at 5, Carmen Lane, but you can't always go by that. Some people never register. Never want to vote, probably.'

Dr Ironmonger had been and gone, and Dr Maltravers and Pansy Watkyn's body had left more or less with him. The SOCO team had gone too.

The pathologist's work had been thorough, deft, and swift. His very provisional opinion on the likely cause and manner of death had corresponded with that of Dr Maltravers's, prompting that reticent worthy's tanned and leathery face to register only the most fleeting sign of satisfaction before his departure, taken only after he had offered a heavy promotional comment to the café proprietor on the superiority of local pork sausages.

Dr Ironmonger, dressed in white SOCO gear, had extracted the knife from the body, examined it, measured it, had it photographed, and turned it over for forensic examination, while dictating a running commentary on his actions into a pocket recorder. The weapon had been a six-inch, single-bladed angler's clasp knife, not a sheath knife. It was new looking, made in France by Opinel, and was intended for descaling and degutting fish.

The pathologist had proffered no binding view on any aspect of the death prior to his performing a postmortem, but he had briskly announced that he would begin that melancholy task immediately after lunch, despite its being Saturday. He had helpfully suggested that Parry might want to telephone him later.

The market had been fully reopened – including the gallery – but only after the quiet removal of the body had been accomplished via the most unobtrusive route the relieved market superintendent could devise. Not that those shoppers who caught sight of the anonymous, but immediately identifiable, oblong box had stared at it for long. A mundane container, with no blood dripping from it, conjured up nothing sensational, only a kind of anticlimax, and, to the impressionable, a disquieting sense of memento mori.

In contrast, many shoppers had been anxious enough to view the *scene* of a murder, and most of them had quickly indulged that whim as soon as they were allowed. As a result, the Popular Café was enjoying a lunch trade that compared to the time when a previous proprietor's daughter had won a beauty queen competition, and mingled amongst the customers, autographing their till receipts, clad only in her crown, court shoes, and a revealing bathing suit – a performance that had kept the café full, and the city pubs empty of male patrons for hours.

Parry and Lloyd were, for the moment, alone in the market superintendent's modest office. This was a room at the west end of the south gallery. It had been gladly loaned to the police by its cheerful incumbent, who was busy elsewhere placating disgruntled tenants. An hour or so's partial closure of the market because of a newsworthy murder, he argued, was nothing compared to the benefit being reaped from the bigger attendance the event was generating. This didn't convince everybody, notably those who insisted, despite evidence to the contrary, that having a killer at large in the market would have a discouraging effect on trade.

The two policemen were seated at an oblong table across

from the superintendent's desk. After earlier giving a short briefing to newspaper reporters, they had separated and had only now come together again to compare notes.

Parry, assisted by Detective Sergeant Linda Johns, had reinterviewed a shortlist of the most promising witnesses, including the girl who had served Sister Watkyn with her coffee, and the young man who had later discovered the dead woman. The chief inspector had hoped that, since their first interviews, one or both might have been able to recall and describe other people they had seen close to the victim: neither of them had.

It transpired that very little ordering or serving was done at the narrow, extreme end of the café counter. Nor was the small open area immediately beyond it much used by customers. It was cramped compared to the space on the other side of the aisle, which had the bonus of its bird's-eye view of the ground floor below.

The counter hand was called Phoebe Wilson. She was short, dark and cheerful, with ear hoops the size of curtain rings, a small chin which she always held high, and very large top teeth. The teeth she kept bared after each statement, and these, together with the ascendant chin and open mouth, combined to give Parry the impression that she was about to burst into song: he had a female cousin with similar facial features who was *always* bursting into song.

Miss Wilson explained that after she had taken Sister Watkyn's money, she had returned to working the long side of the counter from where she could scarcely see the corner to which the nurse had retreated with her order. And, no, she hadn't noticed anything unusual about the customer. 'Well, you don't have time for that, do you? Not on a Saturday. Too busy, aren't you?' had been her last fairly irrefutable sequence of observations. She had left the interview humming quite loudly.

The young man, Eddie Faull, a trainee plumber of frail appearance but bellicose disposition, explained he had only come from across the aisle looking for sugar which had run out at the table he was using. So he hadn't been in the critical area for any time at all, let alone long enough to have noticed the other people there, except some of the café staff. He had only noticed Sister Watkyn because what he had described as her beefy elbow had been between him and the handiest bowl of sugar packets on the shelf. And, yes, he supposed it had been her right elbow. He'd reckoned something was up when she didn't answer him after he'd asked twice if he could have the sugar bowl. She'd never blinked even, or moved a muscle. He couldn't remember anything else, except telling another customer he thought the fat woman looked poorly. The other customer, a lady, had been waiting at the time to be served at the short end of the counter behind him.

It was this lady who had advised the café proprietor to send for a doctor – and she had been the next witness Parry had seen. Although garrulous to a fault, all her words had been delivered hesitantly and with wearing slowness for her listeners. Her name was Doris Peach, and she was a middle-aged housewife and part-time dressmaker, who lived with her husband, a financial services consultant, in a converted ground-floor flat in the Roath Park area. She had come into the city centre by bus, as she often did on Saturdays, but not as early as usual, because the buses had been running late, and her toaster, the German make of which was on the tip of her tongue, had broken, and she'd had to take it to be mended locally at Elliott's, the new electrical store near her who did repairs. Her husband hadn't been able to take the toaster because he was seeing a client. Mrs Peach had been in the market gallery to buy a number of haberdashery items, which she then listed by name, and which were quite hard to come by these days, as she was in a good position to know. All this she had expounded to Parry, with frequent knowing nods to Linda Johns to whom she had explained most of it before.

But, no, Mrs Peach had been too worried about Sister Watkyn's condition, she said, to have noticed anyone else on the customer side of the café counter. This was a pity, Parry thought, in someone who seemed to have noted pretty well everything else that had happened to her that morning. However, after more prompting, it transpired that the lady did remember seeing one other person, though the identity of that person hardly warranted the time it took Mrs Peach to unfold the fact. Nor, as it happened, was she the first to have recalled seeing Mai Lewis.

'Oh, yes. She's the café helper who clears the dishes and does the washing-up. Older woman, she is. Been there for years and years. Oh, yes,' Mrs Peach had offered at her usual funereal pace and length. 'Wearing a white, wrap-around overall like the other staff. And a coloured, polka dot bandana. I do notice things, you see?' Mrs Peach drew breath. 'But she's always there, isn't she?'

Mrs Mae Lewis was indeed 'always there' at the café, and half the time on the customer side of the counter. This was why she was another witness that Parry had deemed worthy of a second interview. She had been one of the café staff also mentioned by Eddie Faull, though all that worthy had remembered about her was her clothes.

The quite tall, gaunt-faced Mrs Lewis was nearing sixty, and thin nearly to the point of emaciation, with deeply sunken, darting eyes, and parched lips, which she was always wetting with the end of her tongue, dartingly, like a snake. From the noise of her breathing, she was suffering from entrenched bronchitis. The only ornament she had on was a man's-size watch on her left wrist which she consulted with unusual frequency.

'Now I've had a minute to think proper, I suppose it could have been nearer ten than quarter past. And I'm not sure it was the lady you said,' she told Parry. An hour or so earlier she had informed Linda Johns that she had cleared up the area where Sister Watkyn had been sitting at 10.15. Now she was perched bolt upright in her chair across the table from her interviewers, and wearing a grieved expression meant to indicate that someone obliged to clear café tables to earn a humble crust deserved indulgence, not blame, for being less than totally accurate in recalling the exact time of events. Which is why Parry found the frequent glances at her wristwatch a touch incongruous.

Mrs Lewis was still wearing her overalls, but she had removed the bandana. She had already explained to DS

Johns that she only wore the bandana on duty because the management insisted staff should have their heads covered, and she didn't care for the uniform cap provided. 'And anyway, you like a bit of variety, don't you?'

Judging by the state and condition of Mrs Lewis's patchily red-dyed hair, Parry thought any covering would do.

'But, Mae, you told me this morning you remembered seeing Sister Watkyn,' Linda Johns had pressed, miffed that the witness was close to making her look an unreliable interviewer in front of her chief.

'Well, that's another thing. I thought I'd seen her, right enough. Sitting in the corner. By herself. But, come to think, that lady was in orange with white stripes, but you did say the sister was in blue with flowers on. I think I'd have remembered that.' In a strangely refined way, Mrs Lewis had then delicately scratched the end of one nostril with an extended little finger.

'The mind can play tricks with colours, of course, Mrs Lewis,' Parry had observed with a smile. 'The important thing is, can you describe anyone at all you saw close to the lady who may have been Sister Watkyn?'

'Well, that's hard to tell again, isn't it? There were so many people there this morning. Millions milling about.'

And it had soon become clear that out of all the millions, Mrs Lewis had been unable to describe even one.

So the only four people who could be classified as having witnessed anything relevant recalled virtually nothing of value to the Senior Investigating Officer. And despite the fact that Sister Watkyn had been such a sizeable figure, nobody else in the whole market had so far admitted to having caught sight of her, let alone anyone who could have been her killer.

This was basically why Parry had been loath to leave the market quite yet, when there was still a possibility that someone would come forward with information. It was also why, after the abortive reinterviews, he had walked through both floors of the building with a uniformed constable, making himself known to stallholders, and repeating that the police still needed all the help they could get in identifying the killer. He was too well aware that in the case of what could prove to be an entirely motiveless murder, the chances of finding the perpetrator diminished drastically as time passed, and the memories of potential witnesses faded.

The chief inspector didn't intend to set up an incident room in the building. The Central Police Station, being so close, was the most practical place for that, though he had sent for a police caravan which was already in place outside the market's eastern entrance: Lloyd had just come from there. The caravan would stay where it was, open, for the rest of the day. Parry was using the market superintendent's office in case anyone came forward who was diffident about being seen in identifiable police premises. It was also a convenient place for him to go on working while eating the snack lunch Lloyd had ordered for them from the Popular Café, and which a constable had just brought in.

'Did you get anything on the knife, boss?' asked the detective sergeant, helping himself to a covered dish from the tray on the table.

'Yes. I went to that sports equipment stall on the other side of the gallery. They sell Opinel knives. In three different sizes. The chap in charge is sure he hadn't sold one this morning, except he didn't know how many he had in stock in the first place. They're quite pricey, but one of the best makes, apparently.'

'So it could have been nicked off the stall? Dr Ironmonger thought it looked brand new.'

Parry sniffed. 'Possibly. The regular stall owner's on holiday. The chap I spoke to is an elderly relative standing in for him. If he was serving someone else, I think a slick operator could have palmed anything without his seeing.'

'The knives are on open display, boss?'

'No. There's a heap of them in a glass case on the counter, but it wasn't locked.'

The sergeant made a tutting noise through his teeth. 'Suppose the owners of fishing tackle shops don't think of angler's knives as weapons. Like expecting Woolworth's to lock up carpet knives, I suppose. Except every kid with a blade seems to be a potential villain these days. Different when I joined the force. Come to something, hasn't it?' he completed, with another tut.

'We can't be sure the knife was new, of course,' said Parry, who was used to hearing Lloyd on the parlous deterioration in public morals. Other senior officers in the unit were often not as tolerant, but Parry liked working with the sergeant, who was a hugely experienced and reliable detective. Although a subordinate, Lloyd was also an old friend, and an unusually understanding one when Parry's wife had died eighteen months before this. 'But if the knife was new,' the chief inspector went on, 'Dr Ironmonger said there'll probably be traces in the wound of whatever the manufacturer puts on the blades.'

'If they put anything on them, boss. Should have thought they'd most likely just give them a last buff-up. Still.' Lloyd had turned to a fresh page in the notebook he had brought out and was writing on it as he spoke. 'We've got the names of twenty-nine fishing tackle shops in the Cardiff area, that's not including general sports outlets, which we're ignoring for the time being. The specialists should be open all day today. We're phoning them now, finding out who sells Opinel knives. We'll call on the ones who do.'

'Have we talked to Sister Watkyn's neighbours in Bryntaf yet?' Parry asked, switching subjects and taking one of the plastic mugs of coffee from the tray.

'No, boss. I've just had a word on the radio with DC Mary Norris, who's up there. Carmen Lane's an unadopted cul-de-sac. There's only the row of three bungalows in it, all on one side. The first one you come to is empty, and Sister Watkyn lived in the third. The people in the middle are out. Married couple, probably. Or man and woman anyway.' The sergeant made pedantic, if grudging, allowance for the increase in unmarried cohabitees. 'There's washing on the line at the back,' he went on. 'A man's shirt and some ladies' things, so they're probably not gone for long, DC Norris thinks. The garage is empty.'

'Intelligent officer, Mary Norris,' said Parry approvingly, while telling himself that he was as complimentary about

64

the less attractive women detectives when occasion offered. 'Is she waiting there for them to come back?'

'No. She's on other calls, the post office and the other shops. They're all in Station Road. So's the local petrol station. She'll go back when she's done that.'

'She hasn't tried to enter the bungalow?'

'We haven't ordered her to, boss. D'you want her to break in?'

'No. The key'll be on the ring in the victim's handbag.' He looked at the time. 'What about Sister Watkyn's car? She had one, did she?'

'Yes, boss. But it's not in the garage. It's a five-year-old red Metro. The nursing home director told us that. We got the number pronto from DVLC Swansea. Uniform are looking for the car in the central city car parks.' Lloyd picked up his fork after removing the cover from a plate of two fried eggs, a thick rasher of bacon, a well-cooked sausage, some sautéed potatoes and a splodge of laver bread. He and his generously proportioned wife were health-food addicts, but, for his part, he made exceptions when he was 'out' – which he was for lunch on most days. The laver bread, the least fattening item on the plate, is made from a species of seaweed, and has nothing to do with bread, having the appearance of puréed spinach, except it's darker, and has a tangy, briny taste popular with the Welsh. 'This is great laver bread,' Lloyd enthused, savouring it first, and slowly. 'They really know how to cook it in the market. You should have had some, boss.'

Parry had ordered a ham and tomato sandwich on brown bread, with an apple to follow. He gave a thin smile that was less genuine even than it looked, and his next comment had nothing to do with food. 'The point is, Gomer, she was here by intention. The diary note for today says "Ten thirty C. Market". The C being the initial of someone she was meeting, probably.'

'Or it could stand for the C in central market. Or in covered market, boss. Some people would put it that way. So it could mean she just got here early to do some shopping.'

'Except there's no evidence she did any shopping.'

'Unless she did, and the killer or somebody swiped her

shopping bag. Funny, in that case, he didn't take her handbag.'

'But no stallholder up here or downstairs remembers serving her with anything. And do people make notes in their diaries about going shopping?' Parry looked up doubtfully. 'I'd say she was meeting someone here. A friend. Boyfriend or girlfriend.'

'But if that's right, why hasn't the friend come forward, boss? Unless it's the one who killed her.'

'And Sister Watkyn hasn't been working with schizophrenic patients?'

'Not in the nursing home. I asked the director that, like you said.'

There was a brief silence as both men sipped coffee and wondered if the nurse might still have been stabbed by a deranged person abroad in the city who might be choosing victims at random, and who was capable of causing more death or injury unless the police acted quickly.

'And there's no criminal psychopath loose anywhere?' asked Parry.

'No, none reported. And we're checking the psychiatric hospitals.'

'For outpatients with histories of unprovoked violence on strangers – or nurses?'

'That's right, boss.' Lloyd put his knife down, and, picking up his fork in the same hand, stabbed some potato with it which he dipped into an egg yolk. 'That diary entry could just be because she had a bad memory, like. Perhaps she always made a note about going shopping. Gracie makes notes to herself to do things. To remind her. It works, too. If she doesn't lose the notes.' Gracie was Lloyd's wife, and the mother of his five children. 'Sister Watkyn didn't actually state she was meeting someone.'

Parry turned back the pages of the diary, shaking his head. Then he stared almost accusingly at the half-eaten sandwich in his hand. 'OK, Gomer, let's finish here in five minutes, and get up to the bungalow.'

Before the chief inspector had finished speaking, Lloyd's radio began squawking on the table where it was lying beside his cellphone and his notebook. It was DC Norris calling from Carmen Lane, and being relayed by central radio control at the constabulary's headquarters in Bridgend.

'Mr and Mrs Slocombe live at number three, sarge,' the woman detective reported. 'They're middle-aged, and moved up here from Whitchurch six months ago, after their daughter got married. They've been shopping in Llandaff this morning. They were in the Bryntaf newsagents and post office, paying their paper bill just now, when they heard me asking about Sister Watkyn. They say she had a live-in boyfriend, but the two kept themselves very much to themselves. The Slocombes only knew Sister Watkyn to pass the time of day with, and they've hardly ever spoken to the boyfriend. They didn't know his name, but the postmistress did. It's Rees, Evan Rees. He's some kind of journalist.'

The chief inspector leaned across and picked up the radio. ''Afternoon, Constable. DCI Parry speaking. Had the Slocombes seen either of these two people this morning?'

'Yes, they had, sir,' the young woman answered promptly. 'Mr Slocombe was cutting his front hedge earlier when he saw Sister Watkyn leave on foot. That was at approximately nine forty. She seemed to be in a hurry, and he said she looked angry, or it might have been upset. He wasn't sure. She hardly answered when he said good morning.'

'Does Mr Slocombe know she's been murdered?'

'He does now, sir. He didn't when I was putting the questions.'

'Well done.' He nodded at Lloyd: more confirmation that DC Norris wasn't just a pretty face.

'The next part may be more important, sir. Mr Slocombe saw the boyfriend leave in Sister Watkyn's car about twenty minutes after her. Around ten o'clock. He thinks there was a suitcase on the back seat.'

Parry swallowed. 'You got a description of Evan Rees?'

'Yes, sir. Separately from the postmistress and Mr Slocombe. They tally. He's early to mid-thirties, five foot ten, black wavy hair, heavily built, but not overweight. Deep voice. Educated Welsh accent. Dishy type, according to the postmistress. Mr Slocombe says he was wearing a dark-blue, short-sleeved shirt, open at the neck. That's all he could be sure about, sir. No identifying marks, either, I'm afraid.'

'Maybe there's a photo of Rees in the bungalow. Where are you now?'

'On Sister Watkyn's front doorstep, sir. D'you want me to go in? The back door would be easy to force.'

'No. Stay where you are, but don't let anyone on to the premises. Including the garden. I'll have back-up with you soon, and I'm on my way with DS Lloyd.'

'Right, sir.'

Parry switched off the radio. 'Right, Gomer. We need all motorway patrols, ports and airports alerted with the description of Rees and the car. If he's been on the road since ten, of course, he could be up to a hundred and fifty miles away by now.'

'Not if he was here in the market, stabbing his girlfriend, at ten thirty, boss. And not if he was driving a five-year-old Metro, either.' He took the radio from Parry as he added. 'Will you want another SOCO team up there pronto?'

'Have we got the people?'

'We will have by now, boss.' Stringent rules dictated that if there was more than one site for intensive examination involving the same serious crime, the police investigating personnel had to be different at each site. This was to avoid possible cross-contamination of DNA evidence. It was also expensive in terms of manpower for a force on a tight budget.

'We'll decide when we get there. If there's signs of recent violent behaviour in the bungalow, very recent, like just before she left, it may be worth combing the place through.'

'That's what I thought, boss.'

'Mr Slocombe said she looked angry –'

'Or upset, boss,' Lloyd interrupted. 'He didn't say battered or anything.'

'That's right.' Parry got up from the table. 'If Evan Rees says he's a journalist, the Cardiff papers may know him. We can check that on the way as well. Let's go, then.'

Parry pocketed his apple as he left. Lloyd could hardly do the same with his, as yet, untouched slice of custard-covered treacle tart, which he looked back at wistfully from the door.

7

Huw Bevan drove the white Mercedes into the three-car garage at Hill House, and glanced at the clock on the dashboard. It was 12.42, a few minutes before the time he had promised Dilys that he would be back for lunch. He felt good about that.

He crossed through the workshop and lobby. 'I'm here!' he called loudly and affably, putting on a smile, and opening the door to the kitchen where he expected Dilys would be busy preparing food. He was followed in by an elderly brown and white Welsh spaniel, who had been asleep under the work bench. The dog was called Tyn, pronounced Tin – a Welsh word meaning fast, except this Tyn's speeding days were long over.

At the best of times, Saturday lunch at home was not an event that Bevan particularly enjoyed. Indeed, he seldom even appeared for it, unless his daughter Barbara was going to be there – and that happened less often than it used to, since she had started at the new school. During the last three weekends he had dreaded even the prospect of sharing the meal with Dilys alone. Today, at least, Barbara was expected to be home. This meant there could be no question of another worried discussion with Dilys on a topic that they had to keep from Barbara at all costs.

It went almost without saying that the chairman of Ely Electrical Contractors invariably went to his office every Saturday morning. It followed, too, that Laura Mathews, his indispensable secretary, went there with him. Normally he picked her up at her home and dropped her back there afterwards. Usually they were together until well into the afternoon – working a good deal of the time, though not all of it.

Saturday was the only day of the week when Bevan insisted he could apply himself to desk work, without interruption from telephone or fax machine. Despite the increasing size of the firm, he still went over the scheduling and costings of all major contracts in detail himself – as well as over quite a number of the lesser ones.

Quite simply, Huw Bevan had been what is known as a 'workaholic' almost since the time he had left the RAF. He pretended that his almost ceaseless labours were essential in providing the wherewithal to keep himself and his family in the style of living which they had come to enjoy. But it had been many years since it had done merely that. He was now fifty-five. If he had chosen, he could long since have sold the company and retired from industry, with enough money to keep several such families in reasonable luxury for the rest of their days.

To be realistic in the matter, which Bevan tended not to be, he worked because he had no other consuming interest. He loved what he did, almost as much, in a separate context, as he loved Barbara Anne, whom he regarded in all ways as his daughter, although she wasn't his daughter in any legal way.

He loved nobody else – or not in the literal sense of the word love.

His wife, Dilys, for instance, he had stopped loving years before this. He felt sorry for her – which in his book was something quite different from love – and protective towards her, which is why he indulged her so freely. In the circumstances, many men in his material and emotional situation would have sought a civilized divorce. But he had too much compassion for that, or so he had persuaded himself – too strong an understanding of what their marriage meant to Dilys. He was uncomfortably aware that if he deserted her, she would take her own life. She had said as much, several times, over the years. This repeated threat was permanently in his mind and he accepted it as fact, just as firmly as a committed believer accepted a religious absolute. But it was an acceptance that conveniently relieved Bevan of making the choice between staying with his wife or leaving her. Divorcing her would have meant the loss of something which, with an icy lack of sentiment, he considered a significant part of his wealth – a component of his success and self-esteem.

He had felt the same way at first about parting with the money for the Pansy Watkyn shakedown. But he had changed his mind about that since concluding that it really would protect the only things he held dear.

Huw didn't love Laura Mathews, either. She had been his mistress, as well as his secretary, for over seven years. She was thirty-six, and a buxom, attractive blonde, well preserved, childless, intelligent, divorced – and undemanding. She told him that she had no particular desire to marry again, implying she accepted that unless – or until – something happened to his present wife, there was no prospect of her becoming the second Mrs Bevan. This suited Bevan admirably. He was far from certain that he would ever want to consider her for that office in any case.

Even so, Laura was well rewarded in both her present roles. And although Bevan kept her, giving her a handsome cash allowance on top of a very substantial salary, he made surprisingly few demands in return for the extra outlay. He was unpossessive primarily because there was no way that Laura could feature as an overt part of his private life. She remained an adjunct to his corporate persona, albeit a pleasingly decorative adjunct, as well as an efficient one, all of which suited his rational, tidy mind.

Because Bevan spent relatively little time with Laura outside the office (and much of that time in her bed, early on most Saturday afternoons), he had never objected to her seeing other men if she wished. In practice, she had no other serious male attachments, and no interest in acquiring any. Like her employer she was content with things the way they were – or the way they had been before Pansy Watkyn had upset everybody's life.

In truth, Huw Bevan's reason for ordering his life the way he did balanced on a both underlying and overruling fact.

His peculiar moral attitude hinged upon his work being his real if inanimate wife and mistress combined.

'Did she phone you, Huw?' his animate wife Dilys demanded anxiously as he came through the kitchen door. He had expected the question, and the urgency in her voice.

'Who?' He knew perfectly well who she had meant, but it was important that she believed the matter wasn't the one permanently uppermost in his mind. He put his hands on her shoulders and pulled her towards him, brushing her cheek with his lips. This was the normal ritual when he came home, like the matching farewell token kiss when he left it again. He knew she set great store on small outward shows of affection – the more so when they were alone. When they were in company such demonstrations embarrassed her acutely.

'I meant Pansy.' Unsmiling, she moved away from him as though the embrace had meant nothing to her, and went back to tossing the salad in a massive wooden bowl. Lunch was laid for three on the pinewood table in the centre of the large, well-equipped kitchen. 'Would you rather eat outside on the terrace?' she asked.

'No, in here.' He bent down to pat Tyn, whose tail wagged with a commendable degree of energy in response – it was now the only part of him that showed such relative animation. 'She didn't ring, no.'

'You're sure? I mean, were you near the phone all the time?'

He suppressed a sigh. 'I was in the stores checking something for about five minutes, that's all. I had my cellphone with me, though.'

Dilys still looked uneasy. 'And if she'd rung the office number when you were doing that, Laura was there to answer it, was she?'

'No, Laura wasn't in today. Anyway, I don't believe Pansy rang the office number.'

'Why wasn't Laura in?'

'She wasn't feeling well yesterday, so I told her to stop at home today. Nuisance. I don't get as much done with her away.'

'Of course.' She tossed the salad with greater concentration showing in her eyes, as though the action was giving her mental relief. 'I don't know how you can be so cool about it all, Huw, I really don't.'

He shrugged. 'What's there to be hot and bothered about? When I last spoke to Pansy, I offered her a deal. Not the one they wanted, but a deal. They have till noon on Monday to accept it. I'm certain they will. They're taking all the time we've given them for effect, not because they have anything to think about.'

'You're certain they'll settle for fifty thousand? And what they have to do to . . .' She stopped without completing the sentence.

'To earn it?' He gave a grim smile. Then he placed the black document case he'd been carrying on the chair next to the one he'd be using at the table. Turning about to face his wife again, he added, 'Like I told you this morning, Pansy knows it's all we're going to give them. She also knows it's a bloody sight more than they'd have got from a newspaper, apart from carrying no risk.'

'You always say "them". You're still sure Pansy's in on it? That she's not just a messenger, like she says?'

'I'm ninety per cent sure. So would you be if you weren't so . . . so good and trusting.' He had nearly said, 'so bloody simple', but stopped himself in time.

'But she's always seemed so honest. So caring. Like she's only got mixed up in the whole thing to protect us. I can't believe she's –'

'A dirty blackmailer?' he interrupted. 'Well, you can take it from me she is, and we should both be used to that by now. The more I think about it, the more certain I am that if there's two of them, she's the active one. The brains. The one who thought it all up. It's what Simon Frankel thinks as well. In fact, he doesn't think now there's a German in it at all.'

'He thinks she's working alone?'

'Not alone, because her boyfriend could be involved.'

'She says he's not. She's told me that twice. That she hasn't told him anything about it.'

He shrugged. 'It could just be true, I suppose. But it's hard to keep secrets from a newspaperman. Anyway, the people Simon's had following them, and watching the house, they still haven't seen any German.'

'Well, I don't believe it's just her idea. She seems so genuine. So fond of Barbara.' Dilys went to the fridge and took out a serving plate already prepared with sliced meats and patties.

'That's while she was pumping Barbara and you for information.'

Dilys sighed. 'So long as she doesn't tell Barbara what she knows. Later on, I mean.'

'You don't need to worry about that. She knows that would cost her a long gaol sentence, and anyone working with her, as well.' Except Huw himself had once been worried about just that, worried desperately that Pansy might tell his daughter the truth about her origins, after the blackmail money had been paid. Or else that she'd have some other person tell Barbara, out of spite, because he'd only paid half the money demanded. It was the unpredictable effect such devastating news would have on his daughter – how it could change her attitude towards him – that had been petrifying him. Well, at least that was off his mind now. 'Barbara's late, isn't she?' he questioned.

'Yes. Her lesson was supposed to end at twelve.'

'So I could have picked her up?'

Dilys shook her head as she brought the salad bowl to the table. 'She wouldn't have wanted you to drive into the city.'

'More likely she'd have wanted to come back in the bus with that boy Alwyn.' He didn't care for Alwyn, but that applied to all the young men who came near his daughter.

'It's possible. But he's a nice lad. I did ask her specially to be on time. I'm sorry, Huw. It's not like her.'

'Well, it's not your fault,' he commented brusquely. If only she weren't always so ready to take the blame for everything, especially things that had nothing to do with her. 'But we'd better start,' he added. 'I've got a lot to do this afternoon.' He glanced at the bulging document case again, then walked over to the fridge and took out a can of beer, before seating himself at the table. The dog had followed his movements, before flopping down at his feet with an expiring kind of grunt.

'You and Simon are sure we shan't be asked for more? On top of the fifty thousand?' Dilys pressed.

'As sure as we can be of anything. Yes, very sure,' he added quickly, to console her.

'I wish we hadn't had to tell Simon.'

'So do I, in a way, but the deal had to be foolproof legally. The documentation he's produced is exactly that. In any case, Simon's not just my lawyer, he's my best friend. If we can't trust him we can't trust anyone.' He began helping himself to cold meats.

'He hasn't told his wife?' She sat at the table, too, bringing a roll of French bread with her that she'd had warming in the oven.

'Annie?' He looked up at her from what he was doing. 'No, of course he hasn't. And not any of his staff, either. I told you, he drafted all the paperwork in his own handwriting for Laura to type out for me at the office.'

'I wish we hadn't had to tell Laura, either.'

'I'd trust Laura with my life,' he answered, too firmly and promptly, because the comment had riled him.

Dilys's cheeks reddened. Normally she avoided discussing Laura Mathews with her husband, except in the most general terms. Confused, she reverted to the subject of the Frankels while she was slicing the bread. 'But wouldn't you have told me if things were the other way round? If Simon and Annie were being blackmailed over their daughter, say?'

'It couldn't have happened. I'm not a lawyer,' he replied, certain, even so, that in those circumstances he would not have told his wife. 'We've consulted Simon in his professional capacity, not just as a friend,' he continued, except that he and Simon shared too many confidences – private as well as business confidences – for their professional relationship to be any different from their personal one.

Dilys's expression showed some kind of comprehension. 'I still don't see how it's going to work. I know you explained it, but . . . but, I keep thinking, we . . . we broke the law in the first place, so how can the law protect us now?'

He breathed in and out heavily as he poured the beer into a glass. 'Before we pay over the money, Pansy has to sign a confession. It'll say we've paid her under duress.'

'That she's blackmailed us?'

'That's right. I read the confession to her twice at the office.'

'She hasn't got a copy?'

'No. Simon won't give her one, till she and the person she says she's acting for is ready to sign it in our presence, and collect the money. If she comes alone, Simon says it'll go a long way to prove we're dealing with just her. And if she ever asks for more money, she knows we'll take her confession to the police. That would mean gaol for her, for certain, and for any partner she implicates then if she hasn't done earlier.'

'Why would she do that?' Dilys asked.

'To get herself a shorter sentence.'

'Except you don't believe there is a partner.'

'I've told you I don't.'

'But if we ever did go to the police with the confession, the story would still come out.'

He hesitated. 'Not necessarily. The police and the courts are very discreet when it comes to prosecuting blackmailers. The hearings take place in camera. That means in private. With no press present, and no proper names used.'

'But the people in the court would know. I'm nobody, but it'd be different for you. You'd be recognized. Other people would get to know we'd been blackmailed and why. In time they would.'

He drank some beer, then gave her his most reassuring smile. 'Theoretically you could be right, love. But it's not likely the case would ever get to court. Or to the police, even. The confession should see to that.'

'So why do we have to pay anything?'

'To get the confession.'

'So why can't we sort of just pretend we're paying, and have Pansy arrested after she's signed. Or am I being stupid as usual?' She was sitting at the table with nothing on her

76

plate still, her hands clasped tightly in her lap, and her brow deeply furrowed.

Bevan wiped his mouth with his napkin. 'You're not being stupid, love. But it's hard to explain. There's a lot of judgement involved in all this, mostly Simon's, but I go along with his thinking because I'm sure he's got it right.' He paused, then went on. 'If we don't pay, or if we trick Pansy in the way you said, then turn her over to the authorities, there'd have to be a trial, yes. And, like you say, there would be a risk of the story leaking.'

'Even with the trial being in . . . in camera?'

'In theory, no, in practice, probably yes, I'm afraid. What we're banking on is that Pansy will be satisfied with what we're paying, and smart enough to know there'll be nothing to gain if she makes more demands in the future, except probably a bigger prison sentence than she'd have got if we went to the police now. That's what we're telling her.'

'So the fifty thousand is really buying her silence for ever, and keeping us safe for ever. So we'll never have to tell Barbara the truth.' Her last words were delivered almost in a whisper.

'That's it, love. You've got it in a nutshell.'

'Then I hope Pansy signs.' As she was replying, the telephone on the kitchen wall began ringing, and she got up to answer it. She listened to the caller for several moments, then her face clouded. 'But she left here as usual this morning,' she said into the telephone. 'I don't understand. And she hasn't been in touch with you saying why she wasn't coming?' She listened again, then turned to her husband. 'Barbara hasn't been to school today. The school secretary's ringing to find out if she's all right.'

'Sorry, what d'you say?' he asked, his voice strained. As she had gone to answer the phone, he had switched on the television set by remote control to see the one o'clock news. He had been too concerned with what he was seeing to have paid any attention to what his wife had said.

The screen was filled with a blown-up, coloured photograph of Pansy Watkyn's face, and the newscaster had just announced that she was dead.

8

'As I've already told the Carmarthen police, I was on my way to Pembroke Dock. To catch the two fifteen ferry to Ireland. To Rosslare. I was on a working trip. It was planned a week ago. I last saw Pansy early this morning. At around nine forty. When she left the bungalow in Carmen Lane. She told me she was going shopping in Cardiff. She was in good health at the time, poor darling. Is all that quite clear now?' Evan Rees, breathing heavily, had slowed his deep-toned delivery, as if the two detectives he was addressing would only comprehend words of few syllables, spoken with especial clarity, in short, tabloid-type sentences, by someone ready to make allowance for the feebleness of their mental acuities – or that was the impression he was giving.

He had been stopped at 12.22 by the alert crew of a police patrol car on the A48 just beyond Carmarthen, sixty-eight miles west of Cardiff, and not far from his stated destination. After a brief interview at the local police station, he had been driven back to Cardiff in a police car. Now he looked around the interview room with a despairing expression, his brawny upper-arm muscles flexing and unflexing under the tight-fitting short sleeves of the shirt he was wearing. He had taken off his seersucker jacket and draped it over the back of his chair. It was just after 2.30. So, whatever else, Evan Rees had missed his ferry.

'All that's quite clear, Mr Rees. Thank you,' said Gomer Lloyd, who was sitting with Parry on the other side of the small table. The interview was taking place on the ground floor of Cardiff Central Police Station, and it was being taped. 'I wonder, can you tell us anything about an entry in Miss

Watkyn's diary,' the sergeant went on. 'It's under today's date, and reads "Ten-thirty. C. Market".'

Rees thought for a moment, then shook his head, a touch wearily. 'I told you, she was going shopping this morning. She used the central market a lot. Usually on Saturdays. That's if she wasn't working.'

'She was also stabbed to death there, Mr Rees,' Parry offered in a level voice. 'What we need to know is, did she tell you she was meeting anyone in the market?'

'No, she didn't.'

'Pity. Would you have any idea what the letter C in the diary entry stands for?'

Rees played with the hairs sprouting above his shirt opening. 'Central, I should think,' he said. 'That's what she always called it. The Central Market.'

The policemen exchanged glances before Parry asked: 'You don't think it could have been the initial of someone Miss Watkyn was meeting?'

'Could have been that, too, I suppose.'

'Can you think of anyone with the initial C she might have arranged to meet?'

'Not immediately, no.'

'If she had been meeting someone, is it likely she'd have told you?'

'Not necessarily. Not if it was someone I wouldn't have been interested in.'

'Or someone you didn't like, sir, or who didn't like you, perhaps? Do any names come to mind now?'

Rees hesitated before replying. 'Not really,' he answered, but not as promptly as before. 'We didn't know the same people.'

'You mean you didn't mix as a couple?'

'Not all the time, no.' He shook his head. 'I still think it's more likely she wasn't meeting anyone. If that's all it says in the diary, it was probably just a reminder she needed something from the market.'

'We thought the same thing,' said Parry. 'But if we're wrong, if she was meeting someone, we have to believe it could have been her killer. Would you think again, Mr Rees, very carefully.'

'I have. I tell you, she didn't mention anyone, and I can't think of anyone she'd have avoided telling me she was meeting.'

'Thank you.' It was Lloyd who had spoken, and who now took up the questioning. 'On another point, sir. Can you tell us anything about the thousand pounds she had in her handbag? All in twenty-pound notes?'

'A thousand? Good God. No, I can't.'

'You mean she didn't have it with her when she left this morning, sir?'

Rees hesitated. 'No. Well, not so far as I know. Not unless she had a hoard of money somewhere she hadn't mentioned to me.'

'Is that likely, sir?'

'No, it isn't. It wouldn't have been like her at all. We, er . . . we tended to share and share alike where funds were concerned.'

'Is there anyone you can think of who might have given her the money this morning, sir? A debt, it might have been? Or payment for nursing services, perhaps?'

'Your guess is as good as mine, there.' Rees took a deep breath, then exhaled it slowly. 'I suppose she could have saved up in secret to buy me a present. It's a possibility.'

'But cash, sir? Wouldn't she have been more likely to have paid for a present by cheque or credit card?'

'Depends what she was buying, I suppose. A lot of people like cash, don't they?'

Neither of the detectives seemed disposed to answer that question. Instead it was Parry who asked: 'Is it your birthday soon, Mr Rees?'

The journalist gave a short chuckle, and rocked back on his chair. 'No. That's in March. It wouldn't stop Pansy giving me a present now, though. She was generous by nature. We were generous to each other, irrespective of birthdays or Christmas,' he ended magnanimously, gesturing with one hand.

'But there's nothing you can think of she might have been planning to get you today, sir?'

'No. Nothing.'

'Nor anyone she might be paying in cash, for an expensive item or service?'

Rees shook his head. 'Honestly, I've no idea.'

'Since you were so open with each other about money, sir, would there have been anyone who, for any reason, was giving Miss Watkyn anything up to two hundred and fifty pounds a month in cash?'

'Who says anyone was?'

'Nobody, sir,' Parry put in, amiably. 'It's just that her bank statement shows these regular deposits of up to that sum, sometimes a lot lower. They were near the end of every month, and always in cash.'

'Ah, it could have been money from me. Towards the housekeeping. I often gave that to her in cash. I suppose what she didn't use, she could have paid into the bank.'

'I see, sir,' said Lloyd, leaning forwards with both forearms on the table. 'Going back to the market again, do you remember her ever arranging to meet anyone there?'

'No ... Sorry, yes, she might have done. She did once meet a schoolgirl in the city for coffee. It was mid-morning, quite recently. That could have been in the market. The girl looked up to her, so far as I could gather. Pansy was good with young people.'

'Do you know how they met, sir?'

'Yes. The girl's the daughter of an ex-patient at the nursing home. Pansy was helping the mother to find a long-lost friend.'

'And when did Miss Watkyn meet the daughter for coffee, sir?'

'About three Saturdays ago. No, come to think of it, it was a Friday, not a Saturday.'

'And you don't know whether it was in the market, sir?'

'No, I don't.'

During this exchange, Parry, who had the diary in front of him, had been flicking through a section of it. 'There's no entry that fits for the last five Fridays or Saturdays, I'm afraid.' He looked up. 'Do you have the schoolgirl's name, sir?'

'Yes. Well, the family name, anyway. It's Bevan. Her father's head of a company called Ely Electrical Contractors, something like that. They live here in Bryntaf somewhere. Look, I don't think the kid could have had anything to do with the murder. It's just that she's the only one that might fit the question you asked.'

'Quite so, Mr Rees,' said Parry, who was inclined to agree with the last comment. 'Going back to your own plans for today, we gather you weren't booked on the Pembroke Dock ferry?'

Rees sighed. 'As I've explained to the police once already, I had a tentative booking on the four o'clock Fishguard ferry before I realized I had time to go from Pembroke Dock. That's closer, so I switched. It meant twenty miles less driving. I was tired and hot. I'd had to change a tyre just after I came off the motorway. There'd been a lot of traffic hold-ups as well. There's never any trouble getting on the Irish ferries this late in the season.'

'Your reservation on the Fishguard ferry wasn't logged, either, sir,' said Lloyd, whose voice was even deeper than Rees's, apart from sounding more ominous.

'Like I said, the booking wasn't confirmed. I rang them yesterday. They said there'd be plenty of room. At that point, I wasn't absolutely sure if I'd be going by car, even. But what does any of this matter?' Rees's face had hardened again. 'I'm a feature writer. I was going to Ireland to do an article on the Wexford Opera Festival. It's irrelevant to Pansy's death which ferry I was using. God, you really are an unfeeling bunch, you know that? I loved the girl, can't you understand? In my own way, I loved her deeply.' He looked from one stony-faced policeman to the other. 'I'm completely broken up by the news. I'd give anything now not to have left this morning. If I'd stayed with her, maybe she'd be alive still. I'm utterly devastated by the news. Utterly. So how d'you think I feel at being hauled back here in a police car like a bloody criminal?' He reached for his cigarettes in his shirt pocket.

'We sympathize, sir, of course, and we're trying not to prolong this,' Parry replied. 'You're not under arrest. You came voluntarily, and you're free to leave when you choose. But you'll understand our position, especially since you're a journalist. Because the lady you admit you've been living with was stabbed to death this morning, we have to make certain you're in the clear. Sorry to be so frank. But it's really in your own interests.'

Rees gave a loud and still-irritated sigh. 'All right. I understand. But let's get it over with,' he snapped.

'The Wexford Festival isn't for another three weeks, of course,' Parry observed, in a matter-of-fact voice.

'I know that. This trip was for background material. Pre-festival stuff.' Rees lit a cigarette and blew out smoke vigorously.

'Were you intending to stay long, sir?' asked Lloyd, leaning back from the table. He had given up smoking two years before.

'No. A couple of nights. Maybe three.'

'Had you made reservations at a hotel?'

'Yes, I . . . well, I'd arranged to share a room in Wexford. With another journalist. An old German friend who's there already. On assignment from a Frankfurt paper. That's how I got the idea. Of doing a similar piece.'

'So it was the other writer who made the reservation, sir?'

'Yes, from Germany.'

'And the name of the hotel, sir?'

'It's just a guesthouse. I've got the address and telephone number here somewhere.' He frowned as he reached into his back pocket.

'And the name of the friend, sir?'

Rees drew in hard on the cigarette. 'Metz . . . Freda Metz. Yes, she's a woman journalist.' He was countering the hardly disguised surprise in Lloyd's expression, as if defying him to make something extra out of the last piece of information.

'I see, sir. And you won't mind if we check with a . . . would it be Fräulein or Frau Metz, sir?'

'Fräulein, she's not married.'

'Thank you, sir. To check that she was expecting you?'

'Sure. Somebody'd better. She's expecting me tonight at the latest. But there's not another ferry till the crack of dawn tomorrow. That's assuming I'll still go over, which I probably won't. Not in the circumstances.'

'You mentioned you weren't sure yesterday whether you'd be going to Ireland by car,' said Parry. 'The car you were driving today wasn't yours, of course.'

'No, it's Pansy's. I don't have a car at the moment. Not necessary, not most of the time. We've been sharing hers. I had to be sure she wouldn't be needing it for anything special while I was away.'

'Like going shopping in Cardiff, sir?' asked Lloyd with studied interest.

Rees stared hard at the sergeant. 'She hardly ever took the car into Cardiff by herself. Too difficult parking. There's a bus stop at the end of our road. Or the station's only a minute further. There are more buses than trains, of course. She usually took the bus.'

'And she didn't ask you just to drive her in this morning, sir? Not since you were leaving so soon after her anyway.'

'Except I wasn't ready when she wanted to leave. I hadn't decided what I needed to take by then. That's because I was on the phone for ages first thing. If I'd driven her, and got snarled up in the Saturday traffic, I could have missed the ferry.'

Parry's eyebrows lifted as if he doubted it could have taken that long to reach Pembroke Dock, even after changing a tyre. 'And, as it was, you got straight on the motorway from Bryntaf in five minutes or so?' he said.

'That's right.'

'So you weren't in Cardiff at all this morning, sir?' asked Lloyd.

'Obviously not.'

'Was there ever any question of Miss Watkyn going with you to Ireland, sir?'

'Yes. We'd talked about it. I was keen for her to come. Trouble was, they've still got staff on holiday at the nursing home. She couldn't be spared. She was very conscientious

84

about that kind of thing. Overconscientious, really. Dedicated to the job.'

'But she wasn't working today?'

'Not today, no. She was going in early tomorrow, though.'

'Was she upset about not going with you, sir?'

'Not upset. Disappointed, perhaps.'

'Someone who saw her just after she left the house said she looked as if she'd been crying, sir.'

'That's not true.' Rees savagely stubbed out the half-smoked cigarette. 'The rubbish people invent. I suppose it was that moron from next door?'

'You and Miss Watkyn didn't have a row of any sort, Mr Rees?' Parry asked, without reference to Rees's own question. 'Over whether you could have the car, for instance.'

'No, we didn't. Nor about anything else. When she left the house she was probably looking determined, that's all – to catch the nine forty-six bus.'

'If Miss Watkyn had gone with you, sir, would it have been embarrassing, like?' Lloyd put in. 'I mean, since you were staying with the German lady?'

'Good God, no. Pansy and I would have taken an extra room, that's all. Look, I'm not sleeping with Freda Metz, if that's what you're getting at. Not currently, anyway. I told you, she's an old mate and colleague. She's on an expenses-paid trip. We agreed we'd share her room and my car. It helped us both with our claimable expenses. I'm freelance.'

'So she could claim nonexistent car expenses from her paper, and you could claim nonexistent hotel expenses from the taxman,' Parry commented with an indulgent smile.

'Something like that, yes.' It was a firm reply, not evasive, and implying that the speaker's relationship with the Inland Revenue was none of the policeman's business, even if that relationship involved some sleight of hand.

'I see, Mr Rees. Could you tell us, did Pansy Watkyn know Freda Metz?'

'They'd never actually met, no.'

'And Fräulein Metz is younger or older than Miss Watkyn, sir?'

'A bit younger.'

'And since Fräulein Metz is a . . . is an old mate of yours, you feel Miss Watkyn had no reason to be jealous of her?' Parry pressed.

'None at all. Look, I've told you –'

'And Miss Watkyn knew you'd be staying with Fräulein Metz. In the same room?' the chief inspector interrupted.

'I don't think I bothered mentioning that, no. Well, would you?' Rees smirked.

'Was Miss Watkyn what you'd call unusually liberal, sir,' asked Parry woodenly, and again ignoring the other's question. 'In her attitude to your other lady friends, I mean?'

Rees's upper lip curled a fraction. 'Not especially. She was just realistic.' He looked from Parry to Lloyd, and back again. 'Pansy was a very sharp lady. Also very committed, to me as well as her job. What we had going between us meant a lot to her. She wasn't likely to spoil it with niggling gripes about ex-girlfriends.'

'Well, that must have been very . . . satisfactory for you, sir,' offered the sergeant, who was strictly a family man. He shifted in his seat. 'Going back to the Bevan schoolgirl,' he said. 'You mentioned Miss Watkyn was helping her mother find a lost friend. What sort of friend would that have been, sir?'

'A German woman who'd been a cleaner or something for Mrs Bevan. But in Germany, years ago. Mr Bevan had been a regular in the RAF when they first married. He'd been stationed there. The woman's name was Resen . . . Carla Resen. That was it.'

'Was Fräulein Metz involved in the search for Carla Resen, sir?'

Rees frowned. 'As a matter of fact, she was, yes. But not for long. Mrs Bevan thought her friend might have been wrongly implicated in a case of baby snatching, in a town called Rheindahlen.'

'Wrongly implicated, sir?' Lloyd questioned.

'That's what Mrs Bevan told Pansy. Except she was wrong. Pansy got me to ask Freda to do some research. Basically to check back through newspaper files. There had been a case of illegal baby trading in the town, that or unofficial adoption.

And it was around the time Mrs Bevan said. But her friend wasn't implicated in it. Freda did translations of the reports. The person who did the trading was a midwife called . . . er . . . Heller, I think it was. Anyway, Pansy passed the stuff to Mrs Bevan. End of story. I don't see what it could have to do with Pansy's death.'

'Neither do I, sir. Not at the moment, at least,' said Parry, folding his arms. 'Would you mind telling us when and how you came to meet Miss Watkyn?'

'Mm, that was two years ago. At a singles night at the Falcon Disco.'

'You're single, too, are you, sir?'

'No, but my wife and I had separated long before then.'

'And you and Miss Watkyn have been living together for . . . ?'

'Just under two years.'

'Did she want you to divorce your wife, sir?'

Rees hesitated before he answered. 'I don't know what any of this has to do with Pansy's killing, either, but . . . yes, she'd have liked me to divorce Kathy.'

'And marry her, sir?'

'We never got as far as that. My wife's a strict Catholic. She doesn't recognize divorce.'

'I see, sir. Where's your wife living now?'

'In the back of beyond. Well, at the far end of the Gower Peninsula. She's a PE teacher in one of the schools in Swansea, or it may be Pontyglas now. She moves jobs a lot.'

'Did she know you were living with Miss Watkyn?'

'Sure. And with other women before that.'

'Does your wife hope you'll come back to her, sir?'

'No idea. We're not in touch at all. She's a bit of an optimist, though, so maybe she still has ideas about a reconciliation.'

Parry leaned back in his seat again as Lloyd asked: 'The bungalow in Carmen Lane, sir, we understand Miss Watkyn owned it?'

'That's right. Her parents left it to her.'

'Do you know if she'll have left it to anyone, sir?'

'Yes. To me,' Rees replied, unblinkingly. 'She had no close relatives.'

Both policemen avoided giving an outward show of special interest in this last illuminating fact. 'You mean she made a will, leaving the property to you, sir?' Lloyd questioned.

'That's right.' Rees had adopted his uppish expression again. 'It's not worth much, but it was one of Pansy's ways of showing her devotion. I was very touched. Of course, we both regarded it as a sort of symbolic gesture. She was hardly at the age to be considering dying.'

'Quite, sir. Did she leave you anything else?'

'I don't think she had much else to leave.'

'Her car?'

'That's not worth much, either. Incidentally, is it still in Carmarthen?'

'No, sir. It's in the underground garage of this building. You're free to take it with you when you leave.'

The red Metro had been brought to Cardiff after it had been searched by members of the Major Crime Support Unit permanently attached to Swansea Police Station. This had been after it had been driven on a low-loader to Swansea, from Carmarthen, courtesy of the West Wales Constabulary in whose bailiwick Rees had been stopped. The searchers had been looking for evidence that the car might have been in Cardiff that morning – for a car park ticket, a petrol station sales receipt, or any other sales receipt issued in the city. But Parry had been notified before he and Lloyd began interviewing Rees that the car had yielded nothing of interest.

'So, can I go?' Rees asked, making as if he was about to rise.

Lloyd looked at Parry, who answered: 'In a moment, sir, yes.' He looked at the time. 'I should tell you that we've had to make a thorough search of the bungalow.'

'You had a warrant to do that, I presume?' Rees demanded sharply.

'No, sir. Because we didn't need one. Not in the tragic circumstances surrounding Miss Watkyn's death,' the chief inspector ended his words solemnly.

9

'Now, would you be Fräulein Freda Metz, by any lucky chance?' asked the rubicund Irishman with the full red beard. His warm if slightly crooked smile had half closed his right eye as he dipped his head to one side, and deferentially touched the peak of his tweed cap with an extended forefinger.

The sturdy young woman, with the sharply silhouetted figure, who the man was addressing, stopped and looked from him to the elfin female at his side with some surprise. 'That's my name, yes. Who are you?' she asked in clear, heavily accented English. She smoothed the fringe of blonde hair away from her forehead, then shaded her eyes from the strong sunlight. The last movement had seemed unnecessary since she was wearing dark sunglasses, but it nicely accentuated the firmness of her bare arm, and the upward tilt of her breasts under the tight-fitting, sleeveless white sweater – at least, it did both these things to the private satisfaction and approval of her questioner.

The lady's well-shaped legs looked powerful, too, which was something the man had registered already. 'I'm Detective Sergeant Paul Mallory from the local force, miss,' he said, 'and this is my colleague, Detective Constable Bridie O'Hara.'

The two police officers produced their warrant cards in unison, like a double conjuring trick. DC O'Hara, dark and diminutive, was turned out in a blue linen coat and skirt, both somewhat creased, as though she had been sitting in them for too long. She had blue, darting eyes with a gaze made more studious by oversized, square-framed spectacles.

The sergeant was dressed more like a farmer than a police-man, in a wool suit of a weight that suggested he was pre-paring for the snap arrival of winter.

'Mrs Gallagher, your landlady, up the road at the Ocean Rise guesthouse, she told us we'd find you here,' Mallory continued. 'And it's a good description of you she gave us, so it was.' He nodded an extra appreciation, more it seemed of the subject described than of the description itself. Then he looked about him with the air of a satisfied proprietor. 'It's a fine exhibition we've made here, at the Wexford Herit-age Park, don't you think, miss? Irish life as it was lived through the ages. And we'll not be keeping you from seeing more of it for a second more than we need, will we, Bridie?'

'No, Sergeant, we won't,' his companion responded promptly with a sober smile, and in a soft but high-pitched voice that fitted her elfin build.

'Especially not on a glorious late afternoon like this one,' Mallory went on. 'Which, since you're a valued visitor, we'd like you to know is typical in this area at the time of year. But first of all we're to give you the message from Mr Evan Rees.'

Fräulein Metz stiffened. 'Evan Rees sends a message through the police? He is not ill? Not in an accident?'

'No, no, he's right as rain, so we understand, miss. Only there's been a change in his travel arrangements due to . . . to unforeseen circumstances.' The sergeant's right eye had half closed again, this time in a conspiratorial way, as he pronounced the hardly specific reason. 'If we could just sit down for a moment over here, sure, we'll tell you all about it.' He motioned her towards a substantial oak picnic table with benches attached, set with others on a sward of grass. The tables, all empty, were in the shade of a spreading copper beech in full leaf. There was a clear view from here across to Wexford Bay in the middle distance on one side, and a closer one on the other of a reconstructed nineteenth-century, thatched farmworker's cottage, which was part of the open-air exhibition.

'We've promised to contact you as . . . as a favour to our Welsh police colleagues,' Mallory continued, when they were all seated at one of the tables. He opened a hand wide and stroked his beard with it. 'As a gesture of more Anglo-Irish cooperation, you might say. And would we be right in thinking you arrived in Wexford earlier this afternoon, miss?'

'Yes. I flew London to Dublin on the one o'clock Aer Lingus flight. Then I drove straight here.'

'Ah, you drove here, miss? You have a motor car then? Fancy that,' the sergeant exclaimed, as though he had never before come upon the owner of such a conveyance.

'That's right. I hired it at the airport.' She gave an interested smile that showed off her faultlessly regular white teeth. 'That's so strange in Ireland? To hire a car?'

'Not at all, miss,' replied the detective, returning the smile, while his colleague made a note of something that hadn't at all agreed with what they'd been told to expect. 'And you flew from London, not Germany? That would be from Heathrow?'

'Yes. I was in England yesterday. To visit Glyndebourne. The opera house. It's been rebuilt, you know?'

'Has it now? Well, I never. And did you visit Cardiff this morning, by any chance?'

She shook her head. 'No. How could I do that? There wasn't time.'

'That's right. How could you do that?' Mallory, right eye closed completely this time, looked reprovingly with the other one at DC O'Hara, as if it was she who had suggested such a preposterously impossible feat. 'And we're right to be thinking Mr Rees was going to join you here, miss?'

'Yes. He told me he would arrive this evening. On the Fishguard ferry. It comes to Rosslare, I think, at six forty-five.'

'You didn't decide to join him in Wales for the journey here? That's instead of flying from London?'

'It was a possibility, but too complicated. Better we came separately. But what are these circumstances that have changed his arrangements? I don't understand. And why am I being told by the police?'

'Ah, now, could we be coming to all that in just a moment, miss? Meantime, could you tell us, had you fixed that you and Mr Rees would be staying together at Ocean Rise?'

91

The woman hesitated for a moment before replying, guardedly this time: 'Yes. He ... he is my ... fiancé, you understand? It's already arranged with Mrs Gallagher,' she completed, giving Mallory a candid, wide-eyed stare.

'That's what Mrs Gallagher told us, miss, but we wanted to be sure,' offered DC O'Hara. 'Mrs Gallagher wasn't certain how long Mr Rees was going to stay,' she added. 'Could you tell us that, perhaps?'

'He's not certain, either. It's partly depending on how long his work will take. Three, four days, maybe. We are both journalists writing background features on European opera festivals. There are also other considerations. Probably I shall be here until Wednesday. I am not too sure whether Mr Rees is staying till then.'

'Thank you, miss,' the woman detective replied.

'But you are still not telling me why –'

'Sorry, miss, I was forgetting,' said Mallory. 'Mr Rees has been delayed by the death of a friend. A Miss Pansy Watkyn. We believe the lady was a nurse, and it's a sad day when we lose one of those, so it is.' He shook his head very slowly, while, in a roughly matching tempo, he wiped his nose in a red check handkerchief, while staring the while at the ground under his seat. Then he looked up sharply with an expression that suggested a new thought had suddenly occurred to him during this quiet period of regret. 'Did you know the lady, by any chance, miss? Was she a friend of yours, too?'

The now stony-faced Fräulein Metz touched one of the pearl earrings she had on. 'No, I do not believe I have ever heard of this friend.' The frown that followed the disclaimer was a touch petulant. 'Do you know when Mr Rees will be arriving now?'

'Ah, well, as we understand it at the moment, he may have had to put off his trip altogether, miss. For the time being, at least.' He glanced at his watch: it was a minute to five. 'I believe he's been trying to ring you himself, only he's been moving about a lot today, and he wasn't sure how soon you'd be getting here. No doubt he'll ring you soon, and meantime we were to tell you he definitely won't be here today.' He knew there had been no chance of Rees calling before this, and that he had been detained by the Cardiff police until five to give the Wexford force time to contact Fräulein Metz first.

'I see.' The German woman opened the white handbag that was slung from her arm by a strap. 'So do you know how this Miss Watkyn died?' she asked, producing a packet of Marlboro from the bag.

'Well, from what we've been told, it seems she was stabbed to death this morning. In Cardiff Central Market, miss.'

'*Nein*?' Fräulein Metz exclaimed loudly. The fingers of her hands seized up tightly – so tightly that she snapped in two the cigarette she had half removed from the packet.

'No DNA findings on the knife, then, boss,' said Lloyd, coming through the open door of the small, half-glazed office Parry was using. The room overlooked the open office area now arranged as the Pansy Watkyn Incident Centre. This was currently occupied by a dozen or so police and civilians talking on telephones, or engaged with typewriters, desk computers, and photoprinters. It was on a floor higher in Cardiff Central Police Station from the room where Evan Rees had been interviewed – and finally released an hour before this.

One of the faxes just received had been from the forensic laboratory in Chepstow, giving a fast indication of what had been gleaned so far from evidence sent there for analysis. Both Parry and Lloyd had been reading copies of this.

'Nothing on the knife, and nothing helpful on her clothing, either. Not so far,' said Parry. He was seated at a small steel desk, the top of which was covered with accumulated reports and messages which he had been doing his best to scan.

'Well, that'll be it till Monday, won't it?' the sergeant offered dourly, as though it ill behoved forensic scientists not to be working through Sundays as well as nights.

'Except I've just talked to Dr Ironmonger at the hospital,' said the shirt-sleeved chief inspector, and without looking up from something he was writing. The room was sparely furnished – the whole contents comprising the desk, a metal side table, three chairs and two telephones. 'His first con-

clusion about the cause of death was pretty spot on,' Parry
went on. 'The single stab went straight to the heart. Blood
built up straight away in the ... the precardial sack, which
stopped the heart beating pretty well instantly. The victim
could have died in seconds, possibly without even a
whimper.'

'And probably did, boss, since no one heard her make a
sound.'

'Incredibly accurate stabbing, even so.'

'Or lucky, boss?'

'No, I don't think so. Neither does Dr Ironmonger. He
thinks our murderer had practical knowledge of human anatomy, or extensive theoretical knowledge of it, at least.'

'Like he was a surgeon or something, boss?'

Parry looked up as he shrugged. 'He or she could have
been a surgeon, doctor, nurse, physiotherapist, you name it.
It's a pretty wide field.'

'And Mr Rees isn't in any of those categories.'

'Not unless he got a badge for first aid in the boy scouts.'
Parry had stopped writing and was leaning back in the chair.
'So what did this DS Mallory of the Garda have to tell you?'

Lloyd, also in shirt sleeves, had just finished talking on the
phone to Mallory. He sat himself in one of the chairs in front
of the desk, while turning back the pages in his notebook.
'There'll be a full report faxed to us tonight, boss. The head-
lines are that Freda Metz is a smashing blonde, who says
she's never even heard of Sister Watkyn. She claims Mr Rees
is her fiancé, and she's pretty miffed about him not being
there to sleep with tonight.'

'If she thinks she's his fiancé, that's not surprising, is it?'
Parry commented.

'Except Mr Rees didn't say they were engaged, boss.
Another thing, she also seemed more surprised than grieved
about the death that's been keeping him here.'

'Well, that's more understandable if she really didn't know
Sister Watkyn, I suppose,' said Parry, though not sounding
convinced. 'But didn't it bother her that Rees was brought
here for questioning?'

Lloyd looked up from his notes. 'It did once she knew

94

Sister Watkyn was murdered, boss. Anyway, more to the point, she was in London yesterday and this morning. Stayed last night at the Bonnington Hotel in Southampton Row. She says she spent this morning in museums after an interview she'd arranged was cancelled. It was with the director of Mercia Opera.'

'Which of them is supposed to have done the cancelling?'

'She said it was he who cancelled after calling off his trip to London. She then left Heathrow for Dublin on the one o'clock flight this afternoon, arriving there at two ten. According to Aer Lingus, it landed a minute early.'

'We're checking with them she was on it, as well, are we?' The sergeant nodded, as Parry went on: 'If she's in any way involved with the killing, of course, she'll deny she was anywhere near Cardiff this morning.'

'She told DS Mallory she wasn't, boss. For the record, she was here earlier in the year. For two nights in June, to hear the Welsh National Opera, she says.' The sergeant paused. 'Would have been difficult for her to have been here this morning, at the time of the stabbing, and then to have caught that flight from Heathrow,' he completed, more thoughtfully.

'Difficult, or impossible?'

Lloyd produced a roll of peppermints from his pocket. 'Not impossible. Not if she's a fast driver.'

'Or if it was worth it for them to have hired a fast driver to take her.'

'Them being her and Evan Rees, boss?'

Parry hollowed his back, and clasped his hands behind his head. 'Could she have got a later flight, Gomer?' he asked, while considering Lloyd's question about his own previous comment.

'Ah, that's why we're checking she was on the one o'clock,' said the sergeant, slipping a peppermint into his mouth. 'The next one's an hour later, which would have given her plenty of time to get from Cardiff to Heathrow after the murder. Except, after she'd landed in Ireland, she still had to drive from Dublin Airport to Wexford. That's nearly ninety miles, and she was definitely at the guesthouse by four thirty. The landlady confirmed it.'

'It's a good road, though. Perdita and I drove a lot of it when we were in Ireland last autumn,' Parry interjected, and involuntarily glancing at the time. Perdita Jones was his girlfriend, and he was meeting her off a London train at Cardiff Central Station, known to all as 'the Gen'ral', at six fifty-three. 'You said Miss Metz drove herself?' he completed with a frown.

'Yes, boss. That's the other thing. She's hired her own car.'

'So the share and share alike, and save on the expenses idea only applies to Rees. He was to get the pleasures of her bed, and presumably her body, but she doesn't get the use of his car, or rather Pansy Watkyn's car.'

'Wouldn't have been a fair trade for her if she had, not by the sound of it, boss,' Lloyd responded, with a lapsed Methodist's half-sanitized leer. 'That's what DS Mallory said, anyway,' he added, this time a touch primly.

'Rees never said anything about the woman being his fiancée, of course. On the contrary, he made their current relationship sound pretty chaste.'

'That's not how Miss Metz regards it, boss.'

Parry gave a grunt. 'Well, whatever their actual relationship, the fiancé bit could have been for the benefit of the Irish landlady, of course.'

'True, boss.' Lloyd adopted his golden yesterdays expression as he continued: 'There was a time when a couple couldn't get a room in Ireland or Wales, not without the woman was wearing a wedding ring. Did I ever tell you about my Auntie Mavis? She kept a bed and breakfast in Mumbles, that's after her husband died, and she used to insist –'

'You did tell me, Gomer, yes,' Parry interrupted, too pre-occupied to want to hear about Lloyd's auntie. 'One thing is certain. Rees can't have told Pansy he was sleeping with Miss Metz. What we don't know is whether Miss Metz knew he was living with Pansy.'

'Because if he really was Miss Metz's fiancé, she wouldn't have liked that at all, would she?' the sergeant commented, with the suggestion in his tone that you could hardly fault her for that.

Parry pinched the end of his nose. 'Do we know yet how

much that bungalow of Pansy's is supposed to be worth?'

'Ah, now there's a real story behind that, all right, boss. Remember Mr Rees told us it wasn't worth much?' Lloyd was busy referring back to his notes. 'Well, like you asked, DC Norris did some checking with local estate agents after we left. Seems whatever the place is worth now, it's likely to double if planning permission for a new housing development goes through there. It'll take place in Carmen Lane and that field at the back. The developers already own the empty third bungalow. If the plans are approved, they'll want to buy the other two in the lane as well, for knocking down. That's because all three properties will be in the way, see?'

'And Pansy must have known about this,' said Parry.

'She did, yes. So did Mr and Mrs Slocombe next door, boss. But they've told DC Norris they don't think the Council will approve the scheme. They've put in a formal objection to it themselves, and they think Pansy Watkyn may have done the same.'

'Some people might still prefer to stay in their homes than exchange them for more money than they're worth, I suppose,' observed Parry.

'Well, it's a point of view, isn't it, boss?' Lloyd responded, his sympathies clearly lying with those whose values put them above the lure of great riches.

'Even so, it sheds a different light on Rees inheriting the place from Pansy, doesn't it?' said Parry. 'What's it worth now, Gomer?'

'Eighty thousand minimum, boss.'

'But twice that just for being in the way of progress?'

'That's what two of the estate agents said, yes.'

Parry got up from his chair, and moved to the single window which faced east. For some moments he silently scanned the rear elevation of the rococo City Hall with its festooned, campanile-like clock tower. The plainer, high-domed National Museum was beyond that on the right, and the University building was immediately opposite him, on the far side of the formal Alexandra Gardens. This was all part of Cathays Park, the Welsh capital's civic centre begun in Edwardian times, and intended to compete in classical grace with Washington DC, and India's Delhi.

The building Parry was in had been a late and hardly worthy addition to the group, but still had to be one of the most serenely sited police stations in the world. He gave a brief professional glance at the already heavy Saturday-night traffic in King Edward VII Avenue immediately below him, before his sobering gaze returned to the University. He had known this well in his year as a student, before he had dropped out on impulse to become a policeman. If he had his life over again, would he have stayed on, eventually qualifying as a lawyer, as his now dead father had wanted? This same thought had recurred often in the recent past.

Perdita had given up medical school to marry, and had later qualified as a physiotherapist. But her marriage now collapsed, she had gone back to medicine proper at twenty-six. Parry accepted that at thirty-eight it was too late for him to –

'You still having some time off tomorrow, boss?' Lloyd broke in on his train of thought.

'Eh? Yes. I think so. Till after lunch, anyway. Unless something dramatic comes up on the case,' Parry answered, turning his back to the window, and tightly folding his arms across his chest. 'Look, Gomer, if it wasn't Evan Rees or Freda Metz, and I'm beginning to think it wasn't, and if it wasn't some loony –'

'Which it probably wasn't, because the stab was too accurate, boss,' the sergeant put in.

'Well, let's assume that, anyway.' A demented, motiveless killer is every Senior Investigating Officer's culprit of last resort. Parry scratched his head. 'I'd rather work on the basis it's someone in a part of Pansy's life we know nothing about yet. Or too little about. And someone maybe even Rees knows nothing about, either.'

'Wasn't much to help there at the bungalow, boss.' The two had spent an hour and a half at 5, Carmen Lane, going through the nurse's effects with a team of detectives.

'Maybe because we didn't look hard enough. Or didn't

know what to look for. Those regular monthly cash deposits on her bank statement, for instance.'

'They weren't that big, boss, and they did vary a lot. Could be plenty of innocent reasons for them.'

'Like what? Nurses don't get paid in cash. Unless it's for moonlighting jobs, possibly. But according to Rees she wouldn't have had the time to moonlight.'

'Perhaps she knitted and sold the results for cash. Something like that, boss.' Lloyd's wife was a copious knitter – of sweaters, scarves and heavy socks for her husband whose stock of mostly unused woollen wear was, as a result, prodigious. The residue of his wife's output was dispersed as presents to friends like Parry himself, and for no financial return.

'OK, but Rees would have known and mentioned anything like that.'

'Only if it was legal, boss.'

'I'm not sure. Let's ask him again, about that specifically. And ask her colleagues at the nursing home, as well. Maybe they won't be as shy as her boyfriend about dishing the dirt on any profitable sideline she had, straight or not so straight. We want to know who could have been paying her two fifty a month.'

The sergeant was making notes. 'Still doesn't help us over the thousand in her bag, though, does it? Whether it was money of her own she'd just withdrawn from some account, or money someone had just paid her.'

'How much was in her current bank account, Gomer?'

'Just over six hundred at the end of August. That was the last statement she had. The balance had been growing over the last three months.'

'Well we can find out on Monday whether she'd paid a lot more in during September, and then taken it all out recently. Could be, of course, there's an account we haven't found yet. Strange that Rees was obviously more surprised than we were about the money in her bag. Perhaps whoever's been giving her the two fifty a month suddenly quadrupled the contribution. And Rees didn't really know about those payments, either. I'm certain he was ad-libbing about giving her cash for housekeeping. But why?' Parry paused for a moment, made a pained face, and then went on: 'We need to go through those itemized call lists again, too. The ones we found with her BT bills.'

'A lot of the calls were his, boss. Rees's.'

'Yes, even though he said he mostly uses a mobile.'

'He probably used that for calls he didn't want her to know about, boss. And the bungalow phone for the rest, because she paid the bill. We know she did that from her bank statements.'

Parry nodded. 'So let's get a list of his outgoing calls on his mobile, plus the incoming calls to both their numbers.'

'That's already in train, boss.' Lloyd had expected a good deal of what Parry was asking for now.

'Have we got hold of Rees's wife yet, Gomer? The PE teacher.'

'Not yet, boss. There's no one at her cottage, and it's very isolated, apparently. A local farmer's wife who hardly knows her says she thinks she's away most weekends. She and Rees have been parted a long time. She doesn't sound promising.'

'But she still needs to be interviewed.' Parry reached for his jacket. 'Right, Gomer, I'm off. Keep me up to date. See you.'

10

'But you passed that exam two weeks ago. That made you a regular medical student again. At the start of your fourth year. Which is where you left off before. You've worked fiendishly hard for it, too. All through the summer. To my great regret and inconvenience, of course.'

Parry completed this delivery of clipped phrases without meaning the final one. It was a fact, even so, that since April, when Perdita had moved to London and given up her house and physiotherapy practice in nearby Tawrbach, their time together had been limited to a drastically attenuated few days' holiday in France in June, a further snatched weekend, and a few single nights. But this was what they had expected – even agreed to accept. He leaned up on one elbow to look at her now as she lay beside him on the grass in the early-afternoon sunshine.

'I passed the exam by the skin of my teeth, that's all,' she replied, pushing the corn-coloured hair away from her face, then breaking off another piece of the dandelion leaf she was slowly destroying with steely concentration. 'I'm positive most of the examiners were just being indulgent to an older student. Overindulgent. They humour a mature student for being so plucky – or something. That'll last till the results of my finals come out a year next June. Then it'll be: "Good try, Miss Jones, but goodbye, Miss Jones."'

'That's nonsense, and you know it. At twenty-six you're not that mature. Not as a student, I mean.' Parry's hand went out to squeeze both hers tightly. 'You've got to go back to thinking positively again. Otherwise, what's the point of all the effort so far?' he countered, seriously this time.

The two were in Pontcanna Fields, part of the nearly two-mile stretch of wide parkland that runs north, inland from Cardiff Castle and up to Llandaff Cathedral. This is a green haven hugging both sides of the River Taff. The city is all around it, but keeps a seemly distance.

After Perdita's arrival by train the previous evening, she and Parry had made hungry love at his Westgate Street flat, before going out for a late seafood dinner at Quayles, the Art-Deco restaurant in Romilly Street. Back at the flat, they had listened to a new Mozart CD, then made love again, less greedily this time, before falling asleep in each other's arms. They had awakened late with the hottest September Sunday for decades already into its stride.

Perdita had prepared a brunch of melon, scrambled eggs, smoked salmon, croissants and strawberries, washed down with a nutty Sancerre. Most of the ingredients had been fetched by Parry from a nearby deli, except for the eggs and the wine of which there had been impressive stocks in the kitchen – though of precious little else that was ingestible. Perdita had remarked that the two items probably composed his staple diet.

Afterwards they had walked up to the Fields through Sophia Gardens. It would have been a perfect day to drive to somewhere quiet along the coast, but Perdita wanted to catch the early-afternoon train back to London to keep a working date at her hospital in the evening. She had spared Parry her serious misgivings about her studies until now – and had not intended to voice them at all until an unguarded remark had prompted him to dig for more. She had then unburdened at length.

Perdita rolled on to her front, bare bent elbows supporting her raised shoulders. Her head lowered, her widely set, big hazel eyes stared into the grass. 'To be absolutely honest, for the last week I've been seriously thinking about chucking it. Coming back. We could get married this year, if you wanted.' She sighed and looked up at him slowly. 'And you'd have to be a saint not to say: "I told you so."'

All of which put him in a dilemma. When, six months before, she had been unexpectedly offered the chance to complete her earlier abandoned medical course in London, he had first done his best to dissuade her from accepting, begging her to marry him instead. Ultimately, though, he had come to realize that he couldn't allow her to pass up the chance because of him. If that happened, and if their consequent marriage had failed (as her previous one had done), he could not have lived with the thought that he had stopped her fulfilling her career destiny, and all to no purpose. This was why he had encouraged her to follow her ambition, although it meant a sacrifice on his part. She had promised to marry him after she qualified as a doctor, but not before, and only then if he still wanted her.

'I never said you'd ever want to chuck it once you began again,' he answered carefully. 'I said the pressure would be hard, but you'd be strong enough to cope.'

'I thought so, too, except –'

'I know so. And there's no except about it,' he interrupted harshly, with an expression to match, and the dilemma resolved at least for him. 'I'm ashamed of you, not just disappointed, ashamed if you're now trying to persuade yourself otherwise. I can't believe there's anything worse facing you than what you've got through in the last six months. Got through with flying colours, too. And if I can put up with another twenty or so months in a good cause, I think you can. I think you owe that much to both of us – and to the other people who believed in you, gave you the chance. A chance in a million, you said at the time.' He paused. 'See, I love you, Perdita. I'm going to be proud as hell when you qualify. And you *will* qualify. There's no doubt about that. None at all. That's if you have the guts to face what's involved.' He waited some moments, then he leaned down to kiss her lightly on the neck. 'So are you ready now to press on? Or do you want the other half of the lecture? Because I warn you, it's more harrowing than the first half.'

So far, Perdita's only reaction to his words had been a marked stiffening of her shoulders. She hadn't responded in any way to the kiss, and she hadn't looked around at him. Then suddenly she pulled herself to her knees, threw her arms around him and hugged him, with tears coursing down her cheeks. 'Darling Merlin, you're so good for me. Just . . . just marvellous,' she whispered brokenly. Then she kissed him full on the lips, in the process toppling them both backwards to the grass. Two elderly ladies and their equally elderly Pomeranian, perambulating on a nearby path, markedly increased their pace and averted their eyes – even the dog's. 'You're right, of course,' said Perdita, stroking Parry's forehead later. 'I needed telling, I suppose . . .'

'Educational chances should be grasped, and once grasped, never released,' he offered. 'Not released voluntarily, anyway. It's a good rule, that. Wish I'd followed it. Might have been a QC by now. Life's too short for anything else. You'll agree with me, a year next June. It's not long.' He sat up, feeling virtuous, and looked at the time. 'Only we'd better stop all this abandoned behaviour in a public park. It frightens the horses. And anyway, you don't want to miss your train, do you? Otherwise you won't be in time for the ward rounds tonight with that consultant. Conscientious sort of chap to do rounds on a Sunday night, isn't he?'

'Yes, very.' She smiled. 'Only it's a she, not a he.'

'I'm so glad. I was worried about that,' he answered, and meaning it.

It was shortly after he had seen Perdita off at the station that a phone call from Gomer Lloyd soon had Parry driving alone the twenty-odd miles north through mountainous country to an isolated, hillside public house called the Valley Head. It was on a side road off the main route to Aberdare.

The pub was open, but looked empty, like its car park. Despite the relaxation in UK drinking laws, locals were evidently not yet given to imbibing alcohol at teatime on Sundays. The chief inspector pulled the open Porsche convertible to a stop at some distance away from the stone-faced building, and at a spot in the car park that offered a view of the twisting River Cynon, some distance below, wending its way down from its source in the Brecon Beacons.

It was some minutes before the time Parry had agreed to be here, but it now seemed possible the man he was meeting was early too. As the policeman switched off the car engine, he watched a mature, red VW Beetle enter the car park, then chug slowly and erratically across the lumpy, uneven surface, coming to rest with a discernible and threateningly terminal sag, two yards or so to the left of the Porsche.

Several moments elapsed before the door of the newly arrived vehicle was thrown open, and a black-suited man of around fifty, wearing a black goatee beard and a clerical collar, began emerging into the sunlight with evident difficulty. The delay was caused by the newcomer's determination to extract his left leg from whatever was seriously impeding it in the bowels of the car, while, at the same time, attempting, with both his hands, to cram a wide-brimmed Panama hat over well-groomed wavy hair, growing to nearly shoulder length. Although there was a cavalier air to the hat, this was more because it was of the cheap variety offered to tourists around St Mark's Square in Venice than a Panama likely to be worn, let alone sold, around St James's in London.

When the double challenge had been met and overcome, the cleric, who proved to be short and plump, slammed the car door shut with a histrionic flourish. This action produced a disturbing rattle from the vehicle, not a reliable sort of clunk. He next stood erect, sniffing the air through a bulbous nose, like a cautious groundhog. Only then did he direct his gaze to the other car, and with an expression suggesting that he had only now become aware of it or its owner's presence.

'Mr Corbin Hooson?' enquired Parry, who had got out of the Porsche, and was now also standing between the two cars.

'Certainly not,' the man replied unexpectedly, with stern but nervous alacrity, and in a heroically strong local accent. He drew back half a pace. Then the sunken eyes, under flaring and abundant black eyebrows, opened wider, purposely signalling an air of shrewdness, if an overplayed one. 'But hold hard. Was that the name I gave to your man on the telephone? I believe it was. Caution was called for, d'you see? You *are* Detective Chief Inspector Merlin Parry?'

'That's right, sir.' Parry moved closer, and showed his warrant card.

The other waved a hand at the card, in what could have been either blessing or dismissal. He then grasped the hat by the brim, as though he was about to sweep it off in a courtly gesture of greeting, until the movement subsided into a simple adjustment aimed at shielding the wearer's study of the policeman from the lowering sun. 'You know your name was on the wireless this morning?' he observed in a school-masterly and admonitory tone, suggesting the matter could probably be overlooked this time.

'Yes, sir. I understand you can assist our enquiries into the death of Miss Pansy Watkyn.'

'I have vital information about that. Vital information.' The cleric looked about him to ensure that they were still alone, difficult as it would have been for anyone to have sneaked up on them unawares across three hundred square yards of totally empty car park. 'Information,' he continued, his mellifluous tone rising a little in a sermonizing way, 'that I am only ready to vouchsafe to you personally, which is not for general dissemination, nor specific onward attribution, and which I am offering only because of my strong sense of public duty. Do I make myself crystal clear?' He breathed in deeply, twice. 'You'll find the air up here is like champagne. Shall we sit in my car?' Without waiting for an answer to either of his questions, he opened the door of the Volkswagen and levered himself inside again, with similar attendant difficulties to those he had experienced getting out, his left leg seeming to be lame, while his intention now to keep his hat on was firm. Sitting inside the car hardly qualified his previous commendation of the quality in the outside atmosphere, although it offered less chance of their being overheard than if they had sat in the open Porsche.

'You explained your conditions to Detective Sergeant Lloyd, sir,' said Parry, after getting into the passenger seat, and wondering how Gomer would have reacted to being described as his man. 'Of course, we'll observe your wishes so far as we can. So long as they don't impede the course of our investigations –'

'They won't do that,' the cleric interrupted with heavy conviction. 'You'll understand when I explain.'

'I see, sir. If it's to do with anything you've heard in the confessional, of course, there are rules –'

'It's nothing to do with Catholic practices, either. I am the founder and presiding minister of the Free Church Mission of Achievers for Jesus. No doubt you know of us. Our mission weeks this summer in Aberystwyth, Llandudno, and Colwyn Bay have been particularly remarked, in the English as well as the Welsh press.' He straightened his left leg by first grasping it just under knee level. Parry assumed the limb was a false one. 'Very successful weeks they've been. Our mother chapel is in Llangarth, of course, from where I have journeyed this afternoon.'

'Ah, yes,' Parry responded. He had heard of the Achievers for Jesus. It was one of the few surviving missionary sects that operated at seaside resorts in the summer months. Llangarth was over forty miles of hilly driving to the west of where they were sitting. He was impressed that the Volkswagen had survived the journey. Taking the age and state of the founder's vehicle into account, it was reasonable to assume also that the Achievers counted their successes in spiritual not material terms – which, he supposed, was to their credit. 'Now then, I wonder would you be good enough to give me your full name and address, sir? For the record.'

'My name is Ifor Dafydd Owen-Pugh, DD, MA. That's Doctor of Divinity and Master of Arts. My degrees were obtained at overseas universities where I have taught as well as studied.' He glanced sideways at Parry. 'The address is the Mission, Corporation Street, Llangarth. I reside there with my wife and children. Four children.' The doctor began smoothing the top of the steering wheel with his fingers, and cleared his throat before speaking again. 'I was a patient at the St Olaf Private Nursing Home two years back. For a week in the September. It was just after our mission that year in Blackpool, which had been a huge success. In most respects, at least.' A discomforted sigh punctuated the last phrase.

Ten seconds or more silence followed until Parry broke in with: 'So you met Sister Watkyn professionally, perhaps, Doctor?' He had wondered if his companion had dried up, or had possibly gone to sleep, since his hands had slipped down to his lap, and his eyes were tightly closed.

'The condition for which I was hospitalized was of an intimate nature. A very intimate nature. I was assured by the consultant that no one other than himself need have been aware of its . . . its true nature.' Eyes still shut, Owen-Pugh stroked his beard gently as he spoke. 'I was admitted ostensibly for a period of rest, due to overwork, you understand? It was a harmless subterfuge with a basis in fact, aimed at protecting my reputation. It was also to protect the physical wellbeing of others close to me.' He cleared his throat. 'I include my dear wife in that group. She knew nothing of my actual medical condition.'

'So you were receiving treatment for an infection? A contagious one?' Parry prompted, when his companion seemed to have lapsed into silence again.

The cleric licked his lips. 'Contagious in certain circumstances, yes,' he replied, quietly. 'It was more . . . more convenient to be hospitalized for the first week of concentrated treatment. Sister Watkyn was in particular charge of the case. An angel of mercy, comfort, and rectitude she seemed at the time. I can tell you, I trusted her implicitly. The consultant assured me, in her presence, mark you, that no other member of the staff was appraised of the . . . specific' – he lingered over the last word, then repeated it – 'the specific nature of my problem.'

'Quite, sir, and presumably –'

'A month after I left St Olaf's,' Owen-Pugh continued, ignoring Parry's intervention, and with his eyes still shut. 'Sister Watkyn came to the chapel in Llangarth at a time when, as advertised, I'm available for private counselling. In a nutshell, she demanded five thousand pounds to keep her mouth shut. Otherwise she said she'd inform the Committee of Senior Achievers about the nature of my ailment, backed with documentary proof. She had taken a copy of the consultant's report made for his own records, which she had borrowed, as she put it, while he'd been in seeing me.'

'So she was a blackmailer? This is very helpful to us, Doctor,' said Parry, with feeling. 'But didn't you think of going to the authorities? To the police, the nursing home management, the consultant – ?'

'She'd thought of all that. She said if I told anyone, she'd pass the information to the Sunday newspapers straight away, anonymously, and deny she'd done it, or ever been to see me.' Owen-Pugh opened his eyes. 'I'd have been ruined, Mr Parry, not that that would have been the worst of it. Think of what would happen to the work of the mission. The faith of our converts. A betrayal of God and the Lord Jesus is what it would have been in the eyes of the mockers. The mission shamed and brought to nought through a single, sinful, foolish act. Times are hard enough as it is.' He sighed loudly.

'So you paid her?'

'That's right, Mr Parry.' There was another sigh. 'Not straight away, though. I didn't have five thousand handy, or anything like it. But she was ready for that.'

'She made you pay two hundred and fifty a month for two years,' Parry supplied, after doing a quick mental calculation. 'Which added a further thousand pounds in what she'd have called interest.'

The doctor blinked. 'That's right. How did you know? Do the police know – ?'

'The monthly cash payments more or less show up in what she's been paying into her bank, Doctor.' Parry thought for a second before continuing: 'I wonder would you mind telling me where you were at ten thirty yesterday morning, sir?'

The bushy eyebrows lifted in surprise. 'Why do you? . . . Oh, I see,' Owen-Pugh gave a bleak smile. 'From nine till twelve, I was conducting a teach-in for three lady novice missionaries at the Llangarth chapel.' He crossed his left leg over his right with no apparent difficulty, which the policeman noted and found vaguely surprising, as the speaker added: 'I think she may have been murdered by someone else she was blackmailing, though, don't you?'

11

'So she was blackmailing him, boss. Well, I never,' said Gomer Lloyd, before ingesting another piece of Cornish pasty brought upstairs on a tray from the canteen at the Central Police Station. 'Over a sexual indiscretion, was it?' he added, gathering up a forkful of peas. 'Or did he have his hand in the till, like?'

'You were right the first time,' Parry answered, eyeing the not especially appetizing ham salad in front of him which had come up on the same tray. The drooping lettuce in particular had a distinctly end-of-weekend look to it.

The two were eating in the small office off the incident room, using the desk as a table. Parry had just returned from the Cynon Valley.

'Well, that's better in a way, isn't it?' the sergeant commented. 'We're all subject to human frailty and temptation, after all. Especially in that department. And clergymen as much as anyone.' It was a magnanimous comment from someone whose marital faithfulness was legend. 'Woman, was it?' He waited for a reply, newly laden fork poised halfway between plate and mouth.

'Yes.'

'Well, that's something, at least.'

'In Blackpool, I gathered,' Parry added. 'On account of the bracing air there, I expect.'

'Ah, he should have stuck to Welsh resorts. Aberystwyth or Llandudno. Cleanest beaches in Britain, as well.' Lloyd nodded to himself as if this last fact was indicative of some deeper spiritual virtue, then he drank some coffee from a plastic beaker.

110

'He's run missions at both of them,' said Parry, grinning. 'Anyway, his defence was he yielded to temptation when he was overworked. But only the once.'

'Well, he would say that, wouldn't he? Bad luck if it's true, as well. Did the girl threaten to tell on him, boss? Report him to the elders, or whatever they have? And Sister Watkyn got wind of it?'

'No. He picked up a social disease.'

'Not Aids, was it?'

'No. Something fairly mild, and curable. Genital herpes, by the sound of it. Pansy Watkyn got to know of it when he checked in at St Olaf's for treatment. It was supposed to be confidential treatment.'

'Go on? That was underhand of her, wasn't it? Unethical, on top of everything else. Had him by the shorts all the same, I suppose. But why did he need to go to hospital?'

'He didn't say exactly. To save embarrassment with his wife, probably. He said that at the time, he was having a near breakdown from overwork.' Parry abandoned the rest of the ham and applied himself to the fruit salad that had come with it. Perdita's brunch was still too appetizing a memory.

'So is that where those monthly cash payments were coming from?' Lloyd asked.

'Yes. She gave him the option of handing over a lump sum, or easy payments over two years. He had to accept the easy payments.'

'Plus interest, of course,' Lloyd offered, knowledgeably. He had been this way before: they both had.

'That's it, yes. The last payment was in August.'

'So why did he decide to tell us everything, boss?'

'Because he genuinely considers murder's a lot worse than extortion.'

'Well, you can't fault that, can you?' Lloyd slurped up more coffee.

'He said Pansy was a misguided woman, but taking a life was worse than anything she'd done to him.'

'Which he probably considered . . . retribution for his misconduct.' Lloyd rolled out the word 'retribution', giving it a power and significance only possible when pronounced by a Welsh bass. 'Must be hard being holy,' he completed.

'And we don't involve him officially unless we have to, Gomer. And if we do, there shouldn't be any reason to admit she was blackmailing him.'

The sergeant nodded. 'Fair enough. He deserves that much. Because of coming forward voluntary, like. And after paying all that money, too, to keep her quiet.' He picked at something between his two front teeth. 'Don't see why we'll need to involve him, do you, boss? Not unless he did the murder himself, of course.'

'Which he couldn't have. Claims to have half a dozen witnesses at least to prove he was in Llangarth all yesterday morning. Conducting a missionary training class at the chapel.'

'We'll check that, then?'

'Yes. As discreetly as possible.'

'Right.' Lloyd pushed his empty plate away from him, made a note, then looked up. 'And his wife couldn't have known about Sister Watkyn and the blackmail? I mean, she didn't do the murder for him?'

'His wife was at the training class as well. I asked. And she certainly didn't know about his er . . . his social disease, either.'

Lloyd returned the other's grin. 'If his payments to Sister Watkyn stopped last month,' he said, 'it means she needed something to make up the shortfall, doesn't it? Unless she was going to ask the reverend for a renewal, like.'

'Which, according to him, she hadn't done. Not up to now, anyway. And for what it's worth, she'd told him she never would. All of which suggests she may have found a new victim, or victims.'

'Who paid by a different method from the reverend. But we didn't find a building society book, or an account with another bank, boss. We'd better have another look in the morning, after we've checked with her bank.' Lloyd made some more notes.

'Since her methods seem to have been pretty amateur, effective but still amateur, she may have phoned other victims from home. Have we got that other list of calls from BT yet?'

'Yes, boss. Right here.' The sergeant produced a British Telecom print-out that had been partly annotated by hand. 'We haven't finished checking through both lists yet, but there's one interesting Bryntaf number Sister Watkyn called three times in the last two weeks. Remember Mrs Dilys Bevan, wife of the electrical contractor?'

'The woman Pansy was helping to find her German home help?'

'That's the one.'

'But she would be calling her. For reasons we know about.' He spooned up the last of the fruit salad.

'Ah, but it happens Barbara Bevan went missing after breakfast yesterday. She's the Bevans' seventeen-year-old daughter. An only child. She was supposed to have gone to school, but never turned up there.'

'When did the parents report her missing?'

'Not till ten this morning, boss. At Llandaff nick. From there the information was passed to missing persons. It came to us because the Bevan name was included on our trawl through the central records computer. Marvellous system.' Lloyd had a healthy regard for the benefits of electronic fact finding – and anything else that reduced legwork.

'And Barbara's their only child?'

'Yes. Apple of her father's eye, apparently. Well, she would be, wouldn't she?'

'So why didn't they report her missing earlier?'

'They assumed she was with her boyfriend. Name of Alwyn . . . Alwyn Price. Lives in Llandaff North.' Lloyd had checked the name in the bundle of print-outs he had brought in with him. 'He's at the same school as the girl, only he's a bit older than her. The school's a sixth-form crammer. Both kids are working to get to university. Alwyn wasn't at school yesterday, either. Mr Bevan rang his mother after lunch. She's a widow. Alwyn had told her he was going to that rock concert in Brecon. Then to a party after. But he never said Barbara was going with him. His mother lent him her car. Party venue is unknown.'

'Acid party?'

'Could have been. But you wouldn't tell your widowed mother that, not when she's lending you her car, would you? Anyhow, Mr Bevan wasn't best pleased. He'd thought Barbara had gone with Alwyn, not telling her parents in advance because she knew they wouldn't approve. Seems it wasn't like her, but he couldn't think of a better explanation at the time. Put it down to Alwyn Price's influence. He doesn't like the lad.'

'And is that what the daughter had done?'

'Can't say for sure. Mr Bevan drove all the way to Brecon himself last night to bring Barbara back. He didn't find her at the concert.'

'What about the boy?'

'Didn't find him, either. At first the organizers refused to page Barbara over the sound system. Said they'd only do that in an emergency.'

'And an irate father looking for a rebellious seventeen-year-old daughter didn't qualify?'

'That's right, boss. In the end, though, Mr Bevan got the attending police involved. Uniformed inspector in charge ordered the girl's name to be broadcast.'

'Just as well if she really *is* lost. And she wasn't found?' Parry leaned back in his chair. 'It was a big concert. We saw a clip of it on the late news last night.'

'Yes. The girl could have been there, and not heard them broadcast for her. But Mr Bevan assumed she and Price had left for this party already. And that didn't please him either because nobody there knew anything about any party. In the end, he came home fuming.'

'But that wasn't when he reported her missing, Gomer?'

'No. He said later he thought you couldn't do that officially till the person had been gone twenty-four hours.'

'That doesn't usually stop distracted parents from demanding police action, does it? And she hasn't turned up yet?'

'No, boss. Nor the boy.'

'Is his mother bothered?'

114

'She hasn't reported him missing. No reason to, really. And he *is* eighteen.'

'Well, it's pretty obvious they're together, which almost certainly means they're all right. In fact, probably having a ball in some motel.' Parry shrugged. 'The girl's beyond the age of consent.'

'It was just they went missing on the morning Sister Watkyn was murdered, boss.'

'I'm thinking about that.' Parry reached for the BT call list. 'Pansy made three calls, you said? Any from the Bevan number to her? Or from his office?'

'We're finding out, boss. Do you want to see Mr and Mrs Bevan tonight?'

Parry looked at the time. 'Probably, but not till we've got something that links the missing daughter with Pansy's murder. I just have the feeling Evan Rees may not have told us all he knows about the Bevans yet, and a few other things as well. So let's go and ask him first.' He pushed back his chair.

'Dilys is going up the wall, of course,' said Huw Bevan, adding Perrier to the generous measure of Scotch he had already poured into a glass. 'This coming on top of the Pansy Watkyn business.'

'The blackmail or the murder?' asked Laura Mathews, his secretary. 'Dilys was relieved surely about the murder? It means the end of the blackmailing, doesn't it?'

'We hope so, yes. But you can't tell, can you? Not for sure. Right now Dilys is beside herself about what could have happened to Barbara. You know how she gets?'

'Well, I think she should stop worrying about Barbara, and count her blessings. You both should,' the woman replied with almost angry conviction.

The couple were in the kitchen of Laura's small, comfortable flat. It was in a modern block in Fairwater, a district a mile to the west of Cardiff centre. Dressed casually in an open-necked white blouse and tight red slacks, she was wearing rather more make-up than was currently fashionable, with heavy eyeshadow, brilliant red lipstick and matching nail varnish. She hadn't been expecting him today, but there had been time for her to make herself presentable in the way he liked after he had telephoned from the car ten minutes before this. Ten minutes was all it took for him to drive here from Hill House in Bryntaf.

He turned to her with the glass in his hand. 'It's hard to explain how I feel. You're right. Common sense tells me Barbara's safe. That she's with Alwyn Price for certain. I've never liked him much, and now –'

'Now you think he's shacked up somewhere with your precious daughter, you feel like murdering him. Except you're grateful as hell that nothing worse is happening to her than being with him,' she had interrupted, pushing past him to pour herself a glass of plain Perrier. 'It's understandable. You just have to be thankful she'll not come to any real harm.' She put a hand over his mouth to stop him saying what he intended as she went on. 'He's the devil you know, Huw. And from what you've told me about him, he's crazy about Barbara, he comes from a good background, he's kind to his mother –'

'Not so kind that he's told her the truth about where they are.'

'Eighteen-year-old boys tell their mothers very little that doesn't suit. He did tell her he was going to the concert and the party. You told me that on the phone last night.' He had called her from the car on his way back from Brecon.

'Except it doesn't look as if they were at either place.'

'That's not necessarily true.' She motioned him through to her cosily furnished sitting room. It had one large window with a view through the open curtains across a wooden-decked, wrought-iron balcony to a small park across the road. 'I told you this morning, they could have been at both places, and just moved on. That's what the police say, isn't it?'

'The police aren't really treating Barbara's disappearance seriously. Not since they found out the boy's missing too. Yes, they say they're together and they'll show up soon. But they can't know that for certain.' He ran a hand across his forehead. 'And where are they? If Barbara's all right, why hasn't she called us, at least?' He slumped into the end space

116

of a long, softly cushioned sofa. He took his cellphone from the pocket of the sports shirt he was wearing to check that the machine was switched on, then took a large gulp of his drink.

'We're back to the shacking up, aren't we?' Laura said, shaking her head, then patting the back of her blonde hair that was cut in a pageboy style. 'Look, she's seventeen. If some boy hadn't got her into bed before this –'

'I'm certain she's still a virgin. Or was till yesterday,' Bevan broke in angrily.

'That's wishful thinking. You can't know.' She sat beside him, putting her glass on a lamp table at the other end of the sofa. 'Look, she's your darling daughter. You've protected her all her life, every way you know. Maybe you've been overprotective to this point. No, hear me out.' She raised her voice to stifle the start of his fresh protest. 'Maybe going away like this, without saying where, it's her way of telling you to ... well, to stop stifling her with love, possession, whatever. Something she couldn't have told you face to face. If they are in bed together somewhere, it'll be with her consent, so accept they're behaving like normal, natural, sexy human beings. In other words, that they're having fun, like you and me.'

'That's quite different. And she's only –'

'Seventeen?' Laura broke in with a low chuckle. 'Come on, Huw, where've you been? Most girls are into sex a hell of a lot earlier than that these days, specially the pretty ones. Be glad she's got a steady. Means she doesn't sleep around like some. I know it's not an ideal situation from your point of view, but it could be a whole lot worse. D'you want some food?'

He shook his head. 'I'm not staying. Dilys's sister came over for an hour. I said I needed some air. They'll call me if there's any news.' Absently he stroked her bare arm, feeling the soft fair hairs along it. 'You may be right. God, I hope you are. If only I knew for sure she's safe.'

'I'm sure. So are the police. They must have cases like this one coming out of their ears. She's OK, believe me.'

He sighed. 'Well, perhaps I don't understand kids.'

'She's not a kid, for a start.'

'That's right, I suppose. I should have spent more time with her. Understanding her.'

'Instead of working your guts out making enough money to keep her in luxury, good clothes, good schools, and everything else.' She was speaking from the heart now, to the man she respected above all others, and who she was ready to protect to the utmost – and not just from himself, as she was doing now. 'Huw, love, you do what you're good at. It's partly Dilys's job to bring up your daughter, too, you know?'

'Sure.' He paused, then took her hand in his. 'You feeling better? Over the tummy upset?'

Momentarily she looked puzzled, then gave another short chuckle – but this time a less than spontaneous one. 'Yes, thanks. I thought you'd never ask.'

'Sorry. Anyway, I'm glad. I missed you yesterday.'

'That's good.'

'Seriously, there was a lot to sort out at the office in the morning. I forgot to tell you, I did ring you here about something mid-morning.'

'Did you? Ah, I went for a stroll at one point,' she offered casually. 'I was feeling hemmed in. Anyway, I'm fine now.'

He leaned across and kissed her on the lips, but not very passionately.

'There's something else bugging you, isn't there?' she said, quietly.

He gave a grunt. 'Good thing you're not the police. You see right through me.'

'The police? Are you thinking they'll find out about the blackmail and figure you killed Pansy? But that's crazy. You –'

'No. That's not what's bothering me,' he broke in. 'Well, not directly.' He finished the rest of his drink with one swallow, and put the glass down. 'It's to do with Dilys. And Barbara.' He paused again, leaned forward, and stared at the empty fireplace, hands clasped between his legs. 'What if Barbara had found out about the blackmail? And the reason for it. About . . . about her not being our child?'

Laura looked puzzled. 'How could she have done that?'

'Through Dilys. Well, possibly.'

'But Dilys wouldn't have told Barbara.'

'Not on purpose, no. But she's so bloody careless. Barbara could have found something.'

'Like what? Everything on paper is at the office, well locked up too.'

'There's a tape. Of that second phone call from Pansy to Dilys. The one I made sure Dilys was ready to record.'

'But that's at the office, too.'

'The original is, yes. But there's a duplicate. I'd told Dilys to make a dupe before I got home on the day. I wanted to give it to Simon Frankel, but then he came to the office and drove home with me.'

'I remember, yes. And you didn't give him the spare tape?' Curiously, she was now sounding a lot more anxious than he was.

'No, I didn't. We listened to the original in my study as soon as we got home. Dilys had rewound the tapes. Both of them. Simon and I agreed I should take the original to the office for safekeeping next day. At the time, I . . . I just forgot about the bloody dupe. I'd meant to wipe it. And Dilys never mentioned it again. She'd left it next to the machine, where I told her. So I suppose it was as much my fault as hers. She must have picked up the dupe later, when she was dusting, probably, thinking I'd wiped it, I suppose. She put it in the end slot of the rack where I keep new tapes. It was still there last Friday evening when I suddenly remembered it. I did wipe it then.'

'So where's the harm?'

'The harm is, it was there in the rack for over two weeks. Barbara sometimes borrows a tape from there if she runs out. It's just possible she took that one. Played it to make sure it was blank and – '

'Heard everything Pansy said? But Barbara would have told you.' Laura hesitated. 'Or, on second thoughts, perhaps she wouldn't. If she played the tape, what would she have learned from it? The lie that she was stolen from her real mother – '

'And the truth that we bought her as a baby,' Bevan broke in heavily.

Laura frowned. 'Also that you and Dilys could still face criminal charges,' she completed.

'All that, yes. Enough to have ... to have traumatized Barbara?'

'No, Huw, that's an exaggeration.'

'Is it? When we've told her nothing about any of it? When she learns in that way we've been lying to her all her life?'

Laura shook her head, making the long, heavy gold ear-rings glisten. 'She's a sensible girl,' she said. 'A bit impulsive sometimes, but highly intelligent. Perhaps she'd have been angry with you. Too angry to turn to you and Dilys for an explanation straight off. Or she could have taken it quite differently. She could have been more angry with Pansy, much more angry.'

Bevan looked up. 'And made a date to see her? That's the idea that's haunting me. Driving me round the twist.' He lunged up from the sofa and went to the fireplace. With his back to Laura, he spread his hands on the top of the low, tiled mantelpiece, leaning on it, head bent, as he went on: 'Did she arrange to see Pansy yesterday in the market? If she did, you know what the police will say? Everybody knows she's impulsive. You said so yourself just now.' He turned about. 'That's why they'll say she murdered the bloody woman.'

'No, they won't, Huw,' Laura put in quietly, going to him quickly, and putting her arms around him. 'They won't say it because she couldn't have done it. Listen, you've got to believe me. She couldn't have done it,' she repeated with heavy conviction.

12

'She didn't have any close relatives. I mean, no brothers or sisters. There's the odd cousin, I think, but she never mentioned any of them by name. Never even exchanged Christmas cards. Not so far as I know. That's why I suppose it's got to be up to me to cope with the funeral. The burial arrangements.'

Evan Rees had admitted Parry and Lloyd to the bungalow in Carmen Lane with some surprise, but no evident hostility, on their arrival at just after seven o'clock. He had led them into the living room while replying at length to Parry's first question about Sister Watkyn's surviving relatives, although this had been offered as more of a social enquiry than a professional one.

Rees seemed to be almost indignant at the prospect of being responsible for Pansy Watkyn's funeral. Parry found this curious in the man who had professed such affection for the dead woman, and, more to the point, who was about to inherit most of her worldly goods. And if Rees's attitude wasn't exactly unexpected – that is, in view of the opinion the chief inspector had already formed of his character – it was an incautious view to expose to police officers who, not long before, had been making few bones about suspecting Rees of murder. Altogether, it was an odd way of reaffirming his devotion to his dead lover.

'There may be a bit of a delay before the body can be released, of course, Mr Rees. Always the way, I'm afraid,' Lloyd volunteered, as the three men stood in the centre of the untidy room. The television set was on, and was presently showing a documentary about the intimate lifestyle of

African lions, but with the sound muted. There was a half-empty bottle of gin, and a wholly empty one of tonic, on the table next to the chair Rees had been occupying before he had been called to the door. The glass, also on the table, was as empty as the tonic bottle. Parry wondered if the liquor was responsible for Rees's garrulousness, the matching mellowness, and his lack of caution.

'How long a delay?' the journalist asked.

'Difficult to say, sir,' Lloyd replied. 'Probably only till the end of the week.'

'It won't hold up probate on the will? That kind of thing?'

'Shouldn't think so, sir. Sister Watkyn's solicitor will be the best person to give you advice about that.' It was Parry who replied, and without volunteering that to execute the will of a murdered person could sometimes take immensely longer than getting the body released for burial, depending broadly on whether the murderer had been identified, and who was to inherit the estate. Again, he found Rees's fixation with the material benefits accruing to him through Pansy's demise more than a bit unseemly. 'Do you think we might sit down, Mr Rees?' he suggested.

'Sure. Sorry.' Rees waved at the sofa and the other armchair, then turned off the television, although a last lingering look at the screen suggested he was loath to exchange the company of soundlessly copulating lions for that of policemen with intrusive questions. 'Like a drink?' he asked.

'Not while we're on duty, thanks all the same,' said Parry, taking the chair on the other side of the fireplace. Lloyd, who had sat on the sofa with his notebook in hand, gave a nod of agreement, followed by a soulful kind of grunt that might just have been a subconscious negation of what the nod had indicated: it had been a long day for the sergeant, notwithstanding the overtime he was earning.

'Two of your people were here this morning.' Rees had produced another bottle of tonic from somewhere before he had resumed his seat, and was pouring himself a fresh drink as he spoke. 'Wanted another look through Pansy's bank statements and her cheque book.'

'Yes. Sorry about that, sir,' offered Lloyd. 'We were

wondering again if she could have drawn a cheque for that thousand pounds she had in her bag. And if she did, how recently.'

'Well, her cheque book wouldn't help you there. She never made a note of the cheques she cashed, even though the cheque book has stubs. But I thought I told you yesterday, the thousand wouldn't have come out of her ordinary bank account. I don't believe she ever had that much in it.'

'But it could have been from some other account, sir? Like with a building society.'

'She didn't have any other account. Or not that I know of. Anyway, your people had a good look. They didn't find anything of that kind.'

'That's right, sir. Of course, no one's been able to see her bank statement for this month yet. We'll be arranging to have a sight of it at the bank in the morning,' said Parry. 'On another subject, did you know about the planning application to develop this area?'

'Yes. Pansy was against it. Those nerds next door are the same. Funny attitude, really. On Pansy's part, I mean. She had some queer notion about owing it to her dead parents to keep the old place standing.'

'Yes, we understand the developers would want to knock it down, sir.'

'That's right. But look at it.' He gazed about the unprepossessing room, which had become much more so through the absence of its previous live-in tidier. 'Not exactly a stately home, is it? And Pansy never had enough money. The deal could have pushed up the value of this no end.'

'It still will, sir. If the plans are approved.'

'Hm. If they are.' At first, Rees seemed to be more interested in rescuing some depleted ice cubes that were floating in a small china bowl, under the side table, and which now contained mostly water, than he was in considering the chances of his shortly-to-be-inherited property doubling in price. Then he looked up suddenly. 'You don't think I'd have done in Pansy so I'd come into this crumby joint, do you?'

'No, sir. But murder has been committed for less. Much less,' Parry commented drily.

'Well, we've been over that ground, and you know bloody well I couldn't have done it. Not time-wise, and not . . . not . . . geographywise.' He beamed at Parry, then at Lloyd. He had encountered some difficulty in articulating the last word, confirming the impressions of both policemen that he had drunk a sizeable amount of gin before their arrival.

'I expect you've been in touch with Miss Metz, sir?' asked Parry, his inflection implying that the question might just have been connected with Rees's last spirited denial.

'Yep. She's as devastated as I am about poor Pansy. Devastated.' Rees sniffed, while pulling at the hairs sprouting thickly along his bare arm. 'Of course, she didn't know Pansy. Not in the flesh, that is. But she knew how much the two of us meant to each other.'

The chief inspector noted mentally that Miss Metz was thus alleged to have developed a better understanding of the relationship between her 'fiancé' and Pansy Watkyn since the day before – an understanding, indeed, that invested the German lady with the same almost superhuman degree of tolerance and forbearance that Rees had ascribed to Pansy during his previous interview. 'Had they talked on the telephone at all, sir?' Parry asked.

'No.' The denial came so fast that both hearers registered the fact in their faces, and Rees realized as much before he went on. 'I mean, Pansy didn't speak any German. Freda speaks English, of course, but Pansy preferred to let me do the talking when Freda rang.' Inwardly, the speaker complimented himself on having put that lie so convincingly.

'That would have been when Miss Metz was helping to find Mrs Bevan's old employee, the home help, would it, sir?' asked Lloyd.

'That's about right, yes.' But Rees's tone had become more cautious than before.

'Could you tell us more about that, Mr Rees?' the sergeant pressed. 'Exactly what information did Miss Watkyn need for Mrs Bevan? I think you said before, it was about a baby snatch in Germany some years ago.'

'Yes. Seventeen years ago, that was. Didn't come to much in the end, though. Freda got the name of the woman accused of the crime. It wasn't Mrs Bevan's cleaner, as she'd thought. It wasn't a baby snatch, either. The accused woman was a midwife. She was supposed to have done a brisk trade in unwanted babies. Buying them from the mothers and selling them on.'

'Selling them on to foreigners as well as Germans, perhaps, sir?' Parry put in.

Rees shrugged. 'I can't remember. That bit didn't seem to matter. Not after Freda established it wasn't the woman Mrs Bevan was looking for.'

'You mentioned yesterday that Miss Metz sent you translated newspaper reports, sir. What happened to them?'

Rees shrugged. 'I gave them to Pansy. I think she passed them on to Mrs Bevan. There's no sign of them here, if that's what you're getting at.'

'I see, sir. Incidentally, is Miss Metz likely to be visiting you here before she goes back to Germany?'

'No. And I've now cancelled my Irish trip altogether.'

'Miss Metz will be disappointed about that, sir.'

'Yes, but she understands.'

'Could I ask, is Miss Metz aware you were living with Sister Watkyn, sir?'

Rees smirked. 'I expect so. But it wouldn't matter to her who I was living with. She's very easy-going.'

'She described herself to the Irish police as your fiancée, sir.'

'Did she now? Good old Freda. Bit of a Calvinist at heart, she is. She was sure the landlady of the Wexford guesthouse would think her a scarlet woman if we didn't put up a front of that kind. Obviously she figured the Irish plods would take the same view.'

'We thought as much, sir,' Lloyd replied, glancing at Parry.

'Anyway, we'll not be upsetting Irish sus . . . susceptibilities after all, since I'm not going there. Too busy dealing with Pansy's affairs, the funeral, and, er . . . and other things.' Rees shifted in his seat, and gave a somewhat shamefaced smile. 'Fact is, I've done an exclusive deal with one of the tabloids. My life with Pansy, that kind of drivel. And I'll be doing inside reports for them on the case as it develops. I'll also be covering the trial, that's if and when you catch the bastard who did for the poor girl. Well, it seemed too good an opportunity to miss. For a journalist. I know Pansy would be the first to agree.' The last comment was more combative than what had gone before. 'Incidentally, did you want to see Freda Metz?' he asked, as though this was an afterthought.

'Not really, sir,' said Parry. 'She was good enough to give very full answers to the questions put to her for us, by the Irish police.'

'She would. Very cooperative lady. She told me they'd seen her.' He chuckled. 'Fiancé,' he added, still chuckling. 'What next?' He cleared his throat, and made an evident effort to be serious as he went on: 'No, she's not coming here on her way home for the good reason she doesn't care to be caught up in a murder. Even remotely. I mean, she's not really implicated at all, is she? But I can see it might look as if she was. Can't say I blame her for staying out of it.' The verbose Rees reached for his glass, which was empty again, glanced at the others, and put it back on the table. Then, with some difficulty, he extracted a Gold Leaf from its packet, prior to experiencing a further problem in bringing his lighter flame to meet the end of the cigarette.

'Understandable, of course, sir.' Parry leaned forward in his chair, adopting an almost confidential style, in manner and tone, as he continued: 'According to the BT log, somebody called the Bevan home three times from this number in the past two weeks. That would presumably have been Sister Watkyn, would it?'

'Well, it certainly wasn't me. I don't even know the people.'

'Quite. And you didn't happen to overhear any of the conversations, sir?'

Rees's head, neck and shoulders moved back woodenly, all of a piece, his face registering something between surprise and moral outrage. 'Not that I remember, and I'll have you know I'm not in the habit of listening to other people's telephone conversations.' Then he let out a guffaw. 'Especially bloody dull telephone conversations. They'd only have been yacking about the baby case, and I was frankly bored with

it.' He waved a hand in the air dismissively, carelessly dropping ash from the cigarette he was holding. 'I mean, I
couldn't understand why Mrs Bevan was so determined to
get all the detail on the case. That's after Freda established
the woman involved wasn't her cleaner.'

'Could it have been that it was Sister Watkyn who wanted
the detail, sir, not Mrs Bevan?'

Rees frowned, and looked from Parry to Lloyd, then back
again. 'I don't follow? Well, I do, actually, and you're wrong
if you think Pansy was nosey by nature. She wasn't. Granted,
she wanted to help the Bevans in any way she could. I
imagine she phoned their house quite often from here, or
from St Olaf's. And called there in person at least once, that
I know of. It wasn't just Mrs Bevan she was friendly with,
you know? From what she told me, she was very close to
the daughter as well.'

'And, in your opinion, the relationship was based on
friendship and nothing else, sir?' the chief inspector asked.

'Yes. That and the fact Pansy and Mrs Bevan had a nurse-
patient relationship which probably came into it somewhere.
I mean, that's how they knew each other in the first place,
wasn't it?'

'To your knowledge, sir, Mrs Bevan never gave Sister Watkyn money.'

Rees inhaled deeply on his cigarette. 'Money? No. Why
should she?'

'And again, so far as you know, Sister Watkyn never asked
Mrs Bevan for money, sir?'

'Of course she didn't.' He paused. 'Oh, if you want to be
ped ... pedantic about it, there was a small professional
payment to Freda. It was for the work she did tracking down
the cleaner. Or trying to. Pansy told me she got it in cash
from Mrs Bevan. I passed it on to Freda, after deducting a
nominal amount for my own involvement, which was not
... not insubstantial.' He had much earlier debated whether
he should explain that, so far as Pansy had been concerned,
their German collaborator had been a male Freddie, not a
female Freda, but he had decided that disclosing the harmless

127

subterfuge invented too many complications. He came to the same decision again now.

'How much was the payment, sir?'

Rees put out the cigarette, and picked up the gin bottle, which he had been eyeing for some time. 'Three hundred quid.' He poured gin into his glass. 'That was quite modest, considering the time and effort Freda had put in.' He looked up with a cynical smirk as he added: 'And what I thought the traffic would bear. Well, the Bevans aren't short of a bob or two, by all accounts.'

'And, so far as you know, that was all Sister Watkyn ever received from Mrs Bevan, sir?' Parry continued.

Rees was adding tonic to his drink. 'Well, I mean, she might have asked her to help with one of her charities, I suppose.' He gazed disconsolately at the bowl, which now contained only water and no vestige of ice. 'Pansy was always collecting for good causes. But I can't think of any other reason. Why are you so interested in the money part all of a sudden?'

It was Lloyd who answered, if obliquely, 'I should tell you, we've now found out who'd been giving Sister Watkyn those cash payments every month for the last two years, sir.'

'What cash payments?' The surprise in the tone, and on Rees's face, seemed almost too prompt to be anything other than genuine.

'The ones you thought could have been part of the money you gave her towards the housekeeping. It seems they weren't, sir.'

'Oh yes, I remember now. Well, can't be right about everything, can you? It was only a guess on my part.' He beamed at the sergeant.

'You really weren't aware she was getting regular cash payments, sir?' Parry demanded. 'Two hundred and fifty pounds a month. We've now had that confirmed.'

'No. News to me. Mark you, I didn't know how many times she blew her nose every day, either. I mean, how would I . . . ?' His voice faltered as he watched Parry's serious expression change into one of irritation. 'The bank deposits were two hundred and fifty a month, you said?' he offered, more slowly.

'No, sir. The amounts were always below that figure, and they varied each month. But as you've just heard, we now know the cash sum she received always began as two hundred and fifty. The deposits she made showed up well enough in her bank statements. I'd have thought you'd have noticed that.'

'But I didn't read her bank statements. Any more than she ever read mine.'

Lloyd stroked his chin. 'You told us yesterday, at the station, that so far as money was concerned, you and Sister Watkyn shared and shared alike, sir.'

'Sure, but that was a way of saying – '

'And since she was getting these payments from one source, in cash, every month, for all that time, it's reasonable to assume you'd have known about them, like.'

Rees drank from his glass, then said: 'Well, tough titty, because I didn't. And the only one of her bank statements I've ever looked at was the last one, yesterday, to see if there was enough to pay any bills she left. I'm her executor, of course.' He looked hard at the sergeant, as though in preparation for a question on the last point. Since there was none, he went on: 'So, who was giving Pansy all this money?'

'You don't know, sir?'

'Of course I bloody don't know, or I wouldn't be asking, would I?' he responded sharply, and now sounding more than just peeved.

Parry sat back again and folded his arms. 'We have evidence to prove the payments were a result of Sister Watkyn obtaining money by threats, sir.'

'Threats? Pansy? You've got to be joking.' He hesitated, brow furrowing. 'Do you mean some kind of blackmail?'

'That's precisely what we mean, sir.'

'Well, I don't believe you. God help us.' Rees looked about the room jerkily, as if in search of actual support, divine or otherwise. 'The idea's totally bizarre. I mean, I'd have known. She couldn't have been blackmailing anyone. It wasn't in her nature. Her make-up.' His native Welsh accent became much more pronounced as he continued hotly: 'She didn't have the . . . the guile, the . . . the artfulness, for a start. Not for that kind of caper.'

'That was the impression we've gathered of her as well, sir. Which is why we came to the conclusion she was possibly fronting for somebody else.'

'For me, I suppose?' Rees's eyes hardened, and so did the veins at the side of his neck. Then he lunged forward in his chair with such energy that he nearly fell off the end of it. 'Well, I'd like to see what evidence you have for that kind of accusation, and I think, while we're about it, I'd better have a lawyer present to –'

'We have evidence that Sister Watkyn was blackmailing someone, sir,' Parry interrupted. 'But we didn't say we thought she was fronting for you. We hoped, once you knew the situation, you might be able to suggest either the name of any collaborator, if she had one, also the names of people she might have been blackmailing.'

Rees groped for the cigarette packet. 'Look, how many times do I have to tell you, I'd no idea Pansy was blackmailing anyone? It's unbelievable. How could I be living with her and not know such a thing? No, I still don't believe it, and that's flat.' He lit another cigarette with a trembling hand.

'I'm afraid the evidence we have is incontrovertible, sir,' said Parry quietly but firmly. 'I realize it must be hard for you to accept. But you'll understand, if our information is right, and I assure you it is, Sister Watkyn's activities as a blackmailer could very likely have a big bearing on her murder. On the identity of her murderer.'

Rees inhaled quickly on the cigarette several times before he spoke, while staring down at the floor. 'OK. I can see that. In fact, it's bloody obvious, isn't it? I may be a bit pissed, but I'm not stupid. But I still want to be sure there's no mistake. And even if your so-called evidence is true, I repeat, I've still no inkling who else could have been involved. One way or the other. Collaborator or victim. And if you tortured me on the rack, God's truth, I still couldn't tell you better than that.'

13

'He'd have to have said that, wouldn't he, boss?' said Lloyd, thrusting a peppermint into his mouth. 'About it all being a terrible mistake that Sister Watkyn was a blackmailer, and that?'

'Perhaps. But he sounded convincing. He was also half cut, of course,' Parry responded, his eyes on the road ahead.

'Drunk, boss? *In vino veritas*, like? Anyway, you believed him?'

'That first reaction was the key one. Either he really didn't know anything about the blackmailing, or he was astonished because . . . because he hadn't expected us to find out about it. Difficult to be sure which, though.'

'But if she didn't tell him she was blackmailing someone, *why* didn't she?' the sergeant asked. He gauged the implications in Parry's tone too well to have any doubt about which of the conclusions the chief inspector favoured, even though the choice exonerated Rees from knowing of Pansy Watkyn's criminal activities. 'You'd have thought a man of the world like him would have been better at extortion than a nursing sister. A lot better,' he added with feeling.

The two were in the chief inspector's car heading away from Carmen Lane, towards the Bevan house in Hillside Rise, at the other end of Bryntaf. The distance was less than two miles, all uphill along a series of prosperous-looking avenues, the properties along the way becoming more affluent the higher the car climbed.

'I think Pansy was keeping him,' said Parry. 'But she would never have intended him to know she relied on crime to do

131

it.' Despite the words, there was still a touch more speculation than conviction in the last sentence.

'I don't see why, boss. He doesn't strike me as being the
. . . the choosy sort, like. Not when it comes to money.'

'But his knowing wouldn't have made for a settled future
for her. I agree, he'd be happy enough to live off Pansy. And
she was probably crazy enough about him to turn to crime
to keep him. But I don't believe he's the criminal type. If
she was into crime, I'm sure he wouldn't have wanted to
know about it. And I'm equally sure she'd figured as much.'

Lloyd pulled a face, and one end of his moustache. He
wasn't given to philosophical speculation about the workings
of the criminal mind. 'Doesn't make him exactly virtuous
though, does it?' he observed, sourly. 'Odd that she was
against that planning application, all the same. Seems to me,
selling the bungalow for a fat price would have solved all
her money problems over getting lover boy to stay around.'

Parry shook his head. 'I'm beginning to think she was
more complex than that. Rees said she felt an obligation to
keep the bungalow because her parents left it to her. That
could be true of a dutiful daughter, I suppose. An only child,
as well.'

'Or one who was conscience-stricken for some reason,
boss. Funny thing, conscience. Gets to people in different
ways, and not always the people you expect.'

'Mm, and remember, she told Owen-Pugh she'd never
ask him for more money. Not after he'd paid what she'd
demanded at the start. He believed her, and it seems she was
keeping her word, too. So she had standards.'

'It's only according to the reverend she was keeping her
word, boss. We don't really know she hadn't come back at
him for more. Good motive for murder he'd have had there,
that's if she had come back at him. Good motive for not
telling us that bit as well.'

'Except his alibi's too tight. And his wife's as well. Still,
you might have a point there, Gomer.'

The sergeant loosened the seat belt around his ample
middle. 'So what did you make of Rees telling us about his
exclusive deal with the newspaper?' he asked.

'Quite a lot. He's letting himself in for extra exposure that way, of course. Either it confirms he wasn't party to Pansy's criminal activities, didn't even know about them, or else he's got a hell of a nerve.'

'And him saying she wasn't nosey, or artful, after we'd told him she was a blackmailer, that's the same thing really, isn't it?' Lloyd offered slowly. 'And either way, he's kind of put himself in control of what's said in the newspapers. All of them. Not just the one that's hired him.' Lloyd sucked loudly on the peppermint, before he added, 'But if Sister Watkyn was going to blackmail the Bevans, like you said when –'

'I said it was a possibility worth looking at,' Parry interrupted. Even so, he had tabled the hypothesis quite seriously, earlier on, when they had been driving up to see Rees. 'But, yes, I think it's more of a possibility now,' he went on. It was certainly the reason he had decided they should call on the Bevans tonight, without delay. 'If Rees really lost interest in the baby-snatch story, when he found there was no snatch, and no involvement by Mrs Bevan's friend and helper either, I wonder was Mrs Bevan herself still interested? Maybe it was then it started to be Pansy's interest.'

'For the same reason we got interested over the daughter's age, and her being born on the day the parents left Germany.' Lloyd frowned as he spoke. 'Fair's fair, though. It was Mary Norris who put us on to that, wasn't it?' It was DC Norris who had pointed out the two facts, gleaned from a newspaper cutting she had come upon while they had been searching the bungalow in Carmen Lane the day before. 'Hillside Rise, boss,' the sergeant exclaimed, as Parry nearly missed the turning. 'Millionaire's Row, they're calling this now. Nice houses, what you can see of them through the trees and fences. Or defences more like. It's the next on the right. Hill House.'

'I'm glad someone senior's been put on to Barbara's disappearance, at last,' said Huw Bevan, as he led Parry and Lloyd through the hall.

'Yes. Well, we're investigating another case that, er . . .

133

that could have a bearing on your daughter's actions, sir,' Parry replied diplomatically. 'And if you take my advice, you won't accept she's disappeared. Or that she's come to any harm.'

'You too?' Bevan stopped at the double doors to the drawing room. 'Your colleagues have been saying the same. You'll have trouble convincing my wife, I can tell you. And me, for that matter. My wife is very upset. You'll need to make allowances for that. Simon Frankel's with us, by the way. He's my lawyer. Through here.' He opened the door wide and let the others through.

'Don't think our paths have ever crossed before, Mr Parry,' said Frankel, as brief introductions were being completed. The accent was public school and Oxbridge, not Welsh. 'My firm doesn't handle much criminal work, and I personally avoid getting tied up in court appearances of any kind. Too time-consuming, and usually unprofitable,' he continued, with a languid affability, and a final short, humorous snort emanating from the very back of his nose. He was tall, well built and loose limbed, dressed casually but expensively in a white, roll-neck sweater over well-cut blue linen slacks and white canvas shoes. His skin had a healthy outdoors tan, and while the black wiry hair was receding a little at the temples, the extra area of exposed forehead added a touch of sagacity to an already impressive and agreeable countenance. Despite their owner's relaxed manner, the deep blue eyes were alert, and appeared to react as swiftly as his brain.

Parry had heard of Simon Frankel, reputedly the sharpest corporate solicitor in the Welsh capital. He knew as well that there was no reason why they should ever have met before, either professionally or socially. It had been polite of the lawyer to suggest that they could have done – polite or calculatedly ingratiating, the policeman wasn't sure which. 'I'm sorry if we've interrupted your meeting with Mr and Mrs Bevan, sir,' he said.

'It's not a meeting, Mr Parry. Just a social call to cheer them up,' Frankel replied promptly, and more pointedly than might have seemed necessary, as though the distinction he was making was important. 'I'm trying to persuade these two good people to stop worrying. I'm sure Barbara's all right. After all, it's still less than thirty-six hours since she left here. Kids are so thoughtless about keeping in touch.' He smiled. 'My wife and I just got back from a sailing weekend. In West Wales. We keep a little boat at Solva. When we heard about Barbara we made tracks earlier.'

'We think she's with Alwyn Price, Mrs Bevan,' said Parry, turning to the red-eyed woman, cowering, shrunken, and occupying, but hardly seeming to fill, an elegant French gilt-framed chair covered in peach silk damask. Head bowed, bent elbows held tightly to her sides, her left hand was clasped over the right which was kneading a handkerchief. 'We gather the boy's mother thinks the same as we do,' the policeman added sympathetically. 'He'll be looking after Barbara, don't worry.'

'Not the way I'll look after him when I get hold of him,' Bevan put in fiercely. 'You said you're involved in a similar case, Mr Parry? What case is that, then?'

'Not similar exactly, sir, but it may have a bearing,' the chief inspector replied, as he and Lloyd seated themselves on the shaped, cushioned seat that skirted the bowed window at the far west end of the room. Frankel was reseating himself on this as well, near Mrs Bevan's chair. The area, softly illuminated now by the setting sun, was altogether cosier and less formal than the rest of the room.

Tyn, the spaniel, who had been in the hall when the policemen arrived, and had followed them in, settled itself at Lloyd's feet. Given a choice, domestic animals seemed to favour being with the sergeant, usually in preference to the close company of their real owners. His colleagues said he fed them peppermints.

'So it's not another disappearance you're on?' Bevan pressed, taking a chair close to his wife's, a match of the one she was using.

'No, sir. I'm Senior Investigating Officer on the Pansy Watkyn murder,' Parry answered, watching the reactions of his listeners.

'What's murder got to do with –?' Mrs Bevan began in a strained, worried voice.

'Let's hear what the chief inspector has to say, Dilys, shall we?' Frankel interrupted gently, but purposefully.

'We understand Sister Watkyn was a friend of yours, Mrs Bevan. And your daughter's,' Parry completed.

'They both knew her, yes. Sad business. Very.' It was Huw Bevan who had answered the question, his eyes on his lawyer, not the questioner. 'They weren't what you'd call close friends of hers, though. More acquaintances. Isn't that right, Dilys?'

There had been little colour in Mrs Bevan's face when the policemen had entered, now there seemed to be none at all as she swallowed, it seemed painfully, and replied, in a near whisper: 'I knew her through the nursing home. St Olaf's. I was there for an operation. Barbara met her there, too.'

'What's the connection with Barbara's playing truant, Mr Parry?' Frankel asked, his tone remaining merely interested, and undemanding.

'We'd hoped Mr and Mrs Bevan could help us there, sir,' Parry responded noncommittally. 'Mr Evan Rees, that's Sister Watkyn's live-in lover, he tells us she was helping Mrs Bevan trace someone's whereabouts. A German woman, living in Rheindahlen.' He turned to Mrs Bevan. 'A cleaner you used to employ when your husband was stationed there, ma'am.'

'It's not true. I never asked her for help of that sort,' Mrs Bevan protested, and speaking a touch louder than before, though she was still difficult to hear distinctly.

'So Mr Rees seems to have been mistaken,' said Frankel smoothly, and before Parry could take up the point. 'Did he mention the name of the woman?'

Parry glanced at Lloyd, who answered: 'Her name was Carla Resen, sir.'

'No!' Mrs Bevan voiced the single word as an exclamation, and as though she had put all her available strength into it. She was also shaking her head quite vigorously.

'Sister Watkyn told Mr Rees she understood the woman might have been involved in a baby snatch many years ago,' Lloyd elaborated. 'She'd said Mrs Bevan wanted her found so she could help her.'

'I didn't ask Pansy about any Carla Resen,' Mrs Bevan

136

protested. 'I didn't know any Carla Resen. I never asked Pansy to trace anyone at all, and . . . and I don't know anything about a baby snatch. It's . . . it's all nonsense. Make believe.'

'Well, that's all right, then. Must have been someone else the sister was helping. Simple enough mistake,' said Frankel. 'Glad we got it sorted out so quickly. Was there anything else, Mr Parry? Anything that might help with the, er . . . the Barbara situation?' he enquired, the implication being that if there wasn't, the policemen might as well be on their way.

'I'm afraid there is something else, sir, yes. According to Mr Rees, there was a great deal of information Sister Watkyn supplied to Mrs Bevan about –'

'But she's just said –'

'About that baby snatch. Alleged baby snatch, at least,' Parry pressed, capping the other's interruption with his own. 'Mr Rees himself helped in collecting the data. That was through a German reporter colleague. There were translations of contemporary reports from Rheindahlen and Düsseldorf newspapers, for instance. Mr Rees said they were required for Mrs Bevan, and sent to her. There's no doubt about that in his mind, even if she hadn't asked for them.'

'Then it's a mystery, isn't it, Mr Parry?' said Frankel, the amiability beginning to wear thin. 'But a mystery you can hardly except Mrs Bevan to be concerned with, not when she has other much more pressing matters on her mind.'

'Funny thing, there weren't any baby snatches, as a matter of fact.' It was Gomer Lloyd who had spoken uninvited. His words were followed by a distinctly expectant silence before he went on: 'It was all about illegal adoptions. Sales of unwanted babies. They were handled by a German midwife called Sonya Heller.'

As soon as the name was uttered, there was a noisy intake of breath from Mrs Bevan, before she thrust her handkerchief to her mouth, and gave her husband a very frightened, then desperately imploring look.

'According to Mr Rees, Sister Watkyn worked out that one of the baby purchases took place on the same day Mr and Mrs

Bevan left Germany,' put in Parry. 'The day their daughter Barbara was born.'

'Quite a coincidence,' commented the lawyer blandly. 'But no more than that, surely? And I still don't see what this has to do with my . . . with Mr and Mrs Bevan.' He maintained his impassive stare at Parry, who had guessed he had been on the brink of referring to the Bevans as his clients, which, in the circumstances, would have subtly altered the complexion of the present gathering. 'Did Sister Watkyn send either of you any information about this . . . this coincidence, Huw?' Frankel completed easily, turning to his friend.

'Certainly not. Isn't that right, Dilys?' asked Bevan, responding to the ciphered message in the way the lawyer had intended.

Mrs Bevan wiped her eyes. 'You said the baby was unwanted, Mr . . . ?' Her voice faltered over the name.

'Detective Sergeant Lloyd, ma'am. That's right.' The speaker bent forward to smooth the dog's head that was now resting comfortably on his left shoe. 'The sale was still illegal, of course. But that's a lot different from stealing.'

'All very interesting, but –' Frankel began, except he was forestalled by Mrs Bevan.

'Did Mr Rees say Frau Heller went to prison, Mr Lloyd?'

'No, ma'am. Could that be something Sister Watkyn told you, perhaps?'

'Really, Sergeant, Mrs Bevan has already said she wasn't given any information,' Frankel admonished.

'Quite right, sir. Sorry. But just to make it clear for everyone, according to the records, Frau Heller served eighteen months of a three-year sentence for arranging baby sales for her own profit. That was after her trial sixteen years ago. Sister Watkyn told Mr Rees that Mrs Bevan wanted to know if Frau Heller had any connection with Carla Resen. But his German colleague couldn't find any mention of her in the reports.'

'You're positive he said the babies weren't stolen?' Mrs Bevan pressed again, somewhat weakly.

'That's right, ma'am.'

'And did he say his contact found out the mother of one of the babies had moved to –'

'Mr Parry,' Frankel cut in on Mrs Bevan, in a very determined voice, 'Mrs Bevan is naturally interested in events that happened in Rheindahlen at the time she was there, or more accurately, it seems a year after she and Mr Bevan left. She's a compassionate lady, and if it's even remotely possible an ex-employee of hers was convicted of some criminal activity, I know her well enough to be certain she'd be the first to want to help with rehabilitation, that kind of thing, even years after the event.' He put a hand out to press Dilys Bevan's arm, then looked across again at Parry as he continued. 'But it really does seem Sister Watkyn, or this Evan Rees, was badly mistaken about Mrs Bevan's possible connection. As Mrs Bevan's legal adviser, as well as her friend, I'd still like to have the details of the matter looked at properly, for her own peace of mind. But at this moment, as you said when you arrived, you're investigating a murder. Unless any of what so far appears to be romanticizing by Sister Watkyn has a direct bearing on your catching her killer, I really feel you should let things lie for now, and respect Mrs Bevan's own pressing, distressing problems. You've seen her condition. Any testimony she gives about anything at the moment would in any case be hopelessly tainted by her emotional state. Her doctor, who was here this morning, and virtually any High Court judge, would accept that,' he added with emphasis on the word judge. 'She's simply not herself. Really, if you've no help to offer over locating Barbara, I suggest we leave further discussions about what Sister Watkyn said she told Mrs Bevan for another time.'

'I'm sorry, but I'm afraid that won't –'

'Hear me out, please, Mr Parry,' the lawyer broke in on the policeman's burgeoning protest. 'Shall we say we'll meet again at, er . . . three o'clock tomorrow afternoon in my office? That's if the time suits you. By then I shall have collected any facts that could have the remotest bearing on the situation so far as Mr and Mrs Bevan are concerned.' He glanced at Bevan, who nodded, then at the now silently weeping Dilys Bevan, before his gaze returned to Parry.

Before Parry had a chance to respond to what had amounted to Frankel's clear play for time, wrapped up in an erudite and telling judicial summary, the cellphone Bevan had placed on the table beside him came to life. The instrument was ringing out with what, in the circumstances, seemed to everyone present to be an especial dramatic urgency as Bevan picked it up. With animal instinct, even Tyn had raised a sleepy head from the pillow of Lloyd's foot.

14

'Poor Daddy, he sounded too relieved to be angry,' said Barbara Bevan, as she joined Alwyn Price in the car, outside Terminal Two at Heathrow Airport. He had been to fetch his mother's Morris Maestro from the car park on their return, while Barbara had been telephoning her parents. 'Anyway, we've only been gone a day,' she went on, pitching the light, white anorak and her small canvas bag on to the back seat – it was the bag that normally contained her school books, and which she had used for carrying the few overnight things she had needed. 'And guess what? Pansy Watkyn has been murdered. In Cardiff Market, yesterday morning.'

'Murdered? Do they know who did it?'

'Daddy didn't say. Well, they probably don't know yet. Anyway, we didn't talk much about that. The police were there with him and Mummy, and Simon Frankel, our lawyer.'

'Oh, God. Was that all because of us?'

'No . . . well, at least I don't think so. More likely because of Pansy. They knew Mummy was a friend of hers. Some friend – the bitch.'

'You told your father where we'd been?'

'That we'd been to Germany, yes.'

'You didn't say why?'

'I said I'd heard the Pansy Watkyn tape, but we'd found out I hadn't been stolen.'

'How did he sound?'

'Relieved. After that, though, he steered away from the subject. Because of the police, I should think.'

'I still think you should have rung him yesterday from

Düsseldorf,' Alwyn offered tentatively. He wasn't decisive by nature – 'highly intelligent but easily led' was the comment his form master had applied to him at his last school. Since then he had been enrolled at the Prince's Academy to cram for even better university qualifications than his previous teachers had expected.

Alwyn was tall, fair and lanky, not unlike Barbara. Indeed, they might have passed for brother and sister, except the girl was a bundle of nervous energy, while the bespectacled Alwyn was a contemplative youth. He was different as chalk and cheese from her father, which was possibly why she got on so well with him: she wasn't looking for a fresh father figure, not yet anyway, even though forty-eight hours before this she had been ready to disown the couple she had suddenly come to believe had only been masquerading as her parents. Alwyn wasn't Barbara's boyfriend in any permissive sense, either. He was good old reliable Alwyn, who she liked to be with, who she allowed to kiss and fondle her in his fumbling way, and who adored her and did everything she asked him to do, and never anything she told him not to. He was scholastically brighter than Barbara. Her German was good, but his was outstanding. It was why she had taken him to Düsseldorf.

'Anyway, you never rang your mother, did you?' she said, countering his last point.

'That's different. I mean, I never do if I'm only away for a night or so. And I told her I'd be in Brecon.'

'Well, up to this morning, I never wanted to talk to my parents again,' she said, as he drove them under the tunnel on the way out of the airport. 'Anyway, I can handle Daddy.'

'I hope so,' he replied with feeling, dread being the feeling currently uppermost in his mind when it came to assessing her father's likely attitude to him. 'Did he ask how we paid for the plane tickets? And the hotel?' Barbara had paid for everything with her credit card.

'Of course not,' she replied. 'Anyway, this quarter I'm still inside the limit he allows me on my Visa. Honestly, there won't be any problems.' She put a hand on the inside of his thigh.

142

He swallowed nervously, which made his prominent larynx even more so. 'I still feel like a . . . a kept man.'

'That's an anti-feminist remark,' she giggled.

'I'll bet your father will think we slept together last night.'

'No, he won't. I told you, I promised him I wouldn't. Not with anyone. Not till I'm eighteen. And probably I won't then, either.' She removed her right hand from his leg, and crossed it with her left over her unprominent breasts as she exclaimed dramatically: 'I may resolve to remain a virgin unspotted till I get married. I'll have to see.'

'You actually talk to your parents about sex?'

'To Daddy, not Mummy.'

'That's even more incredible.'

'Anyhow, the way I felt Friday, after I heard that tape, I could have slept with a whole regiment of Royal Welch Fusiliers, just to spite my father.'

'That was the shock.'

'I'll say it was the shock.' She kicked off her shoes and folded her legs under her on the seat. 'How would you have felt suddenly finding your parents weren't your parents at all?'

'It's no big deal if you love them, and they love you,' he answered quietly, or as quietly as he could over the noise of a car engine unused to being driven at motorway speeds.

'Oh, yes, it's fine to say that if you aren't adopted,' she replied with spirit. 'Or worse, not legally adopted, even, just stolen from your real parents.'

'But, Barbara, you weren't.'

'No, but I didn't know that Friday, did I?'

'Well, you know now.'

'Yes, thanks to my resourceful, handsome Alwyn.' Despite the seat belt, she leaned across, clasped him around the neck, and planted an enthusiastic kiss just below his left ear.

'It wasn't that difficult,' he answered modestly, but inwardly elated, while he straightened his glasses.

'Not after you'd convinced everyone at the newspaper we had a serious school project, tracing a story on a seventeen-year-old baby snatch.'

'They were very helpful, weren't they? Especially Hans

143

what's-his-name, the deputy editor, and the librarian,' he commented, still basking in her compliments.

'And to throw in supper last night.'

'That was because Hans fancied you.'

'He didn't get me, though, did he? He was nice, of course. But not as nice as my darling Alwyn. Do you suppose I'm partial to Germans because I am one?'

'Shouldn't think so.'

She took a deep breath, and then looked solemn. 'Was Pansy Watkyn murdered by someone else she was blackmailing, do you think?'

'We don't know she was blackmailing anyone else.'

'That's true. And she wasn't very good at it, either, was she? So it could have been her first time, I suppose. Want a chocolate? They're gorgeous.' She had leaned over and pulled the packet out of her bag.

'No, thanks.' It had taken him too many years to be rid of his acne to risk a relapse.

'But to con Mummy and Daddy the way she did was freaky. I still don't know why Daddy didn't do what we've just done. Check the facts. He could have put a private eye on the job.'

'Perhaps he did.'

'Not judging from his reaction to what I said on the phone.'

'Well, probably he hadn't wanted to stir up anything. To risk stirring up anything,' he added. 'Your parents' position was very vulnerable. Still is, I should think. And anyway, from what was on the tape, it really sounded as if Pansy was protecting them, not exploiting them. Protecting them from the German reporter.'

'But that was pure con. All her reports were made up. I mean, they were nothing like what really happened, were they? I wasn't stolen. I was sold. OK, that sounds gruesome, but it wasn't really. I think Sonya Heller did a kind of a public service. She thought so as well.'

'The court that tried her didn't.'

She shrugged. 'You have to believe she was helping all concerned. Destitute, deserted mothers. Childless couples desperately needing babies, and . . . and innocent mites like me who she saved from a deprived childhood, probably in . . . in squalid conditions.'

'Yes, her counsel did explain all that,' he answered thoughtfully as he steered the car up from the airport approach road to the M4. 'But there are proper adoption agencies in every country. Well, most countries. Agencies that observe the adoption laws.'

'But they're so slow. The ones here are, anyway. You're always reading they're slow and finicky. Picky. Too picky. That's well known, as well.'

'Picky for good reason, though.'

'OK, but even candidate parents for adoption looking as good as mine, they might have had to wait years. In England they would, anyway. And that's not the end of it. If natural parents want to reclaim an adopted child later, they can.'

'There's a time limit on that. I think it's a year.'

'But imagine Mummy having to give me back after a year? After she and Daddy brought me from Germany, and nurtured me all that time? It would have been too awful for them. Especially Mummy. You know she had two miscarriages before she had me?' Barbara bit her lip, then corrected herself tetchily: 'Well, before she . . . acquired me. She was ill, too. After they came back here. A . . . a serious nervous condition.'

Alwyn pushed his glasses higher along his long narrow nose. 'Still, Frau Heller didn't exactly do it all for nothing, did she?' he offered grudgingly. 'The fee she said she charged for the one baby trade she admitted to sounded pretty steep.'

'But most of the money went to the deserving mother.'

'Or so she said. There was no evidence offered.'

Barbara shook her head. 'I don't believe the newspapers gave enough detail for us to know. But just fancy Pansy inventing all those things she said on the tape,' she added, with an angry snort.

'About your natural parents being witnesses at the trial?'

'Yes. And saying they moved to Zürich after. It all had to be lies.'

Alwyn glanced across at her. 'Do you wish your real

parents could have been at the trial? Identified and everything?'

'So I could find them?' The young woman hesitated. 'No. Not now I don't,' she warranted with sudden resolution. 'Anyway, there probably aren't two of them to find. Just my poor single-parent mother, probably, if what Frau Heller said at the trial was true. Pity the reports didn't give more about the other babies the police thought she might have bought and sold.'

Alwyn looked uncertain. 'Anyway, since Frau Heller died last year, and she's the only person who might have been able to tell you who your real mother was – '

'Except maybe the mother convicted with her,' Barbara interrupted, shifting her legs from under her. 'D'you think we should have tried to find her?'

'Wouldn't have done any good,' said Alwyn. 'She couldn't have been your mother. The birth date of her baby was too close to yours. The real pity is Frau Heller wouldn't admit involvement in other baby sales. It was pretty obvious from what happened locally she'd been in it up to her neck. There wasn't enough evidence to prove it, that's all.'

'If she'd told the police everything, would she have got a shorter sentence?'

'Quite possibly. But she'd have brought a lot of strife down on a lot of people in the process.' Alwyn's facial expression became more authoritative as he continued in a tone that had done the same. 'Look, you said just now you didn't want to find out who your mother was, not any more. And if you ask me, that's right. Looking for her now could be a big operation. And if by some freak chance you did find her, she might not want finding. She could be . . . well, sort of indifferent towards you. Even hostile. Or guilty, more likely. Or she might even have married well without wanting her past . . . indiscretions exposed.'

Barbara nodded slowly, and didn't take umbrage about being described as a putative past indiscretion. 'I don't know why, but I'm sure she's dead. Like Frau Heller,' she observed flatly.

'That's a possibility, too. Anyway, I think it's better to come to terms with the situation as it is. I mean your own situation. Count your blessings.'

'I have. At least, I believe I have. I think more of my parents . . . my adopted parents, than I did before. I mean, what a risk they took. They must have really, really wanted me, don't you think?'

'Sure. I just hope it doesn't all have to come out, though, because of the murder.'

'Why should it? I'm nearly of age. The Germans wouldn't want to prosecute my parents, would they? Not now?'

Alwyn frowned. 'Possibly not,' he said, but without being wholly certain that he was right. 'Depends partly on whether the offence is extraditable. You're right, though. There's probably some kind of limitation on how long something of that kind stays indictable,' he completed, more confidently.

'I hadn't thought of that,' said Barbara, whose respect for him was becoming stronger by the hour.

Alwyn forced a smile. There was something else that bothered him, and it had nothing to do with the baby sale seventeen years ago, or what the German authorities might or might not want to do about it at this late stage.

He just hoped that neither Mr nor Mrs Bevan were responsible for the murder of Pansy Watkyn.

15

Parry turned the Porsche to the right, on to the minor road to Rhossili. Not that the road he had been on since leaving Swansea, twenty minutes earlier, had been exactly major in aspect or width, though the surface had been sound enough: regular maintenance and low usage saw to that. Movements by land in this part of rural Wales were more dedicated to the passage of sheep to fresh pasture, and cows to milking, than to heavy vehicles – that's if you didn't count the school bus. And apart from buses, things hadn't changed much in this regard for several hundreds of years.

The western extremity of the twelve-mile Gower Peninsula is lonely country, except for a few months in high summer when the tourists come with caravans, or tents, or just for the day, to enjoy its stark, ravishing beauty. A salt breeze reminds that the Bristol Channel surrounds the long, narrow promontory on both sides, though the rising ridges inland sometimes obscure any view of the water – and of the scarcely trodden, wide and endless beaches far below. But giddying prospects of the strand are offered from the grass swards running up to the cliff edges, near which occasional steep pathways offer the walker a way down to the sands – and back up again with effort.

Parry liked the Gower for its ruggedness, and because it was still largely unspoiled – green, lush, wooded, and sparsely populated. He had been up at six, and heading westward on the M4 twenty minutes later. It was now barely seven thirty. The interview in prospect might have been handled for him by one of the Unit officers permanently based in Swansea. But the individual he was seeing was the only known member of the supporting cast in the Pansy Watkyn tragedy not yet questioned. If the fresh testimony was going to shed light, he believed it would do so best for him at first hand. On top of this, he had been born and raised not many miles from here in an unsalubrious, steel mill town. The Gower was where he had cycled to camp and swim as a youth. The excuse to visit it on a sunny, early-autumn morning was hard to resist – and at this hour it was not self-indulgent, either, since he was defensibly on his own time still.

The two-storey cottage was not hard to locate from the directions provided, particularly since it was the only building visible for half a mile, along a hundred yards of rutted side lane. Bordered by a hawthorn hedge, the steeply rising lane was punctuated by lengths of rusted iron paling set crookedly in the gaps where the hawthorn, and the rampart of ditch excavation in which it was planted, had been breached by farm animals.

Interesting, lopsided, but hardly picturesque, the building was set to the left of centre on two acres or so of land, the nearer part given over largely to the growing of vegetables and what seemed to be a disproportionate amount of herbs. Behind this there were apple and pear trees laden with fruit. A tethered and wholly preoccupied nanny goat was keeping the orchard grass cropped – assisted by three geese who had appeared from behind the house to make a spirited, noisy advance on the newly arrived car, but giving this up after they stopped to hold voluble exchanges amongst themselves. A large, wired chicken run, with an old-fashioned raised henhouse attached, occupied a prominent position in front of the orchard.

The outer walls of the cottage were mostly of whitewashed stone and rubble, with no-nonsense, square, quartered windows upstairs and down. There was a later, but not too recent, extension on the right. This was lower than the original building, and constructed in unsympathetic red brick, but it, too, was roofed in grey Welsh slate, and with a ridge line a good deal straighter than the older one. A wooden lean-to on the left, near the protruding covered porch to the outside door, appeared to be in the last-but-one stages of disintegration. Despite this, it was providing adequate shelter for a nearly eaves-high store of coke, as well as for the front part of a yellow Citroën Dyane of relatively recent manufacture – at least when compared to Owen-Pugh's VW. Parry, who had once owned a Deux Chevaux, renowned founder of this Citroën line, noted with interest that the vehicle had been fitted with an elementary roof rack of fragile construction, but which cleverly still seemed to allow for the folding back of the traditional soft top.

Although it was quite hot already, a wisp of smoke was rising from the broad-waisted clay pot that crowned the cottage's single concrete chimney. It was the smoke, noted late on the previous evening, that had prompted the local police patrol to report that Mrs Kathleen Rees had arrived home.

'Well, come in, then,' she said, after opening the door to Parry's knock, but not before giving a better than cursory glance at the warrant card he had shown as he introduced himself.

'Sorry to be so early, Mrs Rees.'

'No need. Like I said on the phone, this is early-bird country.' He had called her ten minutes before. 'I'm usually away by eight,' she completed.

'You teach in Pontyglas?'

'That's right. If you call PE teaching. Many don't. They think PE's only physical improvement, not mental. More fool them, that's what I always say.' The smile that followed was an indulgent not a carping one.

He estimated her age as thirty-five or perhaps a year or two older than that. She was above average height, with a thin, taut body – and a healthy, energetic one judging from the way she moved. The sandy hair was cut short like a man's, and the high cheekbones were emphasized by the drawn, freckled skin of her face. There was a recurring hint of suspicion behind the eyes, or it might have been calculation: he noticed she opened her eyelids wider whenever she spoke, making each statement appear more vital. Her teeth were prominent, but remarkably even, behind a wide mouth and full lips. A vibrant woman, with hidden depths, and lots of character, like her cottage, was Parry's assessment.

150

She was wearing a white, short-sleeved shirt, and blue denim jeans: both accentuated the slim outline of her figure.

'You've been away, Mrs Rees?'

'Saturday morning to last night, yes.' The accurate, clipped replies were coming in a slightly husky voice, with a lilting, mid-Wales accent. 'Sit down. Like some tea? I was just making it.'

'Thank you, I'd love some.'

The door had led into the kitchen through a small vestibule hung with coats on both sides. It was a practical, warm room, but hardly modernized, accepting that in addition to a telephone, the isolated cottage had electric power and mains water, evident from the light fittings, and the two taps above the shallow stone sink. A range of battered and unmatching enamel saucepans hung beside the solid fuel cooker in the corner, where a large black kettle was steaming beside a teapot put beside it to warm. There was a scrubbed deal table with wooden chairs in the centre of the room, and a handsome, oak Welsh dresser – the *pièce de résistance* – on the wall opposite the entrance door. A whole crusty loaf of bread was set on a board at one corner of the table, near a glass butter dish, and a jar of home-made jam. The contents and non-commercial origins of the jam were defined by a handwritten label on the side of the jar.

Parry pulled out one of the chairs and sat in it. 'Must be lonely for you here, by yourself,' he said.

'Not in midsummer. I let rooms in the school holidays, and I have campers in the orchard as well then. Only a few. Doing that makes you appreciate the other ten months, I can tell you. But no, I'm not lonely. Anyway, I've got the animals for company. And protection. Nothing gets past my geese, I can tell you.' She had been filling the teapot. Now she brought it to the table, before fetching an extra place setting for Parry from the dresser. 'Not that I'd ever have time to be lonely, really. Always on the go,' she added as she sat down, then, inadvertently proving the point, she got up again to fetch a forgotten teaspoon for the visitor.

'What about the weekends?' he asked.

'Mm. They tend to be quieter for me, I suppose. But I'm

often helping out then at two youth hostels. July and August excepted, of course, because I have to be here.'

'Are the youth hostels local?'

'One is. The other's north of here. Outside Llandovery, where I was born. That's where I was yesterday. Have some bread, if you want. I made it this morning. The strawberry jam is mine as well, and the butter's local. I'm an organic nut, by the way. Self-sufficient as well, as far as I can be, and allowing I have an outside job, too, although that's not quite full time.' She passed him his tea.

'Thank you,' he said. 'Can't resist the bread. Can I have the crust?'

'If you like.'

'I saw the chickens as I came in. Free range.'

She nodded. 'Of course. They're just for the eggs. I couldn't kill one of my own chickens for eating. That's my trouble. I'm too soft hearted to be a livestock farmer. Saw the goat as well, did you? She gives lovely milk.' She was watching his expression. 'No, I haven't put it in your tea. I make cheese from it, and yoghurt. People allergic to cows' milk go for both in a big way.'

'D'you sell a lot of your produce?'

'Quite a bit, yes, including the fruit I grow. It's the health shops, mostly. The herb garden's the most profitable part. People pay fancy prices for fresh herbs. Better for you than dried.'

'And delivered daily by the grower?' he commented lightly. 'I saw a roof rack on your Dyane.'

'Made that myself, for when I'm overloaded inside.' She cut herself a piece of bread. 'So tell me, what do you want to know about Pansy Watkyn?' she asked.

'You knew her?'

'Not really. We never actually met. Far as I was concerned, she was just Evan's latest. Not very glam, by all accounts.'

'He tells you about his, er . . .'

'His girlfriends? Oh, yes. Like a little boy with new toys, he is.' She drank some tea. 'I didn't think Pansy would last, not from what he told me. And that's for certain now, isn't it? She's dead, you said.'

'Yes. Murdered on Saturday. In Cardiff Market. You hadn't heard?'

'Not till you told me just now on the phone. What time did it happen?'

'Around mid-morning.'

'Public sort of place for a murder. You know who did it?'

'Not yet.'

'Well, fancy,' she commented in a surprised voice, then drank more tea. 'No, I hadn't heard. You don't get a lot of news at a youth hostel in the mountains.'

Even so, he wondered why the information hadn't somehow filtered through to her. It had been on the local television news.

'I gather from your husband he couldn't marry Pansy because you wouldn't divorce him. For religious reasons,' he said.

'So that's what he told you, is it?' she grimaced. 'More bread?' In answer to his nod, she cut another slice. 'Yes, I used to be Catholic. Lapsed now. Anyway, it wasn't religion that's stopped us divorcing.' She looked at the knife, then went on cutting. 'I want him back eventually. I'll get him, too. Back here, where he can work properly. Perfect place for a novelist, wouldn't you think?'

'I suppose so, yes. I didn't know he was writing a book.'

'He isn't. Not yet. Still marking time. Doing his little bits and bobs for the newspapers. And he'll go on doing them while there's women stupid enough to support him. When there aren't, he'll come back to me. Mark you, he knows the conditions.'

'Which are?'

'That he gives me babies. Helps a bit with the garden and the animals – that's to keep him fit. Gives up smoking, of course, and spends most of the time writing a novel. He can do it. He's a good writer. Good as P.G. Wodehouse or Evelyn Waugh any day. Mixture of the two, really,' she reflected with apparent seriousness, as she spread jam on her buttered bread. 'Have you read anything he's written?'

'No.' But judging from Rees's limited success as a minor feature writer, Parry assumed that his wife's faith in his potential as a novelist was probably the product of wishful thinking.

'Ah, well, if you had, you'd know he's good. Very good. Workshy, that's his trouble. Workshy, and too good in bed. But he can't go on being a gigolo for ever.'

'He's not that old, surely?'

'No, but it's pride not age that'll get him in the end. Deep down he wants success with his work, not his women. And that's what'll bring him back to me. Quite soon, probably. He's listening to what I say to him. I know he is.'

'You talk to him often?'

'Not that often. But when I do, I make it tell.'

'Has he mentioned a German girlfriend?'

'Freda, you mean? Freda Metz. Oh, yes. She's a one-night stand, not a permanent meal ticket, or even a semi-permanent one. He had plenty of girls like her when we were still together. Used to make all kinds of excuses to be away for a night, or an afternoon. Thin excuses.'

'You were living here then?'

'No, in Cardiff. I came here after. This place isn't mine. It's rented. Very cheap. Evan likes it, too, but won't admit it. He'll be here before long, you'll see.'

It was almost as though she were talking to herself, convincing herself, Parry thought. 'You didn't see him last Saturday?' he asked.

'No. Was he here?'

'He was close by, around mid-morning. Driving to Fishguard.'

'Whose car was it? Pansy's?'

'Yes.'

'But she wasn't with him?'

'No. He was going to meet Freda Metz in Wexford. They're both doing articles on the Opera Festival.'

'Well, there's cosy.' This time the eyes had narrowed as she spoke, instead of opening wider. 'If he was by himself, most probably he did look in. But I wouldn't have been here. Like some more tea? Pass your cup, then.' She refilled both cups as she continued: 'Anyway, he couldn't have had anything to do with Pansy's murder, could he? Not if he was

154

around here mid-morning. You said that's when she was killed. In Cardiff.'

'Around that time, yes.' Parry helped himself to sugar.

'And you said he was meeting Freda Metz in Wexford. You sure she wasn't travelling with him?'

'Quite sure. She flew to Ireland Saturday morning.'

'From Cardiff or Bristol, was that?'

'No, Heathrow. I don't believe there are regular flights from the others.'

'Pity.' She gave him a meaningful, mischievous look over her teacup.

'Would you mind telling me where you were yourself on Saturday morning between ten and eleven, Mrs Rees?' he asked.

She chuckled. 'So I'm on the list of suspects, am I? And that's why you're here. I must be high up, too, with you driving sixty miles for the doubtful privilege. But it's been a waste of your time, I'm afraid, because I didn't kill her, either. Well, why should I? Lot of trouble for no gain, that would have been, and no mistake.'

Parry moved his side plate an inch. 'I'm afraid we need to know the whereabouts of a lot of people on Saturday morning. It's just routine.'

'People who had it in for Pansy? And you think I'm one of them?'

'Not really. Just people who might have a bearing on the case. People who can possibly help us find the killer.'

'By being cleared of suspicion themselves,' she offered with mock earnestness. 'They always say that in the mysteries on the radio. On the telly as well, I expect, but I don't see the telly. There's a waste of time, if ever there was one.' She continued buttering her bread. 'Well, let's see now. Saturday, I got up as usual at five. At first light I was picking apples. Did the same this morning, after the bread was in the oven. I'll give you a few apples to take with you. They're early Cox's. Lovely, but I'll have far too many this year.'

'I really just need to know where you were at say ten thirty on Saturday, Mrs Rees,' he pressed in a patient tone.

'Sorry. Yes, I'd have been just about halfway to Llandovery in the car, I should think.'

'Did you drive direct from here?'

'How do you mean?' She looked up from her plate. 'Well, yes. I took the M4 to where it ends, then the road through Ammanford and Llandeilo. Up the valley. That's the way I always go.'

'You didn't go to Cardiff first?'

'Cardiff? Good Lord, no. Why should I go to Cardiff?'

'And do you know what time you left here?'

'Quarter past nine. Bit after, perhaps.'

'You were by yourself?'

'Yes. All the way. Not that I mind giving students a lift if I pass any, but I didn't this Saturday. I brought two girls back with me nearly to Swansea last night. To where they could get a local bus. They were from the hostel. But that was by previous arrangement. It gave them an extra half day's climbing on the hills.'

'And do you know what time you reached the hostel on Saturday, Mrs Rees?'

'Oh, let's see, about, er . . . quarter to twelve. Or, come to think, nearer twelve, probably. I stopped for petrol in Llandeilo. Anyway, plenty of people saw me when I got there. Plenty of witnesses for you.' She smiled and glanced at the time. 'So is that it? Interrogation over?'

'I think so.'

'Then I'll get you those apples.' She pushed back her chair.

'That's very kind of you.'

He had driven to Llandovery from Cardiff a few weeks earlier. It was a slightly longer distance than from here, but on similar good roads. In the Porsche, he remembered, he had done the journey in much less than an hour. But you had to make allowances, of course.

16

'So my clients, Mr and Mrs Bevan, have decided to give you all the help and information they can, Chief Inspector,' said Simon Frankel. 'Nothing relevant withheld. Nothing at all. And that's quite voluntarily, you understand.' The lawyer was dressed in a dark-blue, impeccably tailored business suit, a quiet, blue and red silk tie, and a white Jermyn Street shirt with heavy gold links visible at the just protruding cuffs. This was a somehow more formidable Simon Frankel than the casually dressed one who had so smoothly wound up the meeting at Hill House on the previous evening – and more formidable not simply because he was now in professional garb and habitat. The manner was still relaxed and courteous, but it was measurably more assured – though Parry wondered cynically if this signified the speaker felt the outcome of the present confrontation was less so.

It was a little after three on Monday afternoon. Parry and Lloyd had appeared, as arranged, at the substantial offices of Goodwich, Frankel & Herbert, Solicitors, which occupied the whole of a converted Edwardian three-storey residence on Park Place in the centre of Cardiff. The policemen were seated across from Frankel and Huw Bevan at the mahogany conference table in the lawyer's elegant, first-floor private office. The thickness of the carpet, the antique partners' desk in the heavily draped, wide bay window, the pair of glazed, English breakfront bookcases, the exquisite Gwen John *Portrait of a Nun* above the carved Italian marble fireplace, all contributed to an ambience of unvulgar, professional affluence.

'What you say is very encouraging, sir,' Parry responded. 'If we could return, perhaps to –'

'Oh, and I didn't consider it a must for Mrs Bevan to be with us,' the lawyer interrupted with a smile, folding his arms, and swaying his straight back a fraction to and fro. 'She's suffered tremendous upset recently, quite crippling, and some of what we have to talk about would be especially painful for her. Should you need her confirmation of anything later, this can easily be arranged, of course, though I doubt it'll be necessary. I was sure this would be acceptable.'

Parry hesitated before replying on purpose, and only because he resented the basic assumption. If Mrs Bevan was to be excused, he should have been asked in advance. 'Quite acceptable, sir,' he said eventually, with pointed emphasis on the first word, something which embodied the veiled advice that no more liberties should be taken.

Both policemen had been producing notebooks as Parry was speaking, and before he could add anything more, Frankel broke in with: 'We need to add one other caveat, Chief Inspector. While Mr Bevan will admit Sister Watkyn was attempting to obtain money from him by extortion, the alleged cause of this . . . this attempted blackmail is not germane to your enquiries about her murder. It should thus remain confidential, and in no circumstances would we allow it to be disclosed in open court. In this last context, of course, my clients are protected under the law.' The smile was this time positively benign. For a lawyer who, the day before, had claimed to be unfamiliar with criminal legal practice, Parry considered Frankel was doing very well. Presumably he had taken advice from whichever member of the firm handled the small amount of criminal work they took, or, more likely, he wasn't nearly as unversed or rusty as he had suggested. Even so, that he had admitted to the attempted blackmail was a huge advance on the day before, and was going to save a lot of time.

'I understand, sir,' said Parry. 'But I'm afraid I have no authority to make deals –'

'In this instance you don't need it, Chief Inspector. As I said, the law's on our side. If it came to it, we could apply to have any court proceedings involving the blackmail heard in camera, and I'm quite sure we'd succeed.' The interruption had been much sharper than the previous one, and the tone even more confident.

'I expect you're right, sir.' Parry was still not prepared to commit himself.

'Even so, we shall need to look to you and to Sergeant Lloyd to exercise personal discretion in other areas,' the lawyer added meaningfully, directing his gaze from one officer to the other.

'You can rely on both of us for that, sir.'

'Right enough, sir,' Lloyd echoed Parry's sentiment. 'Dirty business, blackmail, and you won't find an honest police officer anywhere who'll sympathize with the perpetrators.' He looked about him, head lifted, evidently proud that he had just upheld the probity of the whole British constabulary.

'So if we could just go back to where we left off last evening, sir,' said Parry flatly, and wondering why Lloyd had made such a meal of the last point. 'I take it Sister Watkyn was attempting to blackmail the Bevans over something she alleged happened in Germany more than seventeen years ago?'

'That's right, Mr Parry.' It was Huw Bevan who had answered, with the first words he had spoken since greeting the policemen earlier.

'For an event which, even if it were proved, is unlikely to involve the Bevans in any legal proceedings against them in this country,' Frankel enlarged. He unfolded his arms, and opened his hands before him, palms upwards. It was a gesture indicating the honesty of purpose, already matched by his expression and tone. 'We promised full disclosure, Chief Inspector. So, the facts of the matter are these. The Bevans unofficially adopted a baby girl in Germany all those years ago. It may have been a technically illegal action on their part, but it was perpetrated in good faith. The natural mother couldn't afford to keep the child, and didn't want to. It was brought up, loved and cherished by the Bevans as their own daughter.' The speaker leaned forward in his chair, bent elbows on the arms, clenched fists meeting in front of him. 'Sister Watkyn got hold of the bare bones of the story,' he continued. 'She did this first by deduction, and later by trickery. Then, after embellishing and distorting the one or two genuine facts she'd obtained, she demanded a large sum of money not to disclose what she knew to the authorities. She claimed to be acting as agent in the matter for a German principal, a journalist. We now believe that wasn't the case, that, in truth, she was working alone. Incidentally, she always insisted that her boyfriend Evan Rees knew nothing about any of this. Wasn't involved in any way. This may well have been true since she insisted he shouldn't be told anything, in the Bevans' own interests. It happens no money has been paid to Sister Watkyn, though it would have been if she'd signed our written conditions. These would have made it impossible for her, or any collaborator, to retail the story to anyone else, at least without incurring heavy penalties, and certainly landing Watkyn in prison where she belonged.'

'Could I ask, did Mr and Mrs Bevan consider going to the police in the first place, sir?' said Parry.

'When they consulted me, which they did some time after the business started, I naturally advised that course, Chief Inspector. However, for reasons to do with protecting his wife's frail health, her mental wellbeing, Mr Bevan felt he had to refuse the advice. I should add that I accepted his decision, if with reluctance.'

Parry admired the way Frankel neatly justified his own actions as well as those of the Bevans.

'My wife had a nervous breakdown some years ago, Mr Parry,' Huw Bevan now began to explain, quietly. 'I was sure at the time it was brought on by worry. She was scared stiff about what could happen to us if the way we got Barbara ever came out. It grew to be an obsession with her, the more we both came to think of Barbara as our own, our very own. Funny that, because at the start, Dilys convinced herself she'd actually given birth to Barbara. That's a fact. The real truth never seemed to bother her at that time.' He shook his head. 'Anyway, when the Watkyn business came up, I couldn't risk Dilys going through another breakdown, see? She's not strong. Not strong at all.' He paused and swallowed before adding: 'There was Barbara to think about as well, of course.

You see, we'd never told her she wasn't our own. Well, we couldn't, could we? I was as worried as Dilys about how Barbara would take it if she got hold of the truth. I was right as well.'

'Thank you, sir.' Parry looked from Bevan to the lawyer. 'And it was Mr Frankel, was it, who set out the conditions he referred to just now?'

'That's right,' Frankel answered for himself.

'Did anyone else know what was going on? Anyone in this office, for instance?'

'Nobody, Chief Inspector.'

Lloyd looked up from his note-taking. 'Weren't these conditions of yours typed out, sir?' he asked.

Bevan glanced at Frankel before he answered: 'Yes, by my personal assistant, Laura Mathews. I trust her absolutely. She's the only other person in the know.'

'So, put bluntly, Chief Inspector, it must be clear that the Bevans had no intention of physically harming Sister Watkyn,' said Frankel. 'On the contrary, they were on the point of paying her fifty thousand pounds to shut her up.'

'That's a lot of money, sir.' Parry wondered if it was larger than what they had really been intending to pay – that a higher amount had been mentioned to strengthen the lawyer's argument about the Bevans' position.

As if he had figured what was in the policeman's mind, Frankel got up, went to his desk, and unlocked a drawer there from which he withdrew a document case. 'This contains fifty thousand pounds in used twenty-pound notes, Chief Inspector. Mr Bevan has kept it in our safe here since last Tuesday, ready for the sum to be paid to Sister Watkyn.' He opened the lid of the case and displayed the banded bundles of money. 'And here's a copy of the conditions she had to sign.' He passed a typed sheet to Parry. 'I'd like that back when you've read it, please. Basically, it's a confession, and it names the sum of money she was to get in exchange for her silence.'

The document was quite short. Parry read it, showed it to Lloyd, and then gave it back to Frankel with a nod.

'You said it's a lot of money, Mr Parry,' said Bevan. 'But

it wouldn't have been if it bought sanity for my wife. I'm not a poor man.'

Frankel closed the case and returned it to his desk. Parry gave Bevan a sympathetic smile, and then asked: 'And had either you or your wife arranged to meet Sister Watkyn on Saturday morning, sir?'

'No. Certainly not.'

'Not even to hand over the money, perhaps?'

'The ball was in her court over that, Chief Inspector,' Frankel volunteered, sitting down again at the table. 'We were waiting to hear that what she called her principal had accepted our conditions. We never did.'

'Thank you, sir. So, just for the record, Mr Bevan, can you tell us where you and your wife were between ten and eleven on Saturday morning?'

'Dilys was at home. I was at my office. That's near Michaelston.'

'Michaelston-super-Ely, sir?' put in Lloyd, writing in his notebook. 'So you were about two miles from Cardiff centre?'

'That's right. Bit more, in fact. We're on a new industrial development site above that big Cowbridge Road junction.'

'So there'd have been other people there with you?' asked Parry.

Bevan frowned and rubbed his chin. 'Not really. We don't officially open on Saturdays. Not the offices, or the work-shops. The stores are open sometimes, but not last Saturday. I always go in Saturday mornings. It's a chance to catch up on things. Usually my secretary's there too, but she was ill.'

'You mean nobody saw you, sir?'

'Someone might have. I mean driving in and out. But, er . . . no, I can't be sure of that.'

Lloyd looked up. 'Did you make any phone calls from the office between the times mentioned, sir?'

Bevan considered for a moment. 'Not so far as I remember. Oh, I called Laura, to see how she was, but there was no answer. She told me later she'd gone out for some air.'

'The call will still be on the BT log, sir. Can you remember what time you made it?'

'Probably about ten. Oh, and I sent two faxes.'

'At what times, sir?'

'They were later. The first at about, er . . . half ten. The other was nearer twelve. The times will be recorded on the machine, and on the print-outs, won't they? I can give you the names of the people they went to.'

'That'll be very helpful.' This was Parry. 'And you arrived and left the office at what times, sir?'

'I got in about nine, and left just before half twelve. I remember I was home by quarter to one.'

'It takes you about fifteen minutes, sir?'

'Yes. If there's not too much traffic. It's a straight run north from the office to Bryntaf.'

'And you didn't go to Cardiff at all during the morning, sir? On the way in, for instance?'

'No, and I didn't murder Pansy Watkyn, either. But I wish I had. And whoever did deserves a medal. She very nearly cost me the love of my daughter, apart from . . . from probably taking years off my wife's life.' The response had been delivered quite soberly, but it was difficult to understand what had brought on such a heartfelt pronouncement at this particular juncture. Parry assumed the man was probably under greater pressure than he was showing outwardly.

Frankel shifted in his seat. 'You'll understand how resentful Mr Bevan feels. Justifiably, of course,' he said, making it plain in his tone that he felt the careless comment near the start of the emotive statement would have been better left unsaid all the same.

'You mentioned your wife was at home, Mr Bevan?' Parry questioned.

'That's right. I don't suppose you're going to suspect her of doing in Pansy Watkyn, are you? I think she may have been shopping in our village at the times you mentioned. Plenty of people will have seen her. Talked to her, probably. Bryntaf shops are very social places.'

'Thank you, sir. And we heard your daughter got home two hours or so after we left you last evening.'

'Yes, she did. Of course, you were there when she phoned us from Heathrow.'

'Do you want to tell us exactly why she flew to Germany, sir?'

It was Frankel who answered the question, partly because it had been he who had firmly suggested – almost demanded – the evening before, that since Barbara was safe, the details of what she'd been up to could be given to the police after her parents had heard them privately. Parry had made no objection to this at the time, since, on the face of it, it had no direct bearing on the death of Pansy Watkyn.

'Some time on Friday, and quite by chance,' the lawyer began, 'Barbara had come upon the tape of a phone call from Sister Watkyn to Mrs Bevan. It pretty well covered the whole story of the blackmail. Sister Watkyn had already given the details and her demands to Mrs Bevan, but to get them recorded, we pretended Mrs Bevan had been too upset to remember them clearly. Sister Watkyn was told Mr Bevan needed them repeated, either at his office or on the phone.'

'And she agreed to do it on the phone, sir?' Parry asked with some surprise.

'Yes, Chief Inspector, which showed either that she was a very unsophisticated blackmailer, or that she was very sure the Bevans would be too scared to take a recording to the police.' The lawyer shrugged. 'Of course, Barbara should never have got hold of the tape, but she did. It was a spare one. A copy that should have been destroyed. Naturally she was shocked. No, more than that, she was shattered by what she heard. According to her own account last night, she was outraged that the Bevans could have been party, as she thought, to stealing her from her real mother.'

'She didn't challenge Mr and Mrs Bevan straight away? To ask if the story was true, sir?' Parry interjected.

'No, she didn't. Without telling them, on Saturday morning she flew to Düsseldorf with Alwyn Price, and ended up at a newspaper office there. It's thanks to what they found out we now know Sister Watkyn's story about Frau Heller was mostly lies, built on the slimmest foundation of truth. For instance, she'd said the woman had been tried sixteen years ago for stealing babies from hospitals. She got the year right, but the charge was trading in babies, not stealing them

164

from hospitals. There's a hell of a difference, of course.'

'Could I ask Mr Bevan why he hadn't got this information earlier on his own account, sir?' asked Parry.

'That's a good question,' said Bevan. 'I wish I could give you a logical answer, Mr Parry. Mr Frankel wanted to set up a proper investigation, but my wife wouldn't hear of it. She was frightened to death that no matter how confidential it was, something would leak. That the German reporter Pansy was supposed to be acting for would get wind of what we were doing, and the next thing we'd be exposed, and extradited for trial in Germany. Like Mr Frankel said, there was enough in the Watkyn story Dilys knew was true for her to believe it all was. You just wouldn't credit the state she's been in.'

'That's quite right, Chief Inspector,' said Frankel. 'In fact, we did set up a watch on Sister Watkyn in this country for a bit. Unfortunately for all of us, including you, we called it off a week ago. It was a low-key operation, to see who she met, who visited her house. That was to try to identify the German. We didn't tell Mrs Bevan we were doing it. I suppose we could have done the information search in Germany as well, without telling her, but Mr Bevan didn't want to risk it. For my part, I have to admit I was pretty well convinced that what Sister Watkyn told the Bevans about the baby snatch was true. It was almost inconceivable she'd invented it.'

Lloyd cleared his throat. 'And you never did identify the German reporter, sir?' he asked.

'No. Except we're now of the opinion that there was no such person. And as Mrs Bevan told you yesterday, there was definitely no Carla Resen, either.'

Bevan let out a gruff exclamation at the last remark. 'We never employed home help of any kind when we were stationed in Germany. I was a flight sergeant, not an air vice marshal,' he said.

Parry smiled. 'It was a German woman journalist who researched the Frau Heller trial for Sister Watkyn. Her name is Freda Metz, and she's a friend of Evan Rees's,' he offered. 'Does her name mean anything to you, sir?'

'Never heard of her,' Bevan replied.

'The information she sent through Rees was accurate as to dates and events,' Parry continued. 'We found the stuff, stats of newspaper reports, and typed translations of them, in a second locker used by the sister at St Olaf's. There was a building society pass book there as well, as a matter of fact, which answered another question for us. We didn't know she had two lockers till this morning, when the person in charge of the locker room came back on duty after the weekend. The locker key on the sister's ring fitted both locks. She'd had identical locks fitted to both doors at her own expense a year ago. That was why there was no reason for our people to know she had two lockers. Anyway, it's why the material wasn't found and read earlier. It certainly confirms what Mr Rees told us about the reports on the trial, which he said Sister Watkyn sent to Mrs Bevan.'

'Except I swear to you she never did send them,' said Bevan immediately.

Parry nodded. 'Which strengthens our view that Mr Rees wasn't involved in the invented reports. Strengthens it circumstantially, at least.'

'And you don't think he knows Barbara was adopted?' asked Bevan.

'We don't believe he does, sir. We think he and Fräulein Metz were used by Sister Watkyn. She needed them to follow up her informed hunch that there might have been a trade in babies in that part of Germany at the relevant time. That was why she invented Carla Resen, and pretended to Mr Rees that the enquiries were on behalf of Mrs Bevan.'

'How did the informed hunch start, Mr Parry?'

'We're guessing, but it's logical to believe it was on information she picked up when she was looking after your wife in St Olaf's, sir. Possibly to do with the fact that you and your wife's blood groups make it impossible for either or both of you to be Barbara's parents, apparently. There are other possible related factors, medical factors, we haven't been able to follow through yet.' He would dearly like to have interviewed Mrs Bevan's surgeon, but had already concluded that for the time being that worthy would not be prepared

166

to divulge confidential medical data on Mrs Bevan. The technical information on the blood groups had been provided on request by Dr Maltravers.

'But why should she have handled the blackmail on her own?' This was Bevan again. 'Rees could have helped her. Especially when it came to inventing newspaper reports.'

'Well, apart from our having no reason to think Mr Rees would have been party to blackmail, we think she was aiming to keep any money she got from you for herself, sir.' Parry wasn't prepared to add that if Sister Watkyn had shared fifty thousand pounds with her boyfriend, she might not have kept him for very long.

'Your daughter feeling better about things, is she, Mr Bevan?' Lloyd asked, following a brief silence in the room.

'Yes. She understands everything now. And today, thank God, she seems closer to us than ever she was before. Strange though, isn't it?'

'Not really, sir. Now she knows the truth about how she came to be your daughter, the old bond between you is probably stronger, if that's possible.' The sergeant paused for a moment, and beamed at everybody, before he continued: 'By the way, we'll have to know the time of the flight she and the boy took on Saturday. Like Mr Parry said before, it's just for the record.'

'They went stand-by. She told me they got seats on the eleven-forty Lufthansa flight. I don't know the number.'

'From Heathrow, that was, of course. Thank you, sir.' Lloyd's eyes gave a fleeting indication of relief. There was no way anyone who committed a crime in Cardiff at ten thirty could have caught an aeroplane from Heathrow an hour and a quarter later.

'Would you all like some tea now?' Frankel asked, glancing at the time.

'Not for us, thank you, sir,' Parry replied, closing his notebook. 'We've got what we came for, so we'd better be on our way.'

The lawyer steepled his hands. 'May we assume you won't be taking further action over the, er . . . the unofficial adoption, Chief Inspector?' he asked.

Parry gave a wry smile before replying: 'Our investigation is only into the death of Pansy Watkyn, sir.'

When it was clear that the policeman had no intention of adding to that short but telling comment, Frankel beamed. 'I think we understand each other, Mr Parry. Thank you.'

17

'The answers were too pat, you think, boss?' Lloyd was asking a few minutes later. The two policemen had left Park Place on foot, and were moving along the Boulevard de Nantes, below the National Museum, and back to the Central Police Station on the west side of Cathays Park. The distance between Frankel's office and their destination was barely half a mile.

'They were no more programmed than we should have expected, I suppose,' Parry mused. 'They'd had the best part of a day to get the stories straight, and all the props laid on, after all.'

'Even if they were a bit casual with some of the details. Or was that part of the act, boss?' Lloyd pressed a peppermint into his mouth as he continued: 'I mean, Mr Bevan must have been sure his wife was out shopping on Saturday morning, or he wouldn't have said that, would he? Wouldn't surprise me if all the shopkeepers in Bryntaf were seen first thing today, to make sure they remembered she was in around ten thirty on Saturday.' He sucked hard on the sweet. 'No room for fiddling there, all the same, and it accounts for the movements of one of the principal parties.'

'The fifty thousand quid looked genuine,' said the chief inspector. 'Well, that's without our actually counting it.'

'Doesn't mean to say Mr Bevan didn't murder Sister Watkyn, all the same, does it, boss? As a matter of fact, the money was a pretty good reason to do her in, when you think about it. To save giving it away.' Using both hands, Lloyd gave a tug at his trouser tops. 'Even if it's like Mr Frankel said, they had it there, at the ready, all week,

169

expecting to have to pay her.' He gave another tug at his trousers, except this had as little enduring effect as the first one.

'Could still have been window dressing laid on for us, though. And the ten-thirty fax he remembered sending, and the ten o'clock phone call to his secretary, they were recalled nicely on cue,' said Parry. 'But I expect what he said will tally with those print-outs. Incidentally, have it all checked, Gomer, including the Bryntaf shop staff. Just in case. The shop staff will save us having to see Mrs Bevan again. That'll please Bevan and Frankel, at least. I suppose the reasons for keeping her out of things today were the ones given.'

'Sounded real enough, boss. She was in a bad way the last time. Still, her daughter's back now.'

'That reminds me, Gomer –' Parry's eyes narrowed – 'about that Düsseldorf flight number.'

'He didn't know it, boss. Only the time.'

'Exactly. And why not? I have an idea he hoped we'd take his word for it, without checking the number, or the passenger list. Because we'd reckon it'd be a waste of our manpower to match the time with a number first.'

'No reason why he had to cover for the two kids, is there, boss?'

'None that we know of, no. Anyway, have it checked that they were on the eleven-forty Lufthansa flight, will you?'

'Right.' Lloyd opened his jacket. The afternoon sun was still baking the pavements. 'Of course, you can programme a fax machine to send a message any time you want,' he said. 'Fixed in advance, like. Wonder if anyone's ever used that to fake an alibi?'

'If not, the head of an electrical contractors could be the perfect person to try it,' suggested Parry lightly. 'Except I'm mixing up electrics with electronics.'

The sergeant frowned, which had nothing to do with what Parry had just said: it indicated his increasing physical discomfort. Parry always walked too fast for him. 'Why do you suppose they came so clean over what Sister Watkyn was up to, boss?' he asked. 'They could have held back on that, couldn't they, without giving away the whole basis for the blackmail. The Bevans' big secret.'

'Must have been a big decision, yes,' Parry agreed. 'They did it probably because they weren't sure how much we knew already, or whether Evan Rees had been in cahoots with Sister Watkyn.'

'And if he had been, whether we'd broken him down already? That's possible, I suppose.'

'No, I think Frankel decided they should go for broke with all the information they could give us,' said Parry. 'In the hope we'd reciprocate by overlooking what he calls the informal adoption, seventeen years ago. Let's cross over, shall we, now we've got the chance?' Without waiting on Lloyd's agreement, he headed across the wide and usually busy road, in front of the City Hall, practically at the run. 'Except there's no such thing as informal adoption,' he completed, as they reached the other side.

The sergeant was a pace behind, breathing hard, and wondering why they couldn't have used the pedestrian crossing fifty yards ahead, setting an example to others, and avoiding the risk of a nasty accident. 'Happened in Germany, though, boss,' he offered breathlessly. 'Foreign country. Not our bailiwick, really, is it?'

Lloyd was a sceptic about the European Community. He had yet to forgive the Prime Minister who had taken Britain into the EC in the first place – for deserting 'our cousins' in New Zealand, Australia, and the rest of the Commonwealth, as the sergeant had put it at the time, even though he had no known cousins living further away than Colwyn Bay, then or now: not even second cousins.

'They must have falsified the daughter's birth records, which is a legal offence here,' Parry observed, appropriately enough, since they were moving past the Law Courts, heading north along Edward V11 Avenue. 'But I imagine Master Frankel is aiming to straighten that out once we've solved the murder for him,' he went on. 'Meantime, he's counting on us keeping mum on that one as well. Interesting that Bevan said Watkyn deserved murdering for nearly costing him his daughter's love, and for taking years off his wife's life. Do you think there was any significance in the order he put those in?'

Lloyd's eyes narrowed. 'Probably just the way it came out, boss,' he said.

Parry's nose wrinkled. 'I've got a funny feeling Bevan's more of a minder than a husband to that wife of his. The almost reflex way he protects her seems more like conscience than affection.' He gave a sniff. 'I wonder what his relationship is with his secretary, Laura Mathews? The woman he trusts absolutely. Isn't that what he said?'

'Yes, boss, but –'

'Trusts her so completely, she's let into secrets he believes could put him and his wife in prison. Secrets that to date he'd probably have killed to stop anyone else knowing. That's a very special relationship, if ever there was one.'

'Some secretaries, personal assistants, they're like that, boss. I can tell you, my second daughter's got a friend –'

'Sure,' Parry said quickly, affecting not to hear the start of one of Lloyd's mature reflections. 'But I'm interested to know what this secretary, or personal assistant, or whatever she is, actually looks like. The lady who spends precious Saturday mornings with the boss in an otherwise empty office. If she's in her late fifties, and motherly, I'll buy your upright view, Gomer. If she's young and sexy, I won't. Not without a lot of persuasion. Let's see her when she gets home from work this evening.' He looked at the time on the City Hall clock. 'You got the home address and phone number, did you?'

'From Mr Bevan, yes. He seemed quite keen we should see her.'

'Which means she's well programmed, too, I expect.' They waited to cross the slip road running along the side of the police station which was now in front of them. A patrol car passed them, then swung right, and right again to descend into the garage under the building. A moment later, as they mounted the front steps to the station, Parry added: 'We haven't got any closer to knowing who Sister Watkyn's thousand pounds was intended for, of course.'

'No, but at least we've known since this morning she drew

172

it out herself from her secret account, boss. That it was her money.'

Parry looked at the sergeant. 'I suppose it was secret, yes,' he agreed, as they took the stairs up to the incident room. 'Rees either faked not knowing she had any other account, or else he was telling the truth. On balance, I'd say he really didn't know.'

'Which is why she kept the pass book in the extra locker at the nursing home, boss.' They both gave way to a well-nourished WPC ascending the steps at speed with six copies of the new Cardiff Yellow Pages Directory clasped to her ample bosom. 'Like the press reports she told him she'd sent to Mrs Bevan,' Lloyd completed.

'And never did. So Bevan was telling the truth about that,' said Parry, while absently regarding the WPC's sturdy legs. 'Unless she sent photoprints made at the hospital. That wouldn't have been difficult. But why did she withdraw the thousand pounds on Friday afternoon?' He paused. 'How much was left in the account after that?'

'Four hundred and fifty-two pounds.'

'So it didn't clean her out?'

'No, boss. I'd say it was her nest egg account. Built up regular over the last two years. A bit from her salary, and a bit from the reverend's blackmail money, probably. And she made that big withdrawal because she owed someone a thousand. Or because she was having to pay someone for a service? Or –'

'Because she was bribing someone to do something,' Parry interrupted, as they entered the almost deserted incident room. All but three of the Unit personnel were on outside work. 'Now, who would a blackmailer need to bribe? Pay off?' The chief inspector thought for a second while they both checked the pinboard by the door for news and messages. 'Let's line up some long shots on that. For a start, we'll have all the central city car parks checked for sightings of the Reverend Owen-Pugh's red Beetle, mid-morning Saturday.'

'OK, boss. Except you said he wasn't worth the man hours. Because of his alibi.'

'That was yesterday, Gomer. I gave you the registration number, didn't I?'

'Yes. And I'll have it circulated to uniform branch as well. Are you thinking – ?'

'And do the same on Mrs Kathleen Rees's Citroën,' Parry broke in. 'That's less of a bone shaker. But it seems people connected with this case all own ageing jalopies.'

'Not Mr Bevan, boss. He's got the big white Merc we saw in the garage.'

'I know, and that's the third for your list. They're all distinctive cars in their way. Someone may have seen one of them. Or repaired one of the first two. Try the repair garages as well on them. And the AA. Owen-Pugh was a member. I saw the sticker.'

'You think Sister Watkyn may have had to pay the reverend to keep his mouth shut, boss? About her blackmailing him, when she had bigger fish to fry?' Lloyd questioned doubtfully.

Parry shrugged as they turned away from the pinboard. 'I said we're on to long shots, but –'

'Excuse me, sir.' Detective Constable Lucy Howell, office manager to the incident team, had got up from her desk as the two men had entered the room. 'PC Peter Shaw from local uniform, he's waiting to see you. Says it's important. He's only just arrived. He's over there.'

'Afternoon, Shaw,' said Parry to the uniformed, short and stocky young man standing by the door of the inner office. 'You were on duty at the market Saturday morning, weren't you?'

'That's right, sir.'

'And you played rugby last season for the Police B team. Lock forward,' the chief inspector added with a smile.

'Couple of times, sir, yes.' Shaw's well-fleshed cheeks dimpled with a modest grin.

'So what can we do for you?'

'It's, er . . . it's just you said to let you know anything we remembered later, sir.'

'Yes. Fire ahead.'

'Well, I was present when DS Johns was interviewing some

of the witnesses in the market. Mrs Mae Lewis, for one.'

'That's the Popular Café woman who collected the dirty plates? I interviewed her myself as well, later. What about her?' Parry asked, as he and Lloyd went through to the other office with the constable following, taking off his helmet.

'Well, I had to arrest her at ten past four the same afternoon, sir. Drunk and disorderly, she was. That was at the Gentry Betting Shop in Clare Road. At the bottom.' Until he was capless, Shaw hadn't appeared to be more than about twenty, but once he revealed that he had very little surviving hair he looked considerably older. Premature baldness seemed to be a feature of lock forwards, Parry mused to himself. In a reflex way, he pushed a hand through his own short-cut, full head of hair, and determined to go on playing centre three-quarter, as long as his breath held.

'What's the connection, son?' Lloyd asked.

'She was complaining, well, more than complaining, trying to break up the place, really, Sergeant. That was because she said they'd given her the wrong betting slip for the one-forty-five race at Chepstow on Saturday.'

'So she'd gone to collect her winnings,' put in Parry, with a chuckle, 'only there weren't any winnings?'

'That's about it, sir, yes. We kept her downstairs here on Saturday, till she sobered up, like. Then she was bailed to come before the magistrates this afternoon. It was the last case, as a matter of fact.'

'And you appeared as arresting officer?'

'That's right, sir. She was fined fifty pounds, and another thirty to cover the damage she caused. Only I've got her downstairs here, again. Brought her back with me from the court. I told her she was wanted for more questioning. She didn't object. Well, not too much. WPC Irons is giving her a cup of tea in the canteen. I think I was justified in my action.' Shaw moved his helmet around in his hand in front of him. 'You see, I'm pretty certain she told DS Johns a lie. You as well, I expect, sir.'

*   *   *

'What we're saying, Mrs Lewis, is there's no way you could have been collecting dirty plates in the Central Market at ten fifteen, last Saturday morning, or at ten past ten, or twenty past, as you said in your original two statements to us. And why? Because you've just sworn to the magistrates you were at the Gentry Betting Shop in Clare Road when it opened at ten sixteen,' Parry said to the woman sitting on the other side of the table from himself and PC Shaw in the interview room.

Mae Lewis looked even more of a sad physical specimen now than she had on Saturday, an impression worsened by the crooked application of colouring to her thin, parched lips, as well as the quantities of rouge she had put on her cheeks, and other less suitable parts of her face and neck, on purpose or in error. Her clothes seemed as if they had been retrieved, unwashed, from the unsold residue at a jumble sale. Her dress – a faded yellow cotton affair, several sizes too large for her scrawny figure, and held together near the throat by an oversized safety-pin – was topped by a blue and pink woollen cardigan with most of its buttons missing, and a hole at the left elbow. Her hair, as Parry remembered from his previous encounter with her, was an uncombed, and possibly uncombable, patchy frizz, most of it dyed in lurid and varying gradations of puce, except for the inch or so nearest to the roots which looked not so much a natural grey as a dirty natural grey.

It occurred to the chief inspector that the woman might have created this wretched and nearly destitute appearance simply to enlist the sympathy of the magistrates, but if this was so, judging from the size of the fine, and the costs, her efforts had been in vain.

It was a tribute also to the perspicacity of the magistrates that Mrs Lewis had found no difficulty in paying the penalties in full, in cash, and on the spot, as an alternative to going to prison for three days. As PC Shaw had explained, it wasn't her first offence on a similar charge.

'So I made a mistake,' she said now. 'I could have been there earlier. Minute or so earlier. It was them as made the mistake, wasn't it? Giving me the wrong betting slip, like

176

they did? They could have been wrong about when they opened up, as well.' Slowly, she scratched herself under her right arm as she went on: 'Hundred and ten quid I should have won, Saturday. I never got a penny, and I've had to pay out eighty quid on top in fines. And I've lost a day's pay today, sitting round in the court. Diabolical, I call that.' She stopped scratching, and gave a painfully long, rasping cough, while pulling a packet of cigarettes from one pocket of the cardigan, and some matches from the other.

'But whatever time they opened, Mrs Lewis, that betting shop is a good ten minutes' sharp walk from the market. On top of which, I understand you told the court you had to wait on the pavement outside when you got there.'

'That's what I told you already. They was late opening,' she asserted with feeling. 'They admitted it.'

'All right, and on top of that, you said there was a queue when you got inside?'

'Because they only got the one clerk working, and she was half asleep. Stupid cow.' Indignantly, Mrs Lewis blew smoke across the table, most of it in Shaw's direction. ''Course, if I hadn't been in such a bleeding hurry, because they was so slow, I'd have checked the betting slip at the time.'

'Mrs Lewis, there's a time and date stamp on the slip you showed to the court –'

'Proving they got the horse wrong, as well,' she broke in. 'Curate's Omelette my horse was called. That's what I asked for. Curate's Omelette. Daft name, but it won, didn't it? Romped home, it did. Eleven to one. Home and Wet is what they give me. Come in last, that did.' She fixed the young constable with a stare so withering he dropped his own gaze to his boots.

'Just tell us what time you left the market to go to the betting shop,' said Parry.

Mrs Lewis swivelled the whole of her mouth, now closed over the cigarette it was holding, a full inch to the right, then back again, her eyes squinting against the smoke. Then she removed the cigarette, blew out more smoke, and answered: 'A minute after ten, it was. I was going to catch a bus, but there wasn't none. Never is when the need's greatest. Wasn't none coming back, neither.'

'So what time did you get back to the market?'

She sniffed. 'About half past ten. Only if they'd been quicker –'

'So you were away from the market for half an hour, Mrs Lewis?'

She thought for a moment. 'About that, yes. Wasn't all that busy at ten at the caff. It's after eleven it gets busy.'

'As a matter of interest, why didn't you use a betting shop closer to the market?'

When her silence, and the look on Mrs Lewis's face, indicated she wasn't prepared to answer the question, PC Shaw did so for her. 'She's banned from all of them, sir. Isn't that right, Mae?' he said.

'None of your bleeding business, young man. Bastard betting shops,' she snorted. 'What bleeding right have they got to ban a hard-working woman from –'

'Did you have permission to leave your job for half an hour, Mrs Lewis?' Parry interrupted firmly.

'Who wants to know? You going to tell my boss at the caff?'

'We're not going to tell anyone. Just be kind enough to answer the question, could you?'

'Well, I didn't have nobody's permission, no. Not exactly. But they never notice.' The eyes narrowed. 'Work my fingers to the bone, I do, between eleven and three every day. To the bone.' She looked at her open left hand, then thrust it, still open and upright, across the table in Parry's direction, as if she was stopping traffic. The fingers were quite bony. 'Deserve a break early on, I do.'

'So everything you told us about who you saw at the café between ten and ten thirty was made up?'

She inhaled slowly and deeply on the cigarette. 'Didn't tell you I saw nobody. Well, nobody except the woman in the blue and white striped dress. She was there when I cleared up. Before I nipped out. It wasn't the one who got done in, though, was it? I never said I seen her.'

'If you were back upstairs in the market at ten thirty, you

178

could have seen her, and anyone who was close to her.'

Mrs Lewis shook her head. 'No, I couldn't. I went straight and did the washing-up I'd left before. That's at the back of the caff. I never saw nobody till all your coppers come. And I didn't go looking at the dead one, neither. Not like some,' she ended virtuously, sitting herself more upright, and pulling the two sides of her cardigan closer together.

18

'It's not the people Mrs Lewis said she'd seen, Gomer, and now admits she couldn't have seen,' said Parry, driving the Porsche out of the underground police garage. 'It's the people who say they saw Mrs Lewis who're important now.'

Since interviewing Mae Lewis, Parry had been to Cowbridge and back, to the Major Crime Support Unit headquarters, for an urgent meeting of senior officers called by the Chief Superintendent in charge. Because of this, he had missed the updating session in the incident room at five o'clock. He had come back to pick up Lloyd. They were on their way to see Laura Mathews, but running late.

'Mrs Doris Peach and Eddie Faull are the two, boss.'

'That's right. He's a trainee plumber, I remember. They both said they saw her between ten ten and ten thirty. They even described her. No, that's not quite true. They described the way she was dressed. But they couldn't have seen her if she wasn't there.'

'I've sent a team to see both of them, boss.'

'Good. Both local, aren't they? Mrs Peach was from Roath Park, wasn't she?'

'Yes, and the lad's in digs in Rumney,' Lloyd supplied, settling deeper into the seat with his notebook. There were a number of new developments that needed reporting. 'Apart from the Mrs Laura Mathews item, which I told you about on the phone, there's the two points about Mrs Lewis's clothes. The headscarf thing she was wearing. That, er . . . bandana. She said it was blue with white spots. Mrs Peach said it was red with white spots. I thought one of them had to be wrong. I'm not so sure now.'

'Not if Mrs Peach only saw someone who looked like Mrs Lewis,' Parry agreed. 'And thank God there can't be that many people who look like Mrs Lewis,' he added with feeling. 'Anyway, I did ask her about the colour again. She says she sometimes wears a red bandana, but not last Saturday. Not that I'd really trust her to know what she was wearing. Have we asked the girl serving behind the counter?'

'That's, er . . . Phoebe Wilson, boss.'

'Yes. Nice kid. She seemed all there, as well. She might know the colour of Mrs Lewis's headscarf.'

'We'll try her, boss. But she never mentioned what Mrs Lewis was wearing before.' Lloyd was making notes.

The sides of Parry's eyes and his brow were crinkled in concentration. 'So what's the other thing about Mrs Lewis's clothes?' They were crossing the Taff Bridge at the end of Castle Street, heading west for Fairwater, which was only a few minutes' drive away.

'It can't have been part of her clothes, exactly, boss, but somebody left a long white jacket in the ladies' loo at the market on Saturday. In one of the cubicles. It was found this morning.'

'Who by?'

'One of the cleaners. They don't go in on Sundays. It was the first time the loos were cleaned since the market closed Saturday night. The coat was put in the lost-and-found bin. Nobody thought to report it to us, not till the market superintendent saw it late this afternoon. At least two people had handled it before then.'

Parry frowned. 'Didn't we search all the toilets ourselves, Saturday morning?'

'They were checked for abandoned items, as well as anyone hiding, boss. That was as soon as we closed the market. Around eleven o'clock. They weren't searched again by us.'

'What about the market superintendent's staff?'

'They went round the whole building after normal closing time. They always do, apparently, making a general check. It's part of the fire precautions. That includes the toilets, of course.' Lloyd looked up with a grin. 'To see there's no old ladies locked in the lavatories, like. But the staff don't usually look on the backs of the cubicle doors. That was where the coat was found. If it'd been there when we checked, it would have been picked up. Must have been left there later.'

'It's a coat, not a wrap-around overall?'

'That's the point, yes. Mrs Lewis was wearing an overall. It's standard dress for the café employees.'

'A long coat could look the same to a casual observer. There was no bandana in the pocket? Or in the loo?'

'Afraid not, boss. Nothing at all in the pockets, and no personal identification on the jacket, either. Only a manufacturer's label. The coat's newish. Hasn't been washed very often, not by the feel of it.' Lloyd studied a peppermint, the last of a packet, and brushed something off it before putting it in his mouth. 'A white coat being left could just be coincidence, of course.'

'Not if it was left by someone impersonating Mrs Lewis.'

Lloyd cleared his throat. 'We're checking in the morning with all the people in the market who work in white coats, boss.'

'Which could be most of them. What's happened to the coat?'

'It's gone to forensic, boss.'

'Good. Do we know which of the non-market employees in the frame wear white coats at work?'

'We're checking the list, boss. There's no hospital doctor, or chemist or dentist on it, for instance.'

Parry's eyebrows lifted. 'Plenty of people at St Olaf's wear white coats besides doctors.'

'Nobody from there in the frame though, boss.'

'Well, perhaps somebody from there should be.' Parry was silent for some moments before he went on: 'Would the catering staff in a youth hostel wear white coats?'

'Might do, boss. Is that what Mrs Rees does in those youth hostels?'

'Don't know. Probably not. She helps out, she told me. Could mean anything. I didn't ask for details. I should have.'

Lloyd kept his eyes on his notebook. When Parry started blaming himself for trivial omissions it was a sure sign he had other people's less trivial omissions in mind.

There was a longer silence before the chief inspector broke it with: 'If the murderer really was impersonating Mrs Lewis, knew she dodged in and out collecting dishes, and washed them up out of sight –'

'Or knew she took time off altogether to place bets, boss,' Lloyd put in.

'Then we're talking about a woman murderer for sure. And someone who had to know the victim would be in the market Saturday morning.'

'You don't think that's building too much on two alleged sightings of Mrs Lewis, boss?'

'Two alleged sightings of a woman who wasn't there.' Parry paused briefly. 'In a red bandana, which she sometimes wears, but swears she wasn't wearing on Saturday. A woman who everybody took for granted, who could have reached across Sister Watkyn for used cutlery, and stuck a very sharp bit of unused cutlery through her heart, without alerting anyone, including the victim. Not till it was too late. Who then escaped by simply appearing to go about her normal business.' Parry sniffed, just before his expression changed from earnest to doubtful. 'You could be right, though, Gomer. It's probably too neat. Or too fanciful.'

'Except for the red bandana, boss. And the coat was left in the ladies' loo, not the gents. It all points to a woman, at least.'

'Which narrows things down nicely to half the human race.' Parry gave a grunt. 'Secretaries or personal assistants don't wear white coats at work, of course.'

'They might have hobbies where they do, though, boss. My daughter Gwen, the married one, she wears a white coat for her pottery. Messy business, potting.'

After checking the name on the street door, Parry stopped the Porsche outside the small block of flats where Laura Mathews lived. 'We'll lead with what she wants to tell us about Huw Bevan,' he said. 'When that's done, we'll let her into our medical secret. Right?'

'Right, boss.'

*   *   *

'Please understand, we're not concerned with the reason for the blackmail, Mrs Mathews,' Parry explained.

'But you know about it all the same. Thanks to that stupid Watkyn bitch. She deserved a sticky end, if anyone did,' the woman responded with feeling.

Laura Mathews and the two officers were seated in the living room of her flat. She had been delayed, she had explained when letting them in, and had arrived only a minute before them. She was still in her formal and fashionable office clothes – a short black tailored skirt, and matching jacket worn over a starched white blouse. The frilly lace collar of the blouse was opened to reveal a generous amount of cleavage, and a clutch of expensive-looking gold neck chains. Her carefully arranged hair and make-up were both bandbox, as though they had both just been fixed. Her whole appearance was chic, and businesslike, Parry thought. This, along with her age, the fact that she evidently lived alone, plus what he had recently learned about her, all strengthened his hunch that she was probably Bevan's mistress as well as his secretary.

'Will the Bevans be in trouble over . . . over Barbara. I mean over her origins?' she asked.

Parry shrugged. 'That's not for us to say, Mrs Mathews. Off the record, Mr Frankel's a good lawyer, a very good one. I'd guess he has Mr and Mrs Bevan as legally well protected as they could be. Except for him, you seem to be the only person they ever confided in over the blackmail, or the . . . er . . . unusual way they acquired their daughter. Mr Bevan trusts you totally, he told us.'

She crossed her long, well-shaped legs, in an unhurried, relaxed movement. Her hands remained clasped in her lap. There was no self-conscious, gauche effort to induce the short skirt to cover more of her thighs than it was intended to cover. 'Isn't that what confidential secretaries are supposed to be, totally trustworthy, Mr Parry?'

'I'm sure. But the trust he puts in you, in his private affairs, it seems to go beyond what's normal in a . . . in a business relationship.'

'We're good friends as well as colleagues, if that's what

184

you're getting at. I've been with him a long time.' She was looking Parry steadily in the eye as she spoke.

Lloyd leaned forward. 'Could you tell us, ma'am, did Mr Bevan know in advance you wouldn't be in the office Saturday morning?'

'Yes. I told him I wouldn't be. I went home early on Friday. I, er . . . I wasn't well. Why's this important?'

'So Mr Bevan knew he'd have the whole office to himself Saturday morning?' Parry put in, without acknowledging her question, and before Lloyd could answer it. 'To come and go as he pleased. With no one to say when he was there.'

Laura's eyebrows lifted a fraction. 'There may not have been anyone else in the office, but Michaelston's not exactly in the outback, is it? People would have seen him driving in and out. You should check. Surely you don't think he's the murderer?'

'We need to establish the whereabouts on Saturday morning of anyone connected with Sister Watkyn, Mrs Mathews,' said Parry, again without taking up her own question. 'It's a matter of eliminating those who couldn't have been near her when she was killed.'

'I see. Mr Bevan rang me here at ten. I was . . . I was out, but the call will be recorded by BT, surely? I know he sent out some handwritten faxes, too.'

'The call to you was recorded, all right, ma'am,' said Lloyd. 'Pity of it is, he used his mobile phone to make it. He could have been anywhere in the area at the time.'

She gave an exasperated sigh. 'That's pure habit. It's because he takes his mobile with him everywhere. It's practically joined to his ear. He forgets he doesn't need to use it in his own office, especially if I'm not around to punch the numbers for him. But the faxes –'

'Could have been timed to go in advance, ma'am. Never mind. Like you say, probably someone saw him round Michaelston.' Lloyd shifted in the armchair. 'Now, about your own movements on Saturday?'

'I wondered when we'd get to those, I was –'

'We should tell you we know where you were Friday night, Mrs Mathews,' Parry put in quietly but firmly.

'How d'you mean?' For the first time she sounded and appeared uneasy.

'We learned just before we came here that you were admitted as a patient to St Olaf's Nursing Home on Friday afternoon, and that you left sometime on Saturday.'

'Who told you? They're not supposed to –'

'It wasn't any of the nursing home staff, ma'am. Well, not directly,' said Lloyd. 'We had to be given access to their admission records. We needed to check on all the patients admitted over the period Sister Watkyn worked there, in case any of them was known to have a grudge against her. Again, it was routine. Only –'

'Only my name came up?'

'It was only highlighted when we transferred the list to our computer, ma'am. When we were cross-checking the names on the St Olaf's list with people connected to Sister Watkyn in, er . . . in other ways, like.'

'Through her blackmailing, you mean? But I never even met Pansy Watkyn, in or out of the nursing home. I didn't know what she looked like, even.'

'But you knew she was blackmailing your boss, ma'am.'

Laura swallowed, but made no comment.

'I should explain, we have no details of why you were in St Olaf's, Mrs Mathews,' said Parry. 'No one there would be authorized to tell us, either. Not unless we got a court order. It just seemed odd that neither of the Bevans told us you'd been in a nursing home. Only Mr Bevan said you'd told him you'd been out for a walk when he rang you Saturday morning. I mean, since you're so close to him, we thought at least he'd have known where you really were. Unless you can help us over this, we may need to check with him again. Could you at least tell us what time you left St Olaf's on Saturday?'

It seemed again that the woman wasn't going to answer until suddenly she said: 'The nursing home list gives the name of the doctor or surgeon responsible for admitting the patient, doesn't it?'

186

'Yes, it does, but –'

'So you know bloody well the name of the surgeon who admitted me. You've also been guessing why.'

Lloyd looked up. 'The women detectives in charge of the computer search may have made one or two broad guesses, ma'am, yes.'

'All right. So let me solve your problem for you. I had an abortion on Friday afternoon. But if you tell another living soul, I swear I'll sue you for a packet, you and the police force. For invasion of privacy.' She took a long deep breath. 'Huw Bevan didn't tell you I'd been to hospital because I never told him. And he mustn't know. Or Mrs Bevan.'

Lloyd was showing his embarrassment. 'Could you tell us, was it just coincidence you went to St Olaf's, ma'am?'

'Coincidence, yes, and unavoidable. In the circumstances, I'd have preferred to have gone somewhere else. Anywhere else. But it happens to be where my surgeon does nearly all his private work, and there was no theatre space available at any other nursing home. Anyway, I left St Olaf's after lunch on Saturday, by chauffeur-driven hire car.'

'Like she said when she cooled down, boss, Mr Bevan had enough on his plate not to be bothered by her problems.'

'Their mutual problem, though, if it was he put her in the club.'

'And it's a pound to a penny it was,' Lloyd replied, as Parry headed the Porsche back to central Cardiff. 'Fact remains, we know now she couldn't have done the murder to help him.'

'Yes. I was still surprised she admitted to having an abortion, as if she thought we knew already.'

'That's what she did think, boss. Since we had the name of the surgeon. I told you before, abortion is about all he seems to do for a living,' Lloyd commented in an even deeper sepulchral tone than normal, which could have been implying that he disapproved of the work, or the amount of it, or both. 'Hard decision for her to have made on her own, poor girl,' he added, and indicating a more likely reason for the lowered level of his responses. 'You don't know, she might have wanted to have the baby. She could be going through a difficult time over it still.'

'Of course, she was surprised we knew she'd been in hospital at all,' said Parry.

'That's right, boss. So after that we had her off guard, like. I think that's the other reason she came clean so fast. Otherwise she might have hedged a bit. I don't think she'd have told us lies, though.'

Parry looked doubtful. 'I thought it strange she didn't hint it wasn't Bevan's child,' he said. 'In the circumstances, she might have suggested it was someone else's. To protect him.'

'Ah, she wouldn't go that far, boss. He means too much to her, probably. See, if Mr Bevan found out about the pregnancy from someone else, she wouldn't want him to think the father hadn't been him. Not for definite. It would have meant she'd been unfaithful to him. She'd have thought that one through. No doubt at all.' The sergeant folded his arms over the seat belt and nodded at his own prescience.

Parry decided not to challenge his companion's homespun philosophizing. Instead he said: 'In a way it would have been a lot better for Bevan if he'd spent Saturday mid-morning making love to her at her flat.'

'Yes, like you thought he might have done, boss. Except we might not have believed them. Like one was giving the other a false alibi. Of course, we've no better idea than before about whether he was in the market Saturday.'

'Except we think Sister Watkyn was murdered by a woman.' Parry sneezed. While he was delving for his handkerchief, his cellphone started ringing. It was Lloyd who picked up the instrument.

Seconds later Parry was altering course for the Bevan house in Bryntaf. The call had been from the incident room. Lufthansa had confirmed, and, on being pressed, had just reconfirmed, that Barbara Bevan and Alwyn Price had not been passengers on their eleven-forty flight to Düsseldorf on

Saturday. It was the airline's two-fifteen flight to the same destination the pair had taken.

Routine checking had also revealed that white coats were compulsory for students at the Prince's Academy attending biology classes.

19

'You say you'd forgotten you caught the later flight, Miss Bevan?' said Parry, in a serious, but not badgering, voice. He and Lloyd were closeted with Huw Bevan and his daughter in Bevan's study at Hill House. It was five to seven.

The room, on the upper floor next to Barbara Bevan's bedroom, was unlike the others the policemen had been through in the house. It was unexpectedly small, and far from being handsomely furnished, it was stark and uncosy, with cheap, office fitments, and incongruous pink carperting, badly laid, and looking as though it had been discarded from elsewhere in the house. Drab blue curtains were hanging at the single window which faced north on to a car wash, behind the garage. There were no hanging pictures, and no bookcases, only open shelves, along two walls, stacked with technical journals and brochures, and pieces of unconnected electrical gadgetry. A television set occupied one corner, with a rowing machine across from it. A combined radio and tape recorder was set on the small metal desk beside a telephone, with a rack of tapes behind. Twin speakers were fixed high up on the opposite wall – one of them crookedly.

Earlier on, while Bevan and the policemen had been waiting for Barbara to appear, her father had explained, somewhat long-windedly, that he'd never wanted a study in the house, but had agreed to have one solely to please his wife. He used it, he said, as a kind of workshop-cum-exercise-room, and a place where he could come by himself to watch TV sport or listen to his jazz tapes. He apologized for the disorder. Parry noted the tape rack which had been mentioned in its owner's earlier statement.

The four had ended up in here at Bevan's own suggestion, after he had come upstairs to fetch Barbara who had been taking a shower when Parry and Lloyd had arrived, unheralded. His wife had been out, but he was expecting her back. As always, he was anxious to prevent her being upset, saying she was less likely to think of joining them up here. No doubt she would see Parry's car outside, but she would not be aware that Barbara was in the study with them.

'So I forgot which flight we took. That's not so terrible, is it?' the girl responded with a shrug of her shoulders. Wearing hastily donned blue jeans, a pink cotton blouse and sneakers, she was sitting on the edge of the desk, lank wet hair framing her face. Her father and Parry were occupying the only chairs in the room. Lloyd had propped himself against a cold radiator, next to the door.

'So can you tell us what time you left Cardiff in the car for Heathrow?' Parry continued.

There was another shrug, and the girl's left leg, which was crossed over her right, began swinging faster than it had been doing before. 'I can't remember that, either. Not for sure.' She ran a hand roughly through her hair. 'Why the big deal about times and flights? We flew to Düsseldorf. You know why. End of story.'

'Not quite, I'm afraid, Miss Bevan. You see, if you left Cardiff after ten thirty, you could have reached Heathrow in time for the flight you took.'

'Ten thirty was the time Pansy Watkyn was killed, wasn't it? You saying I killed her?' She looked down at her father. 'Daddy, aren't I supposed to have my brief here when I'm being grilled, like on TV? I mean, shouldn't we get good old Uncle Simon over?'

'I've left a message on his machine, love,' her father put in, it seemed apologetically. He had phoned Simon Frankel as soon as the policemen had arrived. 'But nobody's accusing you of anything. And I'm here to look after you,' he added.

The girl switched her gaze to Parry. 'So you're not saying I killed her?'

'Certainly not, Miss Bevan,' he said. 'But we'd still like to know where you were at ten thirty Saturday morning.'

'To keep you and Alwyn in the clear, like, miss. Out of the picture altogether,' Lloyd volunteered, with an avuncular smile.

'Try to remember what time you left Cardiff, Barbara. It's important,' said her father. His chair was immediately next to where she was sitting, and he put a hand on one of hers.

'I should mention that Alwyn Price is being asked the same questions by colleagues of ours,' Parry offered. 'Perhaps he'll remember times better than you?'

The leg stopped swinging for a moment, and the young girl's face hardened. 'He'll tell you the truth. Alwyn's a really solid citizen,' she responded woodenly.

'I see.' Parry glanced at her father, then continued. 'Perhaps it'd be best if we start at the beginning of the morning, Miss Bevan. You left here at what time?'

'About nine thirty.'

'I assume that's the time you'd have left if you'd been going to school?'

'On a Saturday, yes. We start later then.'

'And you meant your parents to think that's where you were going?'

'Suppose so.'

'And you took the things you usually take for school?'

'I had the bag I take to school, yes. I'd put things for the night in it. And my passport.'

'But you didn't go to school?'

'No.'

'We understand your first lesson on Saturday was biology. Did you have your white coat with you in the bag?'

She frowned. 'I've lost my biology coat.'

'When and where did you lose it?'

'Don't know. I had it at school Thursday. I meant to bring it home to wash. It's probably been picked up in the locker room and gone in the school laundry. Anyway, we don't absolutely need to wear them. Kappy, that's Mr Kapson, our biology teacher, he likes us to wear them, that's all.'

'Good at biology, are you, miss?' asked Lloyd, reassuringly.

'She's top in her class, aren't you, love?' Bevan answered for her proudly.

'I was last term,' the girl replied, with more diffidence than modesty.

'Is that Capson with a C, miss?' asked Lloyd who, as usual, was making notes.

'No, Kapson with a K. I think his family was Hungarian. He's very good, and dishy with it.'

'Does biology involve human biology? Anatomy?' asked Parry.

'Yes. And the human reproductive process. It's very sexy, if that's what you mean. Clitoral agitation, orgasms, and male sperm counts. The lot. Kappy's very thorough.' It was clear the girl had intended to embarrass the others. In the case of her father, she had succeeded. The policemen proved to be less vulnerable. Lloyd, the veteran parent, was looking mildly amused.

'Just tell Mr Parry what he wants to know, Barbara, will you?' said Bevan, his tone showing irritation.

'I thought I just did,' she answered defiantly, without dropping her gaze. She had been doing her best to stare out the chief inspector. When she failed, she began swinging her leg again, this time more energetically.

'So when you left here, where did you go?' Parry asked.

Barbara was watching her moving foot as she said: 'I phoned Alwyn from the box in the village. Asked him if he'd drive us to Heathrow, then go to Germany with me. He said he would. I knew he had his mother's car.'

'Did he ask why you wanted to go to Germany?'

'I don't remember. But I must have said it was important. He aims to please.'

'And you arranged for him to pick you up somewhere? Outside the phone box, was it?'

'Yes. Well . . . no. Not at the phone box. He lives in Llandaff. He had to get some things from school. I . . . I had something else to do as well. At least, I thought I had. On my own. At the other end of the village.'

'Where Sister Watkyn lived?' Parry asked quietly.

She took a deep breath. 'Yes. I wanted to see her.'

Bevan sat up straighter in his chair. 'You never told us that, love,' he said, then turned to Parry. 'Perhaps we had better wait till Simon Frankel gets here before we go on with this?'

'It's all right, Daddy,' his daughter put in quickly. 'I was only joking about wanting Uncle Simon here. There's nothing to tell. Nothing much more than you know already. Only, before, I didn't want to worry Mummy.' She looked at Parry again. 'I was on my way to Pansy's road when I saw her by the shops. She was hurrying to the bus stop. There was a Cardiff bus coming. A lot of people got on. I got on behind her. She didn't see me. When she went downstairs on the bus, I went upstairs, on the left. I watched through the window to see where she got off. She didn't. Well, not till St Mary Street, where nearly everybody gets off.'

'And when she got off, you followed her?'

'Yes.'

'Where did she go?'

'First she just looked in shop windows. Then she walked through to The Hayes, slowly, like she was killing time. After that she went to the market.'

'And you followed her in?'

'No. I was worried about the time. I'd promised to meet Alwyn at half past ten. In St Andrew's Crescent.'

'So what time was it by then?'

She paused. 'I suppose it must have been about ten past.'

'So you're saying you didn't speak to Sister Watkyn at all?'

'That's right.'

'Did you see anyone else you knew when you were following her? Anyone outside the market, for instance?'

'No. No one I remember.'

'Could you tell us why you'd been following her?'

Barbara swallowed. 'I'm not sure. Not even about why I was going to her house at the start. It was . . . it was . . . a sort of compulsion. All I knew was, I wanted her to stop the blackmail.' As she was speaking, she crossed her arms over her chest, and her hands clasped her shoulders. The hands now began pulling towards each other in a self-comforting hug. 'I wanted to talk to her, but if I'd got to her house, probably I wouldn't have rung the bell,' she went on, now

194

rocking her body slightly. 'Deep inside me, I suppose I thought I might just make things worse.'

'In what way?'

She sighed. 'All I had to go on was the tape. I knew I should have talked to Daddy about it, but . . . but I hadn't been able to do that. When it came to talking to Pansy about it, I suppose it was the same, only . . . only for a different reason.' She looked up, pleadingly this time. 'I'm probably not making any sense, am I?'

'What were your feelings towards Sister Watkyn?'

'What do you think they were?' she answered bitingly, confidence suddenly returned. 'I hated her. She'd betrayed us. The whole family. Our friendship. Everything. I loathed her. Wouldn't you have?'

'Barbara, I think you should – ' her father started, but Parry interrupted him.

'You couldn't bring yourself to speak to her, but you'd made up your mind to go to Germany, to get the same information she could have given you.'

'No!' she insisted sharply. 'It was different. I didn't believe what she'd told Daddy. Only I was torn between having her say it was true, and making her say it was lies. I wanted to . . . to prove it was lies for myself.'

'How did you expect to make her say it was lies?'

She breathed in and out noisily before answering: 'I don't know.'

'You didn't believe you were adopted?'

She shook her head. 'No. That bit I could believe. Or accept, anyway. It wasn't so terrible. It was the other. About Mummy and Daddy stealing me from my real mother. Or having me stolen. I thought that was . . . sick.'

'But why hadn't you asked your parents to tell you if it was true?'

Suddenly her eyes were full of tears. 'I suppose because I believed it. I'm sorry, Daddy.' Now it was she who reached for one of his hands. 'Or maybe I was just too mixed up. Couldn't think straight. I just didn't know who I'd believe. Except I had this feeling all the time I should find out the truth for myself. I tell you, I hadn't slept all night. My head was like . . . exploding. It's why I didn't really know what I was doing. Not when I started following Pansy.'

There was dead silence for several seconds, until Parry asked woodenly: 'Miss Bevan, do you own a red headscarf with white polka dots on it?'

'Sort of, yes. It's next door,' she answered, apparently unconcerned, while she concentrated on pulling a tissue from the pocket of her jeans. 'It's got white hearts on it, not dots. Why? I wasn't wearing it on Saturday.' She blew her nose into the tissue.

'And have you ever been to the Popular Café upstairs in the Central Market?' Parry went on, ignoring her question.

'Where Pansy was killed? Yes. Students often go there for lunch. It's cheap.'

'I see.' Parry paused. 'We have a white cotton coat in our possession. I imagine it's like the one you've lost. It was found on the back of a cubicle in the ladies' toilets at the Central Market on Saturday. Did you leave it there?'

Lloyd, looking uneasy, shifted his stance as Barbara answered. 'Of course I didn't. I told you, I wasn't in the market.'

'I should tell you the coat is under forensic examination at the moment. The results will show who's been wearing it,' the chief inspector offered solemnly.

'Well, if it's my coat, someone must have stolen it.'

The two policemen exchanged glances as Parry said: 'All the same, Miss Bevan, I'm afraid I have to ask you and your father to come down to the station with us now. There are some simple tests we need to go through with you. They won't take long.' He looked at Bevan. 'But it might be as well, sir, if you tried to get hold of Mr Frankel again.'

Bevan stood up slowly. 'There's no need for Barbara to come to the station, Mr Parry. There's a much easier way to sort things out,' he said, his voice well controlled. He turned to his daughter. 'I heard your mother's car just now, love. She'll be in the kitchen. Go down and tell her I have to pop into Cardiff, and not to wait supper for me, will you? Go now, there's a good girl. I need to have another word with

Mr Parry and Mr Lloyd before we leave. And don't you worry about anything.'

'I don't understand, Daddy,' she said, clearly worried. 'How can you sort things –?'

'Just do as I say, Barbara, will you?' he interrupted, in a tone now that brooked no argument.

When his daughter had left the room, Bevan went to the door to make sure it was closed, then he turned to the chief inspector, his face showing strain. 'The coat won't have anything to do with the murder, Mr Parry,' he said, then sighed. 'I stabbed Sister Watkyn. At the time I believed she deserved it.'

'But you couldn't do anything else, boss. He's not some nutter off the street, confessing to a murder he couldn't have done. He's been a prime suspect since we found out about the blackmail,' Lloyd was saying, just over three hours later, as he and Parry went through the incident room and across to the corner office.

'Except I'm still not sure he did it, and neither are you, Gomer.'

'At the end, even Mr Frankel didn't seem sure, not either way, boss.'

'That was after he'd heard the case building against the daughter. They both wanted to spare her.'

'Well, that's understandable, isn't it?'

'Understandable or not, tomorrow, if the DNA samples from that coat match with hers, there's no way we can go on holding her father and not her.'

'Mr Bevan was pretty narked about us bringing her down here, after all, boss.'

Parry shrugged as he dropped the papers he was carrying on the desk. 'Making it even more clear why he'd come out with the confession in the first place. And if he really thinks she did it, he could have a reason we haven't got. Or not yet.'

'Not to do with the coat?'

'Father and daughter are close. Very close,' said Parry, taking off his jacket, and draping it over the back of the chair before he sat down. 'She may even have told him she'd done it.'

'And he'd told her if we moved in on her, he'd confess, and draw the heat off, like?' Lloyd slumped down into a chair on the other side of the desk.

'Something like that. In the hope we'd fail to convict him, and then also fail to follow through on her.' Parry smiled ruefully. 'And if one of your daughters was in the same spot, I believe you'd do the same, Gomer. Except you'd do a better job.'

'Maybe.' Two of Lloyd's five grown-up children were girls. 'Except we can't be certain he didn't do the murder, boss. Like he said, he could have driven into Cardiff from his office just before ten, parked in Westgate Street, nipped up to the market, knifed Sister Watkyn, and driven back to his office, all inside forty minutes.'

'If you believe it was he she'd arranged to meet there at ten thirty –'

'We don't have another taker for that, boss,' Lloyd put in.

'But when we do, I guarantee it'll be for a more convincing reason than Bevan's given us for the meeting.'

The sergeant blew out his cheeks. 'He said it was because he'd told her he wanted to talk off the record. With no lawyer telling him what he couldn't say.'

Parry chuckled. 'Frankel didn't like that, did he?'

'Well, that's understandable, isn't it?'

'None of which explains why she had the thousand pounds with her.' The chief inspector waved a hand to stop Lloyd interrupting as he went on: 'All right, I accept the money might not have any bearing. But would a man, intending to get away with a daylight murder, be so plain daft as to park his car on a double line, even for ten minutes, on a busy main thoroughfare, in the centre of Cardiff, on a Saturday morning?'

'He could have got lucky over that, boss.'

'Sure. And if he's telling the truth he did get lucky. But the question is, would he have risked it, with so much at stake? I don't believe so.' Parry picked up the sheaf of new reports that had appeared on the desk during the time they had been downstairs. 'I mean, how would he have looked if there'd been a parking ticket on the car when he got back? Or worse, if the bloody car had been towed away by an ever-vigilant constabulary?'

'According to Alwyn Price, the girl was waiting for him in St Andrew's Crescent at ten twenty, boss, which means she couldn't have done the murder.'

'It could also mean Alwyn Price is lying in his teeth. He aims to please, remember?'

Lloyd combed one end of his moustache with two fingers. 'Except we haven't told him or the girl the exact time of the murder,' he cautioned. 'Not to the minute, like.'

'Assuming we know it ourselves as exactly as we thought,' Parry rejoined. 'When you analyse it, we've only the word of some pretty vague witnesses. And they seem to be getting vaguer by the hour.'

'The till records at the café shows it couldn't have been before ten twenty-six though, boss.'

'Hm.' Parry pulled out three of the call reports from amongst the others in front of him. 'It says here Phoebe Wilson can't remember the colour of that bandana. How can we be certain it really was Sister Watkyn she served, when she said she did?' He sounded as if he'd revised his opinion of the 'nice' kid he had earlier thought was 'all there'. 'And of our other two star witnesses, Mrs Peach isn't certain of the bandana colour any more, and I don't believe Eddie Faull would know if Mrs Lewis was wearing a bandana or ostrich feathers.' He shook his head, then looked up. 'Another thing that still doesn't fit is what Evan Rees told you this morning. About his relationship with his wife.' Parry was studying Lloyd's own report on a visit he had made to Rees, following Parry's phoned instructions when the chief inspector had been on his way back from the Gower.

'Certainly doesn't fit with what Mrs Rees told you, boss. About their little chats, and that. According to him, he avoids her like the plague. And he'll never go back to her,' said Lloyd. 'Either one could be lying, of course. Or both of them. For their own ends, like.'

Parry dropped the yellow report sheets on to the desk, and

looked at his watch. 'Time to knock off, Gomer,' he said, leaning back, stretching his arms high above his head, then clasping his hands behind his neck. 'Look, we've got a prime suspect who's confessed to the murder, and he's safely locked up for the night. We can hold him for at least another day for further questioning before formally charging him. Forensic results will prove in the morning if he's just shielding his daughter, and if he is, it's her we'll be arresting instead, probably. I know you don't like the thought, and neither do I, but we've had other cases involving guilty kids, and this one had a defensible motive, at least.' He was trying to assuage the grim expression on the sergeant's face. 'By tomorrow we may have some evidence to prove Bevan was in Cardiff on Saturday. But on her own admission, young Barbara certainly knows enough anatomy to have hit the right spot with the knife, and I don't believe her father can match that.' Now he leaned forward across the desk, elbows on the arms of the chair. 'Anyway, nobody can say we aren't making progress, *bach*,' he completed cheerfully.

'Is that what the Chief Super was on about in Cowbridge, boss?'

'More or less. So, off you go home to Gracie. I'll be leaving as well in a minute, soon as I've scanned the rest of these reports.'

Lloyd stood up, still looking uneasy. 'Wish I believed it was either the father or the daughter. But I don't.' When Parry didn't seem to have heard the comment, he nodded and made for the door, adding: 'Well, we'll sleep on it, boss. *Nos da.*'

'Good night, Gomer.' The widower, his mind preoccupied, had absently returned the other's identical farewell, but in English, which was always a small disappointment to a Welsh speaker – even a tolerant one like Lloyd.

For once, it wasn't that Lloyd was wishing he too had a wife waiting for him, or that he was contemplating how long it would be before Perdita Jones would formally fill that vacant position – if she ever did.

The sergeant's comment had been perfectly accurate. Parry wasn't nearly satisfied with the state of the investigation, despite what he had said about having a confessed culprit behind bars. That had been an eminently suitable fact to report to a Chief Superintendent who, earlier in the day, had been justifiably concerned to hear about positive developments: but that was all it had been.

It was much later – nearly midnight – when Parry, still at the desk, recalled the answer given to one of Lloyd's questions. It was this that suddenly released a slim piercing ray of light that was to grow into a dazzling beam, starkly illuminating the whole case.

Immediately, though, the recollection only sent Parry into the next room to retrieve Sister Watkyn's diary from its place of safekeeping.

20

More than a day later, on Wednesday morning, the weather had changed dramatically. Instead of the clear skies and bright sunshine that had complemented Parry's excursion to the Gower Peninsula on Monday, today he was pressing the Porsche along the same route through strong winds and pelting rain, with car roof closed, wipers working at maximum speed, and frequent warnings to drivers coming through on the radio about the dangers of road flooding following the driest late summer on record. It wasn't quite broad daylight yet either, partly because of the clouds, but more because it was still some minutes short of six o'clock. He had been up since 4.30, and was now only a short distance away from Kathleen Rees's cottage.

It had not been until late on the previous evening that Huw Bevan had been released from Cardiff Central Police Station. He had been held there for questioning, but not formally arrested, since the same time on Monday, confirming his guilt throughout, though unable to support his contention that he was a murderer with anything more conclusive than his own word on the matter. He had only changed his tune after the results of the DNA tests had come through from Chepstow. The overloaded forensic laboratories there had taken longer than expected to provide scientific proof that Barbara Bevan had not been the owner of the white coat found abandoned in the market. As Parry had expected, once informed of this, her father had promptly retracted his confession, leaving the police with no grounds or hard evidence to justify detaining either father or daughter – as Simon Frankel, for one, had made forcefully clear.

So far as the police were concerned, both Bevans were still suspects, but it would have required a special magistrates' order to detain Huw Bevan any longer without charge. Parry hadn't been prepared to go to that length when no new line of questioning was presenting itself. To detain the daughter, when she had Alwyn Price as witness that she was a mile away at the time of the murder, was pointless – and would remain so unless, or until, other witnesses could be found to prove they were both lying.

So Huw Bevan had been admonished for wasting police time, and warned that proceedings might be taken against him for this at a later time – in short, when the officers concerned weren't so busy trying to find the real murderer. Except everyone involved was well aware that he had made his confession to protect his daughter – and most, including Gomer Lloyd, grudgingly admired him for that.

By this time a fresh and promising line of enquiry was being pursued thanks to Parry's own initiative, begun late on Monday night. Unlike the line linked to the Bevans, the one now bringing the chief inspector west again had been both labour-intensive, and time-consuming. Successive reliefs of detectives, members of the uniform branch, and civilian police employees of the Crime Unit had been at work through Tuesday, adding new data spun off from the accumulated information already collected. It had been a day of hard plod – some electronic, but a lot of it the old-fashioned kind of foot plodding.

Lloyd should have been with Parry in the Porsche now, but before Parry had arrived to pick him up *en route* at his house, Gracie Lloyd had phoned to say that the wind and rain had removed a section of tiles from their roof, and that water was pouring down through the house. A tiler was on the way, and Gomer was meantime on the roof with a neighbour trying to anchor a tarpaulin sheet over the opening. When he had done this he would follow Parry in his own car, and shouldn't be more than half an hour behind.

When the chief inspector swung into the rutted lane to Mrs Rees's cottage, it was like driving into a shallow, fast-moving mountain stream. He urged the car along it, then swung left

203

to stop as near to the front door as he could. He was glad to see a light in the kitchen window. On his previous visit, Mrs Rees had told him she rose at five, but that might have been a piece of countrywoman's bravado. This time she had no warning of his coming, either.

'Well, there's a surprise!' she exclaimed, on opening the door to his knock, her tone more curious than affable. 'Come in quick, out of this storm. Terrible, isn't it?'

The first thing he noticed was the frayed white cotton coat she had on, and then the round-brimmed, soft white cap covering her hair. 'Sorry to call so early, Mrs Rees,' he said, steeling himself to the fact that she was not the only person connected with the case to own a white cotton coat.

'That's all right. But you'll have to wait a bit if you want some of my new bread. I've only just put it in the oven. Why don't you sit down?'

'Thanks. But I haven't come to cadge breakfast again.' He took a chair at the table.

'You'd be very welcome if you had. So, what have you come for? About Pansy Watkyn again, I suppose?' She was brushing flour off the coat as she added: 'Making bread's a dry old business.'

'But you're well dressed for it.'

'That's right. Proper baker's girl, I must look. Did I tell you, my father was a master baker? I worked with him for years as a girl, after my mother died. Strict about the proper clothing, he was.' She plucked at the coat. 'If he'd lived, he'd have been telling me to get a new one of these, too, but I can't be bothered. He was red hot on getting-up time, as well.'

'And old habits die hard,' Parry observed with a smile.

'Oh, right enough.' She nodded at the oven. 'I have to make six extra loaves on Wednesdays. To take to school with me. Standing orders from some of the other teachers.'

'That's quite a compliment,' he said, 'And well deserved. I speak as one who knows the product.'

'Thank you. Flattery's good for you, so long as you don't inhale. That's what our headmaster always says. I'll make

204

some tea in a minute.' She sat down opposite him, her back very straight in the chair.

'I'll enjoy that, but, er . . . but I'm afraid this isn't a social call, Mrs Rees. I'm here on serious business.'

'In that case, we'll probably both survive better on a cup of tea.'

'Perhaps.' He gave her a half smile. 'You mentioned last time, you'd never actually met Pansy Watkyn.'

'That's right.' She took the white hat off, shook her head, then tidied her short hair with her hands.

He thought how lithe and vital she looked, as he asked: 'Had you ever written to Pansy?'

'No, never.'

'Or she to you?'

'No, I don't think so. We talked on the phone once or twice.'

'What did she call you?'

'How d'you mean?'

'Well, was it Mrs Rees, or – ?'

'Oh, I see. No, no. Very chummy. Kathy and Pansy, it was. Well, no reason to be upstage, was there? Just because she was borrowing my husband. She wasn't the first to do that, after all.'

'Is that what your husband always called you? Kathy?'

'Yes. Always. From the very beginning. I should think he's forgotten what my real name is, that's if he ever knew it.'

'It's Kathleen. With a K, isn't it?' It was the first of the two Christian names registered on her car documents at the licensing centre in Swansea – and the same first letter as the surname of Barbara Bevan's biology teacher.

'That's right.'

'It's more usual for that to be shortened to Katy than to Kathy.'

'Ah, there's a reason for that. I had a cousin called Katrin. She didn't like the name at all. Shortened it to Katy. That's when we were kids. In the same class at school.'

'And that's why you became Kathy, with a soft A?'

'Yes. So we wouldn't get mixed up. Why you asking?'

'So it's possible Pansy Watkyn believed your real name

was Catherine with a C, which you'd shortened to Cathy, also with a C.'

'It's possible, yes. Is that what she did?'

'These phone conversations you say you had with her. You rang her, did you? At her bungalow?' It was the second time he had ignored a question from Mrs Rees, and this time the fact seemed to register in her changed expression.

'Not really,' she replied, more slowly than before. 'I'd be ringing Evan there, only she'd come on the line instead. You know how it is.'

'Yes. Although he has his own number. A cellphone. She answered that, too, did she?'

'No . . . I, er . . . I only had the ordinary number. The one in the book under her name. I kept meaning to ask Evan for the other one. I . . . I didn't ring him that often.'

The answer she gave had seemed to embarrass her, Parry thought, clearly because it confirmed a lesser continuing relationship with her husband than she had boasted of earlier. 'I see,' he commented. 'And I believe she rang you, too, sometimes?'

Mrs Rees frowned. 'Not that I remember.'

'Last Thursday, for instance? At lunchtime? Twelve thirty?'

'No, that couldn't be right,' she countered easily enough this time, almost eagerly. 'I wasn't here then. I was at school.'

'The call wasn't to this number. Pansy made it from a pay phone at St Olaf's Nursing Home. It was to your school in Pontyglas.'

She turned her head from side to side several times, as if she were doing neck exercises. 'How d'you know that, then?'

He didn't know it for certain. But he knew a call had been made, and he was ready to bet a month's salary that it was Pansy who had made it. 'Did she ring you to make arrangements to meet?'

'No. Certainly not.'

'When you lived in Cardiff,' he added, and, despite the solid negative in the last reply, keeping the momentum of his questioning going while changing its direction. 'I expect you used the Central Market a good deal, like most people.'

'Quite a bit, yes. When it was ... convenient.' Her tone had become thoroughly cautious now, and she was choosing her words carefully.

'Your husband says you always bought your fish there.'

'Did he now? Well, that's the first time I've ever known him take an interest in my shopping habits.'

'He also told us yesterday you and he sometimes had coffee upstairs at the Popular Café.'

'Once in a blue moon. It was cheaper than taking me to Howell's department store, anyway. He only did that once, before we were married.'

'Anyway, you might still recognize some of the café personnel. One of them, at least. Mae Lewis. She's been there for years. Quite a character. She clears the tables. Wears an overall – white, like the coat you've got on. And she always has a coloured bandana on her head.'

Mrs Rees blinked several times. 'Don't think I remember her, no. Like I said, it's been some time.'

'You mean you haven't been to the market at all recently?'

'No, not for years. I could really do with that tea now, couldn't you?' She had got up already in a movement that had seemed close to compulsive. After sliding the kettle on to the oven hotplate, she busied herself preparing the teapot, and putting tea things on a tray.

Parry watched her for a few seconds, before he asked: 'Did you leave your car in the covered park in Quay Street at ten to ten last Saturday morning? The car park closest to the market?'

She had her back to him still, but he sensed, as well as saw, her whole being momentarily freeze. 'Someone say they saw me there, did they?'

'No,' he answered.

'That's good, because they'd have been lying. I told you, I wasn't –'

'No one's said they saw you, Mrs Rees. Not yet. But no one's had to, really. The ticket you had to surrender to the machine, when you left again, it had your fingerprints all over it. According to that ticket, you left again at ten thirty-seven.' And uncovering that fundamental fact had been a hugely time-consuming operation. Twelve hundred and fifty-seven tickets had been surrendered at the five centrally located Cardiff car parks before eleven a.m. on Saturday morning. They had been collected from the operators and scientifically, painstakingly checked for fingerprints by a team of six civilian technicians working through the whole of Tuesday. It had been the eight hundred and twenty-third ticket examined that had yielded the prints being sought.

'That's absolutely not true, of course. I wasn't there,' Mrs Rees insisted, turning around. 'And how can you know they're my fingerprints, anyway? You didn't have anything to compare them with.'

'I'm sorry, I'm afraid we lifted a perfect set of prints from your right hand, from one of the apples you gave me on Monday.' It had been an afterthought on his part to have had that done – prompted by a presentiment. He was aware also that it would be judged a legally unacceptable way of acquiring formal evidence.

Her face fell a fraction. 'That was sneaky, wasn't it? And are you allowed to take innocent people's fingerprints without them knowing?'

'No, we aren't, Mrs Rees. And that set of prints won't be used for official purposes, because another person might have handled that apple. The next set will be taken from you with your full knowledge. But we both know they're going to match the ones on the ticket, don't we?'

Mrs Rees considered for several seconds, took a deep breath, then swallowed hard. 'All right, I did go to Cardiff,' she said. 'I didn't want to say so. Not after I knew what happened to Pansy. I was there because I needed to stock up with things from the health shop in Church Street. I've been going there for years. They're customers of mine now, as well. For fresh herbs.' Her tone had been relaxed and matter of fact, as though she regretted having been caught out over a harmless and defensible fib. She turned back to the stove, made the tea, and was bringing the pot to the table, with the other things, as she continued: 'Tell you the truth, Mr Parry, I'd heard about Pansy on the radio Sunday night. I thought I might be drawn in if anyone knew I'd been

208

in Cardiff. Jealous, deserted wife. That kind of nonsense.'
She sat down at the table. 'Wouldn't have been true in my
case, of course. But I just didn't want to get involved.' She
sniffed. 'So there, I've told you now. Glad to get it off my
chest, really. Sorry, and all that. About not coming clean in
the first place.'

'But weren't you involved anyway, Mrs Rees?' he asked.

'I don't see how. Like I said before, why should I have
been? I only had to wait for Evan to come back to me.'

'That's not what he says, Mrs Rees. He says you have
delusions about your relations with him. That they're nonexistent.'

'Delusions, is it? There's a nerve for you. He confides in
me all the time. He's always ringing me.'

'He denies that, too, I'm afraid. Says he never rings you.
That you always ring him. And I should tell you, the printed
information we have from BT seems to confirm that.'

'So who cares who rings who? We talk. Frequently. Right?
How d'you think I know what he's been up to? The names
of his girlfriends, the –'

'The way a lot of wives know that kind of thing, Mrs Rees,'
Parry interrupted quietly but firmly. 'You've been employing
a detective agency to keep tabs on him. They're some of the
first people we consult, in circumstances like these. The outfit
you've been using is Bayland Investigations. That was up to
about two months ago, when we believe you found them
too expensive to keep on. They're good, though. But you
must have had to pay them a lot of money over the last
three years.'

'That was all supposed to be confidential.' She spat out the
words angrily.

'The local detective agencies regularly cooperate with us
when we're investigating serious crimes,' replied the policeman. 'It's very much in their own interests to do that, of
course.' Then, after a brief pause, he went on: 'Speaking
of money, how much was Pansy offering you? A thousand
pounds down, and another thousand after the divorce? Plus
the legal costs? Was that the deal? She had a thousand in
cash with her on Saturday.'

'I'm sure I don't know what you mean.' She was staring at the teapot in front of her, but had made no attempt yet to fill the cups from it.

'I think you do know, Mrs Rees. I think Pansy spelled it all out to you on the telephone on Thursday. That's when you agreed to meet her on Saturday morning. It's in her diary. The entry reads "Ten thirty, C. Market". From the start, we thought the C might have been someone's initial, except no one connected with the case had a name beginning with C. Later we assumed the C stood for Central. We were wrong, though. It stood for Kathy, but spelled with a C. We think you kept the date, but not for the reason Pansy expected. She believed she'd talked you into divorcing your husband for money.'

'If she ever thought that, she thought wrong, but I didn't –'

'I agree, Mrs Rees,' Parry interrupted. 'I believe what she proposed made you very angry. Rightfully angry, to your way of thinking.' He paused again, to give emphasis to what came next. 'I believe you kept your date with her, probably with the intention of teaching her a lesson, but not of killing her. You didn't intend taking her money, either, even when you could have, when you knew it was there for the taking, after you'd . . . finished with her. And for your brief appearance, you decided not to go as yourself. You went disguised as Mae Lewis instead. The white coat, the bandana, and some make-up probably did the trick adequately. And you only had to wait till Mae disappeared for a bit, which you knew she did frequently.'

Mrs Rees had been shaking her head in disbelief as he had been speaking. 'That's nonsense. The whole thing's nonsense. God, you must be desperate to cook up garbage like that,' she exclaimed dismissively.

'But it's not nonsense, is it, that before you left the market, you left the white coat in the ladies' loo, where you went to change identities again? Did you leave it there by intention, or mistake? We think mistake. You were under stress. Probably just forgot it. Our people missed it the first time they looked. That's why we've been slow checking it. Well, one of the reasons. But it was a worse mistake on your part than wearing the wrong coloured bandana. Yes, you did that too.' He was watching her face carefully as he went on: 'I'm afraid your fingerprints are on two of the coat buttons. They're not very good prints, but good enough. Good enough for us to know that DNA tests on the coat, against samples from you, will confirm it's yours. And we know already the coat picked up DNA traces from Pansy's arm when she was clutched and stabbed. So, we already have more than enough evidence to arrest you.' He leaned towards her across the table. 'After that, it'll be up to the Crown Prosecutor's Office. It's they who'll decide whether you went to the market intending to take Pansy's life, or for some other reason. We know you killed her. Admitting it at this stage, and telling us why, could affect the wording of the charge. Whether it's murder, or . . . or something less serious. Do you want to tell me now?'

Kathy Rees's face had grown pale, and her body quite still. After Parry stopped speaking, the only sound inside the room was a low crackle coming from the stove, and outside from the frenzied gusting of the wind as, intermittently, it continued to hurl rain against the window.

It was the chief inspector who eventually stood up, reached across for the teapot and filled the two cups. The woman's eyes followed his movements. By the time he sat down, tears had begun to roll down her cheeks.

'I didn't go there meaning to kill her,' she said, in a hardly audible voice. 'I meant to . . . to hurt her. Scare her. That's all. At least, I think so.' She breathed in brokenly, searching for and finding a tissue in a pocket of the coat. 'It was the . . . arrogance. The sheer bloody arrogance of the woman. She was my husband's whore. Nothing more than that. But she had the nerve to think I'd divorce him for her sake. That she could steal the man I loved with my permission.' She wiped her eyes, then rose slowly, and walked to the window. 'Three thousand she was offering for the divorce, plus all my legal costs, on condition I never told Evan she was paying me to let him go.' She clasped her hands and held them beneath her chin. 'I was to get a thousand in advance on Saturday. To show her goodwill. That's what she said. Her

211

goodwill. That's the bit that preyed on my mind.' She continued to stare, but unseeing, through the window as she went on. 'In the end, I agreed to meet her. She thought it was to collect the money. I meant just to spit in her face. Or punch her where it hurts. And every PE teacher knows how to do that. And then I planned to empty her bag of money over the balcony, and watch her go bananas when the people below fought to grab some.'

When Mrs Rees fell silent Parry put in: 'But the knife. Did you take it with you from here?'

She shook her head. 'I got that after I'd seen her the first time. Sitting prim on her stool at the café. I had the advantage. I knew what she looked like. I'd watched her often enough, out with my husband. She'd never seen me, though. Couldn't have said who I was. I didn't want her to be able to, either. That's why I got myself up to look like old Mae.' Now she took several short breaths in and out before she added: 'It was when I was hanging about at that sports goods stall . . .' Her voice had suddenly become less steely before she left the sentence uncompleted.

'Where you were watching for the right opportunity to . . . to confront Pansy?' Parry probed carefully, from his seat at the table.

'Yes. Only seeing her . . . it . . . it did something to me. Made my chest want to . . . to break in half with rage. The knives were there in front of me. The old man was serving somebody. I picked a knife, and walked away from the stall. I suppose it was then I knew what I was going to do. It was as if I was . . . as if I was programmed. I'd been trembling, now I was quite cool again. I just went up behind her, and . . . and . . .'

Without warning, as Mrs Rees uttered the last halting word, she swung around and grabbed for the knife lying on the bread board near where she had been sitting. Before she could reach it, Parry started to lever himself up. He meant to take hold of the table edge and upturn it – only the other player in the game was a split second ahead of him. Her first objective being still out of reach, she used Parry's tactic and upended the table on him. First the table edge crashed on to both his ankles, next, searing hot tea from the now topless teapot scored across his neck, and as he frantically grabbed at what was behind him to pull himself to his feet, he brought the Welsh dresser and everything on it down on top of him.

As Parry pulled himself out of the wreckage, aware already that one of his ankles was not going to stand his weight, wind was rushing at him through the open outside door. As he hobbled and hopped in a painful pursuit of Kathy Rees, the same wind carried in the noise of a motor springing to life.

21

The Citroën had been facing the wrong way to allow for instant flight. In any case, Parry had parked his own car across the drive, purposely leaving no room for anything else to pass.

When the chief inspector dragged himself out of the house, Mrs Rees was already backing the little car from behind the coke store, across the crunching pebble surface, and on to a waterlogged, half-empty vegetable bed. With spinning from the rear wheels, she next swung the vehicle to the right, and then forward below the drive, aiming to regain the hard surface on the far side of the Porsche.

Parry, still in acute pain, was leaning into a sou'westerly wind that was pelting him with leaves and twigs as well as rain. Half blinded by debris and the elements, he heaved himself past his own car, and aware that he wouldn't be able to drive this, used it first as a prop, then as a springboard to thrust him out into the path of the Citroën. There, balancing himself precariously, he stood waving his arms at Mrs Rees to stop. When, predictably, she didn't comply, he crouched ready to throw himself on to the bonnet. In response, with merciless revving of the engine, she slewed the vehicle away as much as she needed to stop the nearly anchored figure from completing his obvious intention, then she swung back again, finding just enough traction to keep movement going in the yielding soil.

For the next few seconds, in contrast to the movement of the wind, the actions of the human players on the scene seemed to be running in slow motion. As the Citroën, struggling in the mud, crawled past Parry, he grasped the handles of both passenger doors, only to find them locked. Still determined not to lose contact with the fugitive, as the back end of the vehicle came level, he stretched out for a hand hold on the slim roof rack, mounted the bumper on his good left leg, and swung himself aboard, finishing with his body spreadeagled across the car's rear end.

Parry had counted on his weight sinking the Citroën's wheels so much further into the earth as to stop its tank-like progress altogether. A fraction earlier this might have happened, but at the moment he became fully car-borne, Mrs Rees was taking compensating action, bringing both nearside wheels up on to a surface that gave solid traction again, effectively ending the slow-motion phase. The car was soon accelerating into the lane, the driver hurling it towards the main road, swaying the oversprung chassis as she took crazy, malicious aim at the worst potholes.

Approaching the T-junction, Mrs Rees applied the brakes just enough to prevent the car veering off the road altogether with the change of direction. Parry had been hanging on grimly to both sides of his flimsily fashioned hand hold, while trying to push his finger ends under the edges of the roof cover. All his lower weight he was putting on his left leg, because there was no way of using the right to help keep him upright. In this way he had so far survived those short, sharp swerves in the lane that had clearly been intended to shake him off. Poised for an expected left turn at the junction – comparatively easier for him to ride out than a right-handed one – he was nearly catapulted off his perch when the swing, at speed, was made the other way.

Instead of heading for Swansea, the fugitive was directing the car towards a dead end. Parry knew well enough that the made-up road stopped a mile ahead of where they were now. There the way was blocked by the wooden gates to a wide grassy walkers' causeway running above high cliffs on either side, and terminating at the famous, rugged Worm's Head – a massive rock landmark that thrust into the sea, emulating the last loops of a gigantic serpent. The gates were seldom opened, and then only to admit farm and maintenance vehicles. He prayed that they'd be closed this morning.

The time of day and the weather had so far combined to allow the Citroën a lonely passage, unobserved and unhindered. As they had joined the main road, Parry had been uncomfortably aware that had there been anything coming from either direction – Gomer Lloyd had been due at the cottage at any minute – a collision would have been almost inevitable. His fingers were now numbing with the wet and cold, while his whole body was wearying with the superhuman strength he was exerting just to keep his mount, as Mrs Rees continued doing her damnedest to shake him off, lurching the car from side to side of the empty road. Nor was it any consolation to her passenger that they were approaching a small cluster of houses where any law-abiding citizen peering from a window would witness the car's irregularly arranged progress and outrider, and be prompted possibly to report both to the authorities.

Any help summoned now would be too late to thwart whatever plan Mrs Rees had in mind. Ever since the unexpected turn westward, Parry had been nurturing a chilling presentiment about what form that plan might take – and quite soon. Nor did it help that he had a telephone in his pocket which there was no chance of his extracting, let alone using.

As soon as he made out the double wooden gates ahead his heart sank. They were wide open, with a Land Rover parked just beyond them. A figure was even now dismounting from the vehicle, probably with the purpose of closing the gates behind him. But Mrs Rees was going to forestall the action. Coaxing the last bit of extra effort out of the Citroën, she accelerated through the opening, and beyond to the causeway, ignoring the angry gesticulations and shouts of the wax-coated farmer who had leaped aside to avoid being run down.

The little car sped on along the rough path, whose surface was crossed and punctuated by spine ricking and wheel buckling, natural rock ridges. Then the driver suddenly swung off to the right, on to the wet and undulating grassland, gathering more speed on a downward slope.

Sure that it was Mrs Rees's intention to drive herself over

the cliff edge, and he with her if he didn't choose otherwise, Parry prepared now to leap off. It was then he discovered that his right shoe had jammed between the car's rear end and the bumper during an early, heavy encounter with a rocky extrusion. Painfully, he drew himself up straight in an attempt to pull his injured foot out of the shoe. As he did so, the car stopped its downward race and with a sickening lurch was suddenly ascending the steep face of a high ridge. In a moment there was a glimpse of the sea ahead, then the beach a thousand feet below, sights that temporarily disappeared again as the ridge was topped and a fresh drop began almost immediately down the dip on the other side. Despite the undulations, the Citroën's overall progress was a definitely descending one, as the grass drew ever closer to where the land would give out.

Desperate, Parry leaned down as far as he could, while still holding the loosening roof rack with his upper hand. He grasped his trouser leg around his right calf, and pulled hard in a final effort to free his foot. The action was dangerous, the pain excruciating, and the result negative. After that, he only had time left to brace himself for the inevitable. But then, only seconds before the car, with both its occupants, seemed fated to take its terminal plunge over what appeared to be the very edge of the cliff – the unpredictable occurred.

Out of the grey mist and rain immediately ahead, four fat mountain ewes hove into view. They were wobbling along, at a busy pace for sheep, in line abreast, coming up from a last narrow, grassy plateau beyond and below what proved to have been the penultimate, not the final, rising ridge. There was no way forward the careering car could take to avoid all the frightened animals. The driver braked hard, and made a drastic swerve – but so did the now stampeding sheep, and in the same direction. In consequence, the car was steered away from them even harder, and then went out of control, swinging around completely at a dizzy speed on the wet declining surface. The rear off-side wheel smashed hard against a protruding rock with an impact so tremendous, it sent the whole vehicle into the air.

After this brief and quickly stalled takeoff, the little car crashed down sideways on to a cluster of significantly larger rocks, bounced off them as lightly as an empty tin can. Then it slid on its side beyond the ridge – and up to and over the cliff.

Parry's foot had come loose at the first impact, and he'd thrown himself sideways as the car had been levitating. He caught the sound of a woman's piercing scream, followed by an urgent shout from a familiar male voice. After this he hadn't been able to prevent himself slithering helplessly towards where the grass gave out, while he attempted desperately to make hand holds in the turf. Then, without warning, a great weight descended on both his legs from behind, an instant before his head hit something very hard, and his world went black then blank.

'Funny about animal lovers, boss. They'd rather hurt a human being than a rabbit. Or in this case, a bunch of sheep. It's instinctive with them, as well. Lucky for you Mrs Rees reacted the way she did. Not that it did her any good, poor misguided soul. Difficult to tell whether it was an easier death she had than the one she'd planned. I'll never forget the look on her face as the car disappeared from sight with her in it, on her side, going backwards.' Sergeant Lloyd sighed, then folded his arms. 'Sorry again I landed on that foot.'

'Don't worry, Gomer. The bone was broken already. You stopped me going over. That saved my life.'

'Well, pity I hadn't stopped you hitting that rock as well. If I'd been a bit quicker –'

'Can't have everything,' Parry interrupted, and made an awkward shoulder movement. He didn't feel as lucky as Lloyd had implied. There was a large plaster bandage covering the stitches in the left side of his forehead, his right arm was in a sling, and his right foot was heavily bandaged to protect a fractured metatarsal bone. Dressed in pyjamas and dressing gown, he was sitting in a chair, at Swansea's Singleton Hospital, in a four-bed ward, where, at present, he was the only patient. He was also aching all over, feeling trapped and more than a touch sorry for himself.

It was early on Friday morning, two days since Kathy Rees

had been propelled over the cliff, not in the classic, heroic way she had intended, though with the same end result.

Parry had been rushed to the hospital by ambulance, recovering consciousness on the way. He had been detained after his injuries had been treated because there had been a risk of delayed concussion.

Lloyd had been personally very much involved in what happened after leaping from his own pursuing car – it was his shout that Parry had heard. At no little danger to himself, the sergeant had hurled himself and his formidable weight through the air on to Parry, stopping what had seemed to the other as his inexorable progress towards oblivion. The sergeant had stayed at the hospital on Wednesday until it was known that the chief inspector was out of immediate danger. Earlier on in the present visit he had collected the taped report Parry had been making of his interview with Mrs Rees, plus the chief inspector's notebook which had survived the ordeal, dampened but still legible.

Parry glanced at the time. 'The neurologist promised last night he'd be here first thing,' he complained.

'Ah, I expect that's why you woke up too early, boss. In eager anticipation, like. It's always the way,' Lloyd responded philosophically, eyeing the unopened box of chocolates he had brought with him. 'Anyway, he'll be here soon, I expect. Then we'll, er . . . we'll be on the road,' he completed, fidgeting with his chair.

'I hope so.' Parry didn't sound confident. 'The head scans were clear yesterday. I don't know why they couldn't have let me go then.'

'Ah, they like to be sure, don't they?' The sergeant had continued to study the chocolates in a compulsive way, but now steeled himself to look at the flowers arranged in the corner, on the other side of the bed to where they were both sitting. 'Who are all those roses from, then? Perdita, is it?' he asked.

'The Bevans,' Parry answered sharply. 'I haven't heard from Perdita since yesterday morning. She was hoping to get here to see me. I've said she shouldn't. Work wise, it's a terrible time for her,' he completed defensively, but only a touch so.

'I see.' Lloyd looked as if he had something further to add, paused, cleared his throat, and then changed the subject with: 'Mr and Mrs Bevan are very grateful to you.'

'So the note with the roses said. Simon Frankel brought them when he came to see me last night.'

'That was good of him, boss. Coming all this way, I mean. Not that you don't deserve his thanks, and the Bevans'.'

Parry sniffed. 'He's pretty confident he can keep them in the clear. So far as serious charges are concerned.'

'Like murder?' Lloyd gave a grim smile after he had spoken.

'They obviously weren't involved in Sister Watkyn's death,' Parry replied. 'Frankel was more concerned about the . . . irregular adoption, which is what he's calling it now. He knows they still risk minor charges over that in this country, but he doesn't think the Germans will need to be involved – or want to be.'

'Well, let's hope he's right. For young Barbara's sake, at least. Bright girl. Funny the murder had nothing to do with the Bevans buying their baby, after all. Or the blackmail. Looks like Mrs Rees was as fixated about having her husband back as Mrs Bevan was about getting a baby in the first place. Both very neurotic women. And Mrs Rees more than the other, of course, doing herself in, rather than face the music for what she'd done. Crime of passion, they'd have called it, I expect. Wouldn't have got life for that, I shouldn't think. I suppose she thought it'd be all up with her husband after she'd killed Sister Watkyn. That he'd never take her back after that.' The sergeant made a tutting noise, as his hand went slowly to the pocket where he kept his peppermints – very slowly.

'Would you like one of your chocolates, Gomer?' Parry asked, picking up the box.

'Oh.' The sergeant's head and neck drew back in righteous surprise. 'Oh, no.' He paused. 'Well, not unless you are. But don't open them just for me.' He watched closely as the other's fingers broke the cellophane wrapping and removed the cover. 'Well . . . if you insist,' he said, his tongue wetting his lips, as his hand reached out to the proffered box, then drew back. 'After you, then. Gracie said you liked chocolate Brazils.'

'I do. But it's a bit early for me.'

'Ah.' Lloyd nodded at the comment, but had difficulty understanding what, if any, time of day would be considered too early to consume chocolate.

'Of course, keeping off this foot for eight weeks means no exercise to speak of,' Parry continued. 'They say I'll have to ration myself with fattening things. Not to put on weight.'

'Well, the chocolates will keep, I expect,' Lloyd replied, munching happily on one that wasn't going to. 'My Gracie never buys cheap stuff.'

'Quite. Have another, Gomer.'

'Oh, I shouldn't.' He swallowed. 'Just the one more, then. Ta.'

Parry leaned back again in his chair – slowly and carefully, as if he was afraid of breaking more bones. 'Kathy Rees certainly did live in a dream world,' he said.

'I saw Mr Rees yesterday, boss. He still insists he'd never encouraged her to think he'd ever go back to her. It's like he said to you, she fantasized.'

'Delusions leading to criminal acts. Sometimes judged as temporary insanity?' Parry reflected.

Lloyd rubbed a hand across his moustache. 'You think she might have been committed, boss? Not imprisoned?'

'Possibly. It's academic now, of course. But if I hadn't let her get away –'

'Which you wouldn't have,' Lloyd put in. 'Not if I'd been with you, like I should have been, instead of climbing round my roof to no good purpose. In the end I broke more tiles than a rioting convict.'

The chief inspector smiled, then his expression hardened as he said: 'Rees is still a bastard, in my view, and cool with it.'

'Because he might still have given his wife some encouragement, boss? Despite what he says?'

'We'll never know that, either, will we? I think it's highly

221

probable, yes. Kept her on a string, in case he ever needed her for bed and board. Did he seem sorry or grieved about her death?'

'No, not at all. Very matter of fact, he was on that. Seemed to be most bothered that he'd be expected to pay for another funeral. I mean, since she was still legally his wife.'

'That's pretty typical of him, I'd say,' Parry observed. 'Even though he'll presumably inherit everything she owned.' He winced as, unthinkingly, he put some pressure on his right foot. 'When you think of it, she probably earned as much as Pansy. But owning her own house would have given Pansy priority for his attentions.'

'The two women were in the same line of work, in a way. Similar, anyway,' Lloyd remarked ruminatively. 'Keeping people healthy. It was smart of you to figure Mrs Rees would have studied anatomy. For her PE qualification, like.'

'Physiology, as well,' Parry responded. 'But it was Perdita who told me that. On Sunday. Yes, Kathy Rees probably knew exactly where to aim the knife. She still got lucky, though.'

'Making such a clean kill, boss?'

'Yes.' Parry's nose creased in distaste. 'Not that she'd have waited about for the victim to scream. Or fall over, and bleed to death.' He paused, and glanced through the window. It was cloudy but dry outside now. 'Did you contact Mrs Thomas for me?'

'Yes, boss. She's very concerned about you.' Mrs Olwyn Thomas was Parry's once-a-week cleaning lady, who tended to mother him. 'She's ready to come for two hours every day. More if needed. Well, till you're properly on your feet, like.' Lloyd looked at his watch, something he had been doing surreptitiously at regular intervals since shortly after his arrival. He was also trying to veil his own growing impatience over something he couldn't explain to Parry.

'It won't be necessary for her to do that,' replied the reluctant invalid. 'I'll cope. Once I've got the knack of these crutches. Should be back on the job in a week. Less, probably. I'll need a driver, that's all. I tell you something, Gomer, a cleaning lady in the flat makes more –'

As Parry had been speaking, the door behind him had opened, and Perdita Jones had appeared, pushing a wheelchair. 'I'll tell you something else, Detective Chief Inspector,' she interrupted. Leaving the wheelchair at the end of the bed, she moved quickly to Parry's side, hugged him, kissed him gently on the lips, then stood back, assessing the state of his injuries. 'A cleaning lady in the flat won't be nearly as handy as having your not-quite-qualified, devoted personal physician there instead. Also, I'm a completely qualified physiotherapist. And I'm all yours for the next ten days,' she announced, putting her hand over Parry's mouth to stop his impending protest. 'It's all approved and arranged. I'm doing my theory work in Cardiff for a bit, and so far as the practical is concerned, you're my assignment for the period. You're signed off here –'

'Who said?' demanded Parry.

'Your consultant, boss. Last night,' Lloyd put in, glad at last to be owning up. 'Only we weren't sure then Perdita could get here today. And they wouldn't have let you out otherwise.'

'But she's here now, with the Porsche outside,' said Perdita. 'So let's get you dressed. And don't think you're going to spend long in a wheelchair. It's just to get you down in the lift and out to the car.'

Lloyd got up quickly. 'You won't need me any more, then,' he said, sidling towards the door.

'Gomer, I haven't said thank you for saving his life!' exclaimed Perdita, throwing her arms around him, and hugging him hard. 'You're the best friend we'll ever have, and there's no way we can ever reward you for what you did.' As she was speaking, she noticed the box of chocolate Brazils. 'But these can be a token to be going on with, can't they?' she added with a smile, thrusting the box into his hands. 'My patient's on a strict diet till he's walking normally again. No booze and no chocolates.'

'No booze –' Parry began in protest: no chocolate was one thing, no evening whisky was quite another.

'There'll be plenty of non-fattening compensations,

darling,' Perdita interrupted archly. 'And I'm sure whoever sent you the chocolates would understand.'

Lloyd looked embarrassed, and a bit crestfallen. Then he adopted a kind of martyred smile as he put the box under his arm. 'Well, if it's doctor's orders, of course,' he said.